#10 SUMMER 2023

edited by

JOHN LINWOOD GRANT and DAVE BRZESKI

CATHAVEN
PRESS

OCCULT DETECTIVE MAGAZINE #10

ISBN: 978-1-9160212-8-0

http://greydogtales.com/blog/occult-detective-magazine/
occultdetectivemagazine@gmail.com

Publishers: Jilly Paddock & Dave Brzeski

Editors: John Linwood Grant & Dave Brzeski

Logos & Headers: Bob Freeman & Mutartis Boswell

Cover by: Stefan Keller (https://pixabay.com/users/kellepics-4893063/)

Interior design by Dave Brzeski and Jilly Paddock

Published by
Cathaven Press,
Peterborough,
United Kingdom
cathaven.press@cathaven.co.uk

CONTENTS

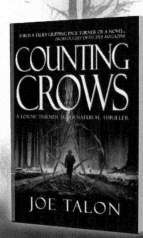

INTRODUCTION

Goodness me — we made it to ten issues, and it's all thanks to you. Unless you stole this copy, or are reading over someone else's shoulder, in which case Boo Hiss. But of course, we know that all our loyal readers are as honest as the day is whatever it is, and we would like to thank everyone who has supported us this far. Gold stars all round.

We say ten issues, but we've also put out various extra publications along the way. One of those, our first ODM Mythos Special, should be available right about now, with an intriguing range of tales drawing on aspects of Lovecraftian, Mythos and King in Yellow roots. Featuring new and reprint tales by some excellent well-known authors, you should have a look. It's darned good stuff, and we have a second Mythos Special coming in a few months.

But back to Occult Detective Magazine #10, which you have before you. We are particularly pleased to shake things up a little this time by presenting no less than FOUR brand new substantial novelettes, along with the usual short stories and reviews. Without giving too much away, we have what we believe is one of our finest longer tales so far, a subtle and moving piece by Simon Avery which might well fit into any anthology of folk-horror stories. To complement this, we offer Joe Talon's story of the popular Lorne Turner and a terrible past, John Paul Fitch's very dark return of his 'Anna and Turk' characters, and a classic psychic investigation with a nasty core from Nancy Hansen, featuring Chandra Smoake.

As for our more 'regular' contents, we offer our usual wide-ranging selection of just what occult detectives, psychic investigators and those who dare to explore the abnatural can get up to. Naching Kassa brings us a first delightful tale of Lady Dahlia Battleroost and her less-than-normal butler, Robert Runté has an investigation at a distance in a time of viruses, and Mike Adamson digs deep into England's Anglo-Saxon past.

Rhys Hughes, a master of wry humour, lets his investigator Nathan Gesture interpret chandeliers and tiramisu, Steven Philip Jones provides one of our rare werewolf stories but with a twist, and Michaele Jordan has a 'powerless' PI who nevertheless knows how to deal with the dirty side of magic. We also recommend our substantial non-fiction article by Maria DeBlassie, in which she looks at representation in this sub-genre.

We hope you enjoy the above, and that you stick with us for another ten issues — should your editors stay vaguely functional and/or sane that long...

John Linwood Grant

1

SOMETHING OLD, BORROWED, BLUE AND CURSED

A Lorne Turner Supernatural Mystery

JOE TALON

This story takes place after The Alchemist's Corpse, *book six in the series, but can be read as a standalone.*

The Wedding

I stood in front of the mirror and realised the nausea swirling in my stomach didn't come from the impromptu stag night I'd endured the evening before. It came from nerves. I'd spent twenty years of my life throwing myself into impossible situations with nothing more than an assault rifle, a thin sheet of body armour, and the rest of my unit. I'd tramped through deserts, over mountains, swamps and jungles. I'd killed more people than I could remember, carried the body parts of my comrades so their families had something to bury, and been shot, stabbed, blown up, and beaten bloody. Apparently, walking down the aisle of the familiar church in Luccombe to be married actually terrified me. I'd rather do a HALO jump without the parachute.

A soft knock at the door forced a curse from me.

"Come in," I snapped.

Eddie Rice peered through a narrow gap, looking as blurry as I felt. He and another old friend, Paul, had taken it upon themselves to end my bachelor life in style. We'd sat outside in Eddie's garden, become very drunk, while swapping war stories. Eddie from his police career, me from my service in the British Army's Special Forces, and Paul from his career in MI6. We must have breached several parts of the Official Secrets Act, but with only a little owl and a hedgehog to hear us, I doubted we'd be found out.

"Hi Lorne. Ella rang, she said they're ready for you down at the church. Heather's in a bit of a panic."

My bride was panicking? That didn't bode well.

"Maybe it's too soon," I murmured to my reflection, not entirely sure what I meant.

Eddie came fully into the room. He no longer resembled a bag of soggy and depressed spanners. Retirement, fresh air and sleep, pulled the years of service off his back. The pot belly had gone, and despite the rest of his hair vanishing with it, the life inside the ex-policeman shone. "You look good."

"I never look good. I've looked fit, strong, but never good."

He chuckled and a warm hand held my shoulder. The quaking deep inside me stopped for a moment.

Eddie said, "It's not too soon. You've been engaged for years now. She wants this. You want this. Neither of you handle change well. It'll be fine. You'll love being married, just as much as I love being married."

I snorted and tried to tackle my tie with hands more interested in shaking like a maraca controlled by a child on a sugar rush, than doing their job. Eddie came around me and took over.

Looking at him calmed me. He and Lilian were the vision of married life I hoped I could emulate with Heather. I'd been through some tough times with that woman, and she'd never let me down. I trusted her with my sanity and my life. She kept me locked onto the future, one I never thought I'd have, one I doubted I deserved.

Eddie finished with the tie, the colour, not chosen by me, brought out my eyes. It couldn't hide the scars or the bald head, but then only a burka could do that, and I'd seen quite enough of those in my life.

How our friends had pulled this wedding together in five days I'd never figure out. The aftershocks of the terrible violence that ended the control of the *Watchers of the Light* cult in the nearby town still reverberated. Heather and I had been lucky to escape with our lives and, most importantly, our liberty.

I slipped on the suit jacket, the cut perfect for my lean frame. My dress shoes were polished to the point moths would mistake them for candle flames, and I looked, on the outside at least, ready.

"Let's do this," I said.

Eddie mumbled, "Anyone would think he was facing a firing squad."

For the last time, I opened the front door to my family's farmhouse an unmarried man. I glanced up the hill, towards Dunkery Beacon and stood for a moment looking at the tiny, old church next to my land. Under the scrubby grass, shorn by sheep more than a mower, were my parents and grandparents. I closed my eyes for a moment and allowed the cool, clean air coming off the nearby hilltop to roll through me. No dust and sand, just damp moorland graced by the beginnings of spring. Snowdrops littered the hedgerow, their white petals like tiny skirts belonging to fairies.

It made me smile. Romance bloomed in my chest and sang in my blood.

I'd never been more scared or more perfectly happy.

* * *

The big church in Luccombe contained an odd assortment of people, most of them from the events that had overtaken our lives since I'd been medically discharged from the 22nd Regiment of the Special Air Service. I stood before the altar; my closest friend, in full vicar regalia, had an expression of smug benediction on her face because she'd managed to pull the wedding together in record time.

Ella grinned at me, hazel eyes sparkling. "You look like you're going to puke."

"I feel like I am," I muttered. I fiddled with the borrowed cufflinks for the thousandth time. "Where is she?"

"Willow's with her, it's fine."

I grunted. Leaving my ex-girlfriend with my wife-to-be didn't feel wise, but still, we'd all been through a lot together.

The door to the church opened, and the organist started playing the ridiculous music. I sucked in a breath as Heather appeared. I genuinely couldn't find the words to describe how beautiful she looked. A few weeks before this, she'd shot a man in the chest to save my life, while I'd been lain on the floor crippled by some mystical bullshit hidden deep in my psyche.

Walking towards me in a gown of soft autumnal colours she smiled and those blue eyes danced with merriment, making them shine like a summer twilight sky. I noticed that she wore a necklace I didn't recognise, with a pendant which sat on her chest, below the small gold Celtic cross Ella had given her a few years before. The blue gem matched her eyes, and shards of coloured light from the stained glass windows hit the surface of the sapphire, sparking fire deep within its core. Who had given her something so over-the-top to wear?

The now familiar sensation of hard black feathers being dragged over my scalp made me shiver. I half expected to see rows of dead people in the pews.

Instead, as I glanced into the crowd, I saw Heather's mother sat with Tess, a runaway we'd helped, in the second row of pews. Iris had returned to Exeter with the death of Heather's father, but we weren't sure what the future for the woman would be. After years of coercive control ending with such suddenness, things for her were difficult.

Heather stood beside me at last, her small, strong hand in mine. Words fluttered around us like bright kisses from butterflies, but I didn't really hear them. I just fell into the magic I always felt around my wife-to-be. At some point Ella asked me to repeat things, which I did. At other points I had to make a statement, which I did. Then, having been blessed with a wife-to-be who didn't need mad statements of love to know I meant it, I repeated some vows Ella spoon-fed me.

Eventually, I was told to 'kiss the bride'.

Which I did.

A soft kiss. One felt deep inside. A soul shifting kiss that changed me from one state of being to another.

As it ended, rather than the soft fragrance of warm light and fresh wind I usually smelt from my bride, a foul stench rose to engulf me. I coughed and my body retched.

"Lorne?" Heather called.

Ella rushed forwards; I saw her white alb from the corner of my eye. Holding my hand up prevented her from touching me.

The air around me stank of rotting flesh and wet earth. I felt maggots in my skin and I wanted to pull it off. Slough it like a snake. Dig them out of my muscles. Breathing became impossible and from a distance I heard voices.

Ella, the new Deliverance Consultant for the area, called out the first prayer of exorcism, The Lord's Prayer.

I grabbed the necklace around my wife's neck and yanked hard. Visions of rotting, tumbling bodies filled my head. I hated this. The 'gift' of psychometry. I wanted to release the damned jewel, but I had little control over my physical body in this state.

Flesh covered skeletons, wasted by starvation, and disease, white flesh tight to the bones, heads covered in tatty shaved hair, eyes too big and empty as more bodies and dirt filled the huge hole. A hole dug by the hands of the desperate. Men in uniform stood over them – us – barking orders to hurry. Fences, high, and sharp with layers of barbed wire, felt like the tight walls of an oubliette.

A hard, sharp intake of breath and the world flicked back to the wide, open space of the beautiful church in the small Exmoor village of Luccombe. I didn't stand in the dirt and filth of a land I didn't recognise.

Ella held the pendant by its silver chain.

"I'm sorry." I breathed in the soft scent of beeswax, candles, and the ever-present damp in these ancient churches.

Heather, who knelt in her beautiful gown so she could look up at me, smiled. "It wouldn't be us without some kind of weird drama. Let's walk back down this aisle, soldier. We'll talk about it at the reception." She rose with dignified elegance and helped me up.

I straightened and looked out at the concerned faces of our friends. "I'm fine. Sorry for scaring you."

Paul, my best man, said, "Mate, we've all seen you have a 'moment'. Let's just try to keep the psychic crap gone for the rest of the day."

"Never mind the day, Mucker, I wish I could ditch it forever." Feeling stronger and more centred, I took Heather's arm and laced it over mine. Together we walked, my new gold ring an unfamiliar weight on my finger. It shone with the light of the future.

* * *

We'd used Paul and Willow's cottage as the Head Shed for the reception and it worked out well. The short walk gave everyone a chance to mingle, and by the time we reached the venue, my odd behaviour had been politely ignored. British pragmatism at its best.

Food, alcohol, toasts and speeches came with laughter and silliness. Heather's colleagues from the National Park authority mingled well with the odd assortment of people we'd helped in the last few years. I'd chosen to keep all those I'd served with away from the celebrations. The man I was then had died in the sands of Syria. They wouldn't understand this version of Lorne Turner and I didn't want to be reminded of the old version.

The day began to close, and I finally had a chance to ask Heather about the necklace.

"Where'd it come from?" I poked the small velvet box she'd returned it to the moment she could. I refused to touch the box. Instead, I jabbed at it with a wooden spoon, as if it were a live wire.

"Iris," Heather said, glancing at her mother. "She said I needed something old, blue and borrowed. It's a family heirloom."

"You sure it's not a trap?"

Heather laughed. "Maybe. She's not exactly fond of you."

"Why's she here?" I asked. "And where's your brother? I expected him to put in an appearance."

Heather had been estranged from her family until the previous summer, when her father had arrived at the farm making demands, which led me to meeting her drop-out brother, Barny.

"Iris said Barny's in rehab. She came because Ella mentioned the wedding to Tess, during one of their conversations, and for some reason Iris felt like she had a right to be here. I didn't have the time to argue with her."

"What made you wear the necklace?"

Heather shrugged. "It's shiny?"

I kissed her soft dark hair. "I love you."

"So what happened when you touched it?" Her shrewd eyes fixed me in place like a laser dot over my heart.

The smile dropped from me, a stone plunging into the darkness of a bottomless lake, to lie forgotten and alone in the silt and the black.

"Nothing good. We don't need to talk about it now. I just want to know where it came from."

Heather nodded and pushed away from me. "I'll see if I can find out later. She'll never say in front of you, anyway."

True enough – the woman thought I was responsible for her husband's death. I'd admit, I probably didn't help matters, and I had provoked him, but it was his actions that brought him into a room full of killers.

Ella wandered over. "You okay now?"

"Happiest man alive."

She gazed at her new girlfriend, Caroline, who chatted happily with Lilian about running bakery sessions for the St Decuman's Rest residential home. A soft voice said, "Maybe it'll be me one day."

I glanced at her in surprise. "That's quick for you."

"I know," Ella said, sounding shocked. "She's..." Ella shrugged. "I've never met anyone like her."

"I'm pleased for you." Seeing Ella happy would be amazing. She threw herself into her parishes, and she'd been beside me for some of the worst, and best, moments of my life. For her to find a partner she could share her life with? It would be wonderful.

"Christ, I'm the most romantic bloody idiot on the planet today," I muttered.

Ella laughed. "Good, you deserve it. Now, go and enjoy yourself."

* * *

The following morning I rose early and made breakfast for my wife and our dog. As I set the tray down on the bed, Heather grinned at me.

"I could get used to this," she said, picking up the toast.

"Our first anniversary, you're making me breakfast," I said.

"Sounds good," she murmured.

The toast lay forgotten for a while.

When we made it downstairs, I saw the box containing the necklace sat on the old sideboard in the living room. Just looking at the damned thing made my skin crawl with the sensation that leeches wanted to suck me dry, growing fat on my flesh. The thing needed to leave my house.

Or maybe you need to man-up and find out what's wrong? my inner voice carped at me.

"It's person-upped," I muttered aloud, arguing with myself.

Still, I wasn't wrong. Whatever lay trapped inside that gem needed freeing. The terrible image I'd seen, those starving dead... I had a duty to set those feelings free.

"Heather?" I called, still eyeing the box.

"What?" she asked, our dog, Ghost, on her heels.

"Do we know anything more about this thing yet?" I pointed to the box.

A gust of wind tore around the corner of the house and rattled the windows, just to add to the effect of something portentous about to happen.

"Well, as I said, Iris lent it to me. When I asked her yesterday, she just said she wore it on her wedding day, and it came from her mother."

"Where do they come from? Your mother's family?" I asked.

Heather shrugged. "I'm not sure. I guess I can ask, though I'd rather not."

I looked at her and didn't bother to hide the apology in my expression.

She sighed. "Fine, I'll ring her now. Get it over with."

I found my jacket and pulled out the lightweight gloves I wore on the coldest days, when the wind on the moor gave the wind in the Hindu Kush a run for its money in the cruelty department. The fine weather of the day before was a memory in the tug-of-war between winter and spring.

Pulling on the gloves, I returned to the box and picked it up. I was a retired sergeant-major of the SAS; a box couldn't scare me unless it had wires sticking out of it.

The innocent object felt heavy for its size, just a little larger than my palm. I examined it closely. The faded red velveteen exterior had badly worn in places, revealing the soft boxwood underneath. The clasp appeared to be aged brass and had a little nipple button to press, releasing the lid. I pressed. It flicked open, the hinges still doing their job after all this time.

The gem glittered in the storm-dark light leaking through the large bay window. It would rain soon. I forced my eyes away from the finely cut sapphire and its tiny diamond companions. In the lid of the box, I saw a maker's name: *Ludlows of Bond Street, London. Established 1856.*

I fished out my phone and did a quick internet search. The company no longer existed. Not really a surprise.

Heather came back into the living room, tapping her own phone against her bottom lip. "Well, that was illuminating."

"Why?" I asked.

"Apparently, Iris's family came from London. My father," she almost said it without grinding her teeth, "he brought her down to Exeter. They met when he took a position at my grandfather's firm after finishing his law degree at Oxford. That necklace comes from my grandmother who picked it up in an auction during the late fifties. So it's not had a long history with my family, though that's not the impression my mother gave when she suggested, or rather blackmailed me into, wearing it."

"There's something terribly sad trapped inside this thing. You shouldn't ever wear it again," I said.

"Do we need to find out what?" she asked, eyes lighting up with the mystery and adventure.

I shrugged. "We could just bury it somewhere and forget it." Though my dreams last night had circled around that damned pit and those blank, starved eyes gazing at the brutal cold of a foreign sky. Would I be allowed to forget it?

"I have the name of the family from which it came…" Heather said with temptation written in every line of her body.

I narrowed my eyes. "Why so interested?"

"Well… If the family are in London we have to go there to investigate and I am kinda owed a holiday…" She sidled up and gave me the full charm offensive.

I was rendered powerless instantly. Just as well enemy combatants couldn't do this to us tough, old soldiers.

"London?"

"Yes…"

"I hate cities."

"I know, but, I've already been on the phone with Ella, and she'll be our tour guide."

I chuckled. "You want to bring the vicar on our honeymoon?"

Heather frowned. "Oh, I hadn't thought of it like that. She just said we could save petrol money by going up together. She says we can stay with a friend of hers making it even cheaper. I've hardly ever been to London."

Despite understanding her excitement I felt trepidation. Over-stimulation of the senses often triggered my PTSD and London would be full of sounds, smells, people… Lots and lots of people with their noisy heads contained within the concrete and brick canyons of a vast city.

My heartbeat started to increase, but the words out of my mouth were, "Of course we'll go."

The Honeymoon

We stood in Highgate cemetery. The wind blew, the rain fell, and I wanted to be at home. While I'd driven into the city, needing to keep control, Ella directed us to a large vicarage we'd be staying in for as long as this investigation took. I kept my mind on the present, tried not to overreact every time someone cut me up, and worked hard to maintain the calm necessary to be surrounded by vulnerable people. Walking the streets disturbed me, too many men with that vacant, thousand mile stare I recognised lived in doorways and alleys. I hated how unprotected this tumult of humanity made me. At least when I walked the streets of Baghdad I'd had an assault rifle to keep me safe.

Now, though, I felt a measure of calm. We stood in a quiet corner of the graveyard. Ella's dog collar helped us gain access to areas usually off limits to the public. On the way up the busy M5 motorway, Heather had searched for Ivy Winslow, the woman who'd owned the necklace before Heather's grandmother bought it. The only reference we found about her final resting place, for her body at least, was on a site dedicated to graves. It made sense to have such a website, I supposed, for genealogists, but I found it disturbing. Still, most genealogists didn't live with the dead in quite the same way I had to on a regular basis.

"I'm feeling underwhelmed," I said.

"You're not seeing anything?" Heather asked.

I peered around, vague wisps of phantoms lurked, but they were memories trapped in a loop that had no meaning. Like a sound wave caught and held in the atmosphere, despite the object that made the sound having moved on. They weren't spirits able to communicate, unlike some I'd known. No consciousness lived in this place.

"I'm sorry, but there's nothing here," I said. "I think we've wasted our time."

Ella stepped forwards and onto the grave. In this corner of the vast cemetery the ivy had control over everything. Its verdant leaves healthy and pungent in the warm spring air. The nearby yew tree spread its dark branches over the area, offering a somewhat sinister shade among the old headstones. Many of these were unreadable due to lichens devouring these last impermanent markers of a human life.

As I watched, Ella crouched and pulled the ivy away, the crackle and snap a noisy protest at the damage done to the plant. The birds fell silent.

Heather looked up. "Oh, that's not good."

I followed her gaze. A large crow sat in the yew tree watching us with its gem-like black eyes. The black beak snapped at the air. It made me shiver.

"She was Jewish," Ella whispered. She rose and turned, pointing to the beautifully carved Star of David. "She was Jewish. Ivy Winslow was Jewish. She died in nineteen-sixty-four, mourned by her son."

Heather removed the box containing the necklace from her pocket. "Do we leave it here?"

I barked a laugh. "I'm not sure your mother would appreciate that."

Heather grinned. "She'd be furious."

I shook my head. I didn't understand her relationship with her family, or lack thereof.

Turning to leave, my foot caught in the ivy crawling over the path and held my boot tight. The crow screamed its rough protest, and rose from the tree in a loud flurry of black wings. I glanced up. The world turned, and I hit the gravelled path. Heather yelled, but her voice dissolved into the raindrops. The crow's caw sounded far more real. My mind followed it.

The light slithered through the dense clouds as if ashamed of being present. She watched the rise and fall of swirling black birds high overhead. Night dark birds. Omen birds.

A rough voice, full of hate, barked an order. Too exhausted to understand the words, she merely gazed at the shovel in her hand and the blood on the handle from her torn palms. Another voice, softer, kinder, spoke with the same instruction. She had to keep working, pushing soil over the bodies. The ones in the pit. She worked hard not to see them. Not to remember those faces, even though she knew she had a duty to her lost brethren. Buried without prayers, without ceremony. Where was their God in this horror? How many of them had asked that question before they'd died?

The naked flesh, paper thin and sagging from starvation, blurred as she tipped the soil over the hole, trying not to see, not wanting to remember. Oh, and the smell...

I sucked in a hard breath. Trembling and anguished. The crow cawed as it circled, its sky-dance mad in the rising wind of the coming storm.

She wandered through the maze of buildings, croaking a name held silent in her heart for months. Isaac. Isaac. Isaac.

So many lost faces, hollowed out by fear, dread, hunger.

Isaac.

She shuffled from child to child, suddenly terrified she wouldn't recognise her son among these tiny, living corpses. That he wouldn't know her. Men in uniforms she didn't recognise tried to move her away, but she clutched at them, begging, begging, begging for her son, her Isaac.

A single figure held her. Wrapped his coat around her thin shoulders. Took her into a different shed. He called out for her son, his voice strong, full of pain borrowed from her.

"Mama?"

I came to, the wet sky overhead soaking my face, and very damp gravel under my backside, leaking through my jeans.

"Wonderful," I muttered.

"What happened?" Ella asked.

I sat up, and tried not to vomit. These messages from the grave hurt, and I didn't like the sensation of being stolen from my life. The grief though, the grief and the fear, the pain and the hate, they were more real than the gravel under my palms. "You're right, she's Jewish. She was at a camp."

Heather, who helped me off the ground, hissed. "Oh, that's not good."

"No. I don't know where the gem comes into it, but she found her son. They both left the camp." I nodded at the grave. "But the things she remembered..."

Ella gazed at the headstone for a moment. She picked up two small pebbles and placed them on the surface with a quiet prayer. "We need to go to the nearest synagogue. I bet they'll know more."

"She died a long time ago," I said.

"They'll have records of Holocaust survivors. We need to help this woman," Ella said. "Whatever is left of her lives in that necklace, and she deserves peace."

I looked out over the old cemetery, and thought about the images I'd seen of the woman and her terrible fate. Even the brief glimpse of her finding her stolen son didn't give me much relief. No one walked away from war unchanged. No one. The horrors of the Nazi regime should never be forgotten, and as a soldier, a part of me still felt I had a duty to its victims. To all the victims.

I shied away from thinking about the prisoner of war camps in the deserts. On quiet nights, usually when we'd had to do sentry duty, we'd share the rumours in low voices of what might be done to our enemies. Few of us were fully aware of what was happening in these hidden places, many of us were deeply confused by the thought of what *might* be happening. Were we taking revenge or seeking justice? Deep down, I still wondered. We were not the good guys in those prisons. I owed unquiet souls in deserts all over the world.

Bowing my head, I whispered, "You're right. We have to do something." We had to know this family's story and find them peace.

I followed in Ella and Heather's wake as they led me north from our current location. They'd found the nearest synagogue, Highgate United. The story behind the gem worried me. How much did we really want to uncover? Where would it take us?

The smell of traffic and humanity, even as the rain eased, overwhelmed the senses. I longed for the fresh air of the moor, or the smell of the sea. This shifting, heaving, unpredictable mass of humanity swamped me. Every sharp noise felt like a threat. Each scream of brakes from a taxi shot through my mind and it hurt, like a blade of tinnitus after being blown up. My skin felt grimy, and my lungs ached. I'd always struggled with cities, from Baghdad to Helsinki – I'd endured them rather than enjoyed them. Understandable in Baghdad considering the circumstances, but I'd disliked Helsinki just as much. The mountains and rolling deserts, empty of humanity except for my comrades and the enemy, those places I could handle.

"Lorne?" Heather tugged on my arm. "We're here."

I'd been wool gathering so long I hadn't noticed. This place had me on hyper-alert so much so that one moment I was seeking potential enemies in every doorway, or rooftop, the next I felt I needed to escape so badly I just drifted off, unaware of my surroundings, in the hope we'd be gone when I came round.

Now we stood in a narrow road, off the main drag and the noise level had dropped considerably. A magpie perched on a security camera with a high, iron fence around a modern, brick building. The magpie chattered at us, then flew off as Ella approached the gate.

"It's sad," Heather murmured, her fingers lacing with mine.

"What is?" I asked.

Heather gazed at me for a moment as if confused by my lack of understanding, then said, "Churches don't need high end security, but these places do." She peered at me. "You're really not doing well are you?"

I squeezed her fingers. "Sorry, I'm just finding all this overwhelming. And you're right, of course, no place of worship should need security."

Ella spoke into the small white box, explaining who she was and why we'd come to London. Nothing about the gem and me being a nut-job, but she told them we'd found a necklace that might've belonged to a woman who'd survived the camps. It took a while, but she convinced them we were credible.

The gate opened on a buzz and a man stood in the doorway of the brick building.

"Welcome to the Highgate Synagogue," said the young man. "I am Rabbi Samuel." He held out his hand. Taller than me, but not quite six feet, he sported a wild, slightly red beard, but no moustache. A black kippah adorned his fading red hair and he wore a dark suit. The wide smile made his pale face friendly, and the clay-coloured eyes remained warm even as he assessed my scars. A small pot-belly made him soft in the middle.

Ella shook his hand. "I'm the Reverend Ella Morgan and this is Mr and Mrs Turner."

Wow. That gave me a moment. I felt Heather's jolt of surprise as well. We were a married couple.

"Come in, come in. You look as if you've been too long in the rain." His north London accent softened as he ushered us out of the damp day. We stood in a large entrance room, very clean, slick, and modern. "I take it none of you want to convert to Judaism, so how can I help?" He eyed Ella's dog collar.

Ella opened her mouth to explain, but before she could mire herself in half-truths, I found myself speaking.

"Ivy Winslow is buried in Highgate cemetery, and we'd like to know more of her history. We thought we'd try the local synagogues hoping she lived and worshipped in the area."

The rabbi's eyes narrowed. "I see." Though he clearly didn't. "One of my duties is the protection of our people, so I'm afraid I'm unable to give out personal details." He glanced at Ella. "I'm sure you feel the same way about your congregation."

Ella nodded. "Of course, but Ivy died in the sixties, and we'd like to trace her family if possible. We have something that belongs to them. They might want it back, or they might be able to give us a little of her, or the object's, history."

The rabbi frowned. It aged his face, matching more with my notions of a Jewish leader. During my military career I'd met many more Muslims than Jews, for obvious reasons.

Heather put her hand in her pocket. "My mother gave me this necklace to wear during our wedding. She said it was a family heirloom, but it isn't, not really." Heather took the box out of her daysack and held it up.

I gasped and stepped back as a wave of anguish flashed outwards like a sonic boom. The world folded in on itself.

The cattle car rattled and bounced on the track. The noises from the creaking metal, screeching brakes, and the endless cold wind ripping through the wooden slats, were a disjointed cacophony underpinning the helpless prayers and sobs of the overcrowded occupants. She cradled her five-year-old son to her thighs. His woollen coat was done up tight, his hated gold star horribly clear on his little chest. She tried never to touch the one on her chest. As if it alone contained all the hate now aimed at her and those of her kind.

Her one belonging, it meant everything to her, nestled between her breasts. She felt her fingers stray to it often, its shape reassuring even through the layers of fabric. The colour, a deep blue captured in the heart of the sapphire, she held in her mind as a talisman to a more beautiful time. One that existed before the death of her family, and her beloved husband, during the initial invasion of Warsaw. Now, she and her son, Isaac, had run and run, trying to keep away from the Nazi hordes, but they'd been betrayed. Handed over in exchange for food and other privileges.

Her terror came in waves over the hunger and exhaustion. They'd all heard the rumours of the resettlement camps. She had no illusions.

Her boy nestled into her body, silent and uncomprehending. No one spoke in the overcrowded space. They'd shuffled around, trying to give the children space, trying to find a place for those who needed to pass water, empty their bowels, their stomachs, as the journey and fear overwhelmed many. The humiliation of such acts, adding another layer to the cruellest of journeys.

The train began to slow and stop. Silence became complete until the shouting of men outside began. Icy fear wriggled through her limbs turning them to water. The sliding door rattled on the rail and grey light poured through the opening, bathing the pale faces, making them mask-like even before death.

She couldn't help but whisper, "Is this what a cow feels like?"

An old man, his face a grey mask of resigned horror, nodded. "It is, my dear. We all feel fear at the end. But God will greet us when our time comes, remember Him." He pointed upwards, as if the all-knowing deity lived in the roof.

She stared at the old man, wondering how God could be in this place. Surely He, Yahweh, had finally forsaken his chosen people? The despair of this thought made a tear slide down her filthy cheek.

People moved around her, and she knew if she didn't obey the shouted commands, it would be instant death. Perhaps a mercy, but something inside her kept the flame of hope alive. She might survive this, and she had to protect Isaac. She'd promised her husband.

A rough hand grabbed her and yanked her off the train. She stumbled, the skin on her hands and knees splitting on the hard gravel. Isaac yelped as a blow caught his head and she pulled her boy under her body as her back received the hard butt of the rifle meant for the child.

Before the second blow came she glimpsed the wire. Miles of twisted metal. A vast cage.

As the vision turned dark, my world swept back. The air cleared and smelt of warm offices the world over.

"Fuck..." I murmured, tears pricking my eyes. "I can't keep seeing this stuff." My stomach rolled and with it my body.

A metal rubbish bin appeared under my nose.

"Use this," Heather said. "We're in the rabbi's office. Ella is trying to explain why you collapsed and started talking about Nazis."

I sucked in more air and swallowed, wanting to keep control of my stomach. "Don't tell me, he thinks we're taking the piss, and we're Holocaust deniers, or something equally terrible?"

"He's not best pleased, but it's hardly your fault." Heather rubbed my back.

"Some honeymoon," I grumbled.

She chuckled. "If I wanted normal, I'd never have married you in the first place."

I managed a smile.

Her eyes clouded. "Oh, love, is it terrible?"

I shook my head, trying to control the rising horror of what I was witnessing through the gem's trapped memories. "It's worse than anything I've ever seen, Heather." Which told her all she needed to know.

* * *

The rabbi, being as polite as possible under the circumstances, wanted us gone. However, Ella, in full Church of England Deliverance Consultant mode, managed to convince him to find any records related to Ivy Winslow. He agreed and we now stood in Jackson Lane. A postcode that had eye-watering price tags for Victorian houses, and cars parked on the road that probably cost more than I earned during a twenty-year service for the British bloody Army. Me, bitter? Never.

On the left stood a beautiful, red brick terraced house, the wooden windows painted a clean white, the front garden graced with a privet hedge trimmed to within an inch of its existence and a neat, low iron railing in shiny black. The net curtains were white lace and hung with regimental straightness behind bright glass. A sense of quiet dignity pervaded the three-storey home.

On the right the property told a different tale. One of woe and neglect. The structure, on the outside, mirrored its sister in shape and size, but that's where the similarities ended. The narrow front garden contained weeds and old forgotten, blown in or thrown, plastic bags and bottles. The windows had been boarded up and painted matt black. The pointing between bricks sprouted the occasional plant, and the gutters, though still in place, had large rusted patches creeping through the degraded paintwork. The front door, raised from the pavement by a series of stone steps, had industrial metalwork and locks in place. This house didn't just look derelict, it felt broken. Whatever dreams the occupants once had, they'd been smashed like a piece of expensive Waterford crystal hitting a tiled floor.

"Can I help you?"

The three of us turned to look at the property on the left. A man stood in the doorway, perched in case he needed to retreat quickly, staring at us with owl-like intensity.

Ella unwrapped the scarf around her neck, once more using the magic of the Church of England clerical collar, and smiled. "Hello. I'm sorry if we've been staring, but we're looking for the Winslow family and the local synagogue pointed us in this direction."

The man relaxed enough to leave the safety of the doorway. I kept back, knowing my scarred face often made Ella's job harder if we needed to gain a stranger's trust.

"My father knew the Winslows, but as you can see, the place has been empty for years."

I felt another wave of Ivy's distress flash out from the necklace in Heather's daysack. I stepped back, into the residential road, trying to avoid the backlash of history. This time my barriers held. The person who drove down the street, his temper did not. Still, he missed me and everything else in the narrow street.

"Are you alright?" the man in the house asked, his accent heavier suddenly in his concern.

"Fine," I said. "Sorry, I didn't mean to startle anyone. Could we ask you some questions about the Winslows? An item of their property came into our possession, and we need to find some answers."

As the man stepped down away from his front porch the light fell on him. No other word than dapper suited this gentleman. He stood only a little taller than Ella and not much wider. He wore a cream shirt with an embroidered waistcoat, buttoned neatly. Pale moleskin trousers and slippers of blue wool. His dark hair owed a great deal to his hairdresser's skill, so that a little looked like a lot. Clean-shaven, warm skinned, and with large, dark eyes softened by kindness.

He studied us for a long moment. "Well, I suppose it's been a few centuries since the Church of England last stole anything from a Jew, so I'm thinking you're probably safe."

Ella gasped, then burst into laughter. "Wasn't it mostly the Catholics?" she asked.

He shrugged. "You religious gentiles, you're all the same to me. Catholic, Protestant, Lutheran, what do I know? Modern faiths are indistinguishable." By now his Jewish accent had become thick enough to make Heather giggle. He grinned and winked at her. Then he peered at me. "There's a story in that face. I'm a writer." He pointed at his house. "I'm a successful writer. You tell me your story and I will tell you that story." Next he nodded to the sad monolith next door.

"Your story first?" I asked.

He grinned. "You have yourself a deal, my boy." He now spoke with a heavier Jewish accent than a badly performed Shylock would have used.

We entered the man's home, removing our shoes at the door, and I stepped onto a carpet so thick and soft I thought I had a case of vertigo for a second as I sank into it. Heather mumbled something about London being too big and we'd done too many miles on foot.

"My name is Andrew Weiner," he said, showing us to a small sofa and an armchair among the expensive tables and desks.

Ella made the introductions and explained why we'd been standing outside his house. Andrew watched me with a peculiar intensity. While Ella spoke, I began studying the books on the shelves that I could see. More than a few revealed an interest in the occult, especially the Kabbalah, and several held the name of Andrew Weiner on the spine.

Sometimes I had to wonder how much fate liked to fuck with me.

Putting a hand out to touch Ella's knee, I brought her to a halt. I gave Andrew all of my considerable attention. "I think we need to be a little more honest than we are usually," I said.

Ella looked confused for a moment before Heather pointed to the bookshelf behind her. Ella mumbled, "Oh, I see. Well, that was a waste of breath."

I said, "Andrew, we're here because we've been led. My wife was given a necklace to wear during our wedding, and I've had the psychic equivalent of an allergic reaction."

Heather removed the necklace from her daysack and put the box on the low coffee table.

I pointed to the box. "The gem in there is—" I considered my options for a moment. "— full of someone else's memories and they aren't happy. We've tracked the previous owner to Highgate cemetery, then the nearest synagogue pointed us to this address. Do you know anything about the house next door and its previous owners?"

Andrew sat back in his chair, fingers steepled under his chin. "It's a sad tale."

"I already know she was in a concentration camp during World War Two. I've seen a little of what she suffered. She found her boy, but all I'm getting now are glimpses backwards and there doesn't seem to be anything nice. I'm guessing her grief and pain has been trapped in there." I pointed to the box.

"May I look?" Andrew asked, his face serious.

Heather pushed it towards him. Leaning forwards, Andrew took the box and pressed the little brass button. I sucked in a hard breath, half expecting something terrible to happen. Nothing. The room remained the same, not even a shift in atmosphere.

"It's beautiful," he murmured, stroking the sapphire. "My father was a gem merchant; he valued this piece. I remember it well. Even then I could pick up on something in there, but I've never had the sensitivity you do." He glanced up at me, but seemed unable to remove his gaze from the necklace for any length of time. "I know its story."

"What happened to Ivy?" Heather asked.

Andrew sat back, closing the lid of the box. "Ivy and her husband tried to leave Poland as the Nazis began to ghettoise the Jewish population. They lost everything at the border and had to return to Warsaw. During the trip Ivy, a very beautiful woman, was attacked by German soldiers. Her husband was killed trying to defend her. Ivy and her son, Isaac, managed to escape and made it into the city. Once there, she took what little they'd managed to save and bribed her way into a house that promised to protect the Jews in its care." As he finished speaking the enormous weight of history filled the room.

"They sold her out?" Ella asked.

He nodded. "The people in the house were scared. It wasn't just the SS they were scared of, it was their neighbours, friends… For those who tried to help our people life could be just as terrifying as it was for the Jews. That kind of pressure can damage a person's soul." He tapped his chest. "Given enough of an incentive the pressure can make even the best of intentions feel like a mistake."

"They came for them?" Heather asked.

"Yes. They came for Ivy and Isaac. The only thing of value she had left was the necklace. It had been given to her husband's grandmother as a wedding gift and passed through their line. She hoped she might be able to use it to bribe her way out of the camp. It didn't work, of course, they merely took it."

"I saw them in the train," I whispered and Heather slipped her hand into mine. "It was terrible. Beyond anything I've seen in war."

Andrew nodded, but seemed to be holding himself locked up. "My father, who heard the story from Ivy during the years they were friends, explained it all to me as a young man so I could always understand the sacrifices our people endured. The guard took the necklace and took Ivy's son. Then, one day, she saw the gem sitting on the chest of another woman. A camp wife of the commanding officer. One of the privileges of power. She was a Gypsy woman and proud of her position in the camp. During the process of liberation, Ivy first went in search of Isaac. Once reunited she decided to find her necklace." Andrew shook his head. "I have no idea why she thought she'd find it, but it was the last thing she had of her husband's and that meant a lot to her."

"She found it then?" Ella stated.

"She did. Still on the throat of the Gypsy woman. Ivy took a knife from a dead soldier. Cut the woman's throat in a fight and took the necklace back. How she found the strength I don't know. My father found a box that matched the original one as closely as possible. She never wore it again, but she wouldn't sell it either. When she died, Isaac sold the contents of the house, but couldn't sell the building. He said his mother walked the rooms. He's in Israel now and an old man. I still hear from him sometimes. He has a big family and is grateful he left Europe behind with its history, but he's never been able to sell the house."

I felt like arguing the deserts of the Middle East had a fair amount of history, but didn't think it would help.

"Do you have a key for next door?" I asked.

He nodded.

"Then we need to take Ivy back her necklace." I knew, I just knew, that's why the gemstone kept lashing out at me.

"Mum won't be pleased if we leave it here," Heather said.

I shrugged. "What's she going to do? Not speak to you?"

Heather chuckled. "Bonus."

Gathering his things together, Andrew decided to come with us into the house. It certainly couldn't hurt having another person who understood the story, and the occult, along for the ride.

When we walked up to the abandoned front door, I took the key from Andrew. Ella stood at my elbow and murmured St Patrick's Breastplate. Drawing up the barrier I'd learned to use for protection, the white and blue as solid as I could make it, I stepped over the threshold. Darkness filled the place; the windows were blank eyes onto the outside world denying the light. We all switched on our phones, and I took out my Maglite as well.

The house reverberated with laughter. A woman, with long dark hair chased a small boy around the newel post of the stairs, sliding on the hallway rug. They raced off towards the kitchen.

I took another step forwards.

Weeping came from the room on my left. Weeping and a horrible cough. The same woman shuffled into the hall, barely able to stand up. A young man appeared from a different room and rushed to help her. They moved back towards the kitchen.

I described what I saw in short, staccato sentences, fighting to keep the emotion out of my voice. The walls sang with loss.

"This way," I said.

Together, in silence, we walked to the back of the house. We found the kitchen down a shallow flight of four steps. Andrew, curiosity washing off him in tsunamis of vibrant energy, managed to hold his tongue. I gazed around. The place had been stripped. Nothing remained, not even a cooker. The shell of cabinets, without their doors, gaped. Rat droppings littered the surfaces, but with nothing to eat even these were old.

Andrew broke the silence. "I come in a few times a year to make sure it's structurally sound. Nothing leaking. To be honest, I don't like it."

Heather's hand in mine tightened, and she pointed. Shadows began to gather before the empty void where a cooker once sat, the grease stains on the floor making its location obvious. A vague shape formed and became a slim woman. Andrew gasped in shock. Ella signalled him to silence.

Heather handed me the box containing the necklace.

"I don't know what to do now," I whispered.

The woman, wearing a dress that reminded me of a nineteen-fifties style actress, kept her back to us.

"Give it to her," Heather suggested.

I held the box, the yearning inside it like a coating of mercury sliding up my arms. The shade of a boy rushed into the room and threw himself at the woman's legs. She bent down, picking him up and finally turned to face me.

The years in the camp stole her beauty, but not her dignity. I marvelled at her courage. When those dark eyes dropped to the box in my hands, they widened. Feeling a little foolish, and a lot awed, I stepped closer.

How would I give a ghost a box?

Refusing to overthink the physics of my weird life, I opened the box and held it out. A perfectly formed and elegant finger reached out and stroked the sapphire. She gazed into my eyes, and a tumble of memories washed through my mind too quickly to grasp, too quickly to share. The shadow-form began to fade, the boy first, then the woman. Her large dark eyes the final aspect of her to vanish.

"Put it down," Heather whispered.

I placed the necklace on the floor. "It's time to leave," I said. Turning back to the others I added, "We'll bless this place. I don't think the rabbi will help, and it needs doing now."

"I know enough," Andrew said, his voice quavering but his determination strong.

Together, we walked around the house, Ella with her holy water and prayers, Andrew giving his quiet rendition of the *Mourner's Kaddish, El Maleh Rachamim*. The combination of faiths sounded beautiful to my uneducated ears, but then, I'd always quietly found some peace in the call to prayer as well.

Returning to the kitchen, we all stared at the valuable necklace. "What do you want to do with it?" Andrew asked Heather.

She shrugged. "I don't want it. It's not mine."

"It was bought in good faith, it is yours," he pointed out. "It wasn't stolen and sold to your family."

"My family are not good people," she said.

"But you are." Andrew crossed the room and bent to pick up the necklace. "Take it home, sell it, keep it, I think its pain has left this house, don't you?"

Heather took the box back and studied the gem. "The money would be handy," she admitted. "It'll pay for a new car. We're rather desperate."

Andrew patted her arm and smiled. "Ivy was a practical woman. I think that sounds like a good idea. I know some dealers here in London. Leave it with me, and I'll see you get a good deal."

"In exchange for a story?" I asked.

"In exchange for all your stories," Andrew said.

I laughed. "Alright. I'll start talking, but I warn you now, it gets weird."

"I love a bit of weird," he said, laying on the Jewish accent.

* * *

We spent several more days in London sharing stories with Andrew who scribbled down our experiences thus far. I confessed about Al-Ahmar, my desert djinn. I talked about events in Culbone, Scob and more. Ella and Heather shopped until they dropped and raced around museums with glee. I knew Andrew would steal my life to create his stories, but it felt good to share and when we left London, one necklace lighter, we had enough in the bank to buy Heather a new car and replace my father's old truck if we were careful.

Leaving Andrew's house for the last time, I glanced up at the abandoned property next door. Someday it would become a family home again, but for now, the shades and shadows would own its still and quiet hallways.

SECRET OF THE LARK

MIKE ADAMSON

The long, level countryside of Norfolk and Cambridgeshire is the quiet heart of England, and the perfect place to retreat from the pace and conflict of today. My husband Derek is a property developer specialising in the Fen District, and when one of the new lodges came available at the Isleham Marina, on the River Lark, we snapped it up. It was central to his work and provided the perfect atmosphere of peace to foster my own career as an artist. We moved into this idyllic spot in the spring and loved it, but it was about then my dreams began to turn dark, and I first saw the ghost.

I specialise in landscapes in something of a classical style, having studied the great English scenic painters at university, and after we settled in I turned out a few canvases inspired by the farm country all about. But, inexplicably, I began to feel my creative impulses drawing ever more firmly toward the *oeuvre* of John Constable – the ancient manor houses, water meadows and river locks of centuries gone by, and always, it seemed, under the most brooding of skies.

Some called them inspired, some frightening, for my skies came to dominate, the landscape ever more secondary until, in a fit of creativity inspired by a storm in early summer, I churned out a piece in less than a day, in which almost the entire canvas was towering black thunderheads. A ribbon of terrain crossed the foot, lit in sunshine from behind the viewer's perspective, buildings half-glimpsed amongst forest seeming metaphorical for human insignificance before nature.

Cathy, my agent, told me I was going too far, that buyers expected dignified, pleasant views of the English countryside from a Lacy Cantwell piece – not to have their philosophy of being challenged. But as any artist will tell you, inspiration comes from within, and I could no more deny my new-found tendencies than explain them.

Dreams were part of it, and I wondered sometimes – in the mornings when Derek had left for an early appointment – if I needed help. Why would a normal, rational graduate of a London university, happily married, be dreaming of times long ago when scant villages were the only human habitation and hard, ruthless men rode the land? The feelings caught me up – apprehension, yes, fear of the wild days that had been; yet also wonder, pride in the indomitable human spirit, which alone bridged from one generation to another in defiance of the still-triumphant wilds.

One such morning I lay in bed for a long while after I heard Derek's car go, and listened to birds in the trees. I sighed into the cream sheets and thought of my work in hand. My dreams had been particularly dark, and so very realistic. Bands of horsemen, clad in sheepskin and leather, their ponies hardy and spirited, wandered trackways between the ancient lakes; I remembered details of harness, the patterns on shields, the very smell of horse and man. How could I be dreaming these things? Why? And why with such vivid clarity?

As always, there were no answers forthcoming from the mild morning air, and I rose to shower, a cool, lazy spray that had the illusion of rinsing away my cares. Long, dark hair greeted me in the mirror, with pale skin and features that had been called attractive often enough for me to believe it. A hair dryer, a silk robe, then hot rolls and tea on the balcony overlooking the canal at the foot of the garden, where our boat was moored, and I could set aside my apprehensions.

Today I would walk the two kilometres into Isleham to visit shops, the necessary exercise to offset hours spent over my work, but first I wanted to tackle the next stage. The canvas was a panorama of the fens at sunset, this time an upbeat sky of reds and golds over waterways shining brightly among the reaped fields of summer, with bailed hay and swallows on the wing – something I was sure my agent would like. The dark visions called, and I had begun sketching for a portrait of my wild horsemen against an angry sky, but income came first.

I changed into jeans and shirt, made fresh tea and went barefoot into my studio. I opened a window to release the odours of paint, dryers and linseed oil, and took in the project, which stood propped on a special timber frame. Two metres was the widest I had worked to date, and the long horizon never failed to impress the eye. I opened oils, took palette in hand, selected a red sable from a jar on a side bench, and was soon engrossed, laying on the underpainting for the waterways to reflect the sky.

I thumbed a remote control and some soft jazz floated quietly in the air. This was my most productive time, when I had the place to myself and could submerge in the project, feel the finished image, making my way along the road to completion. A final painting is never quite as seen in the mind's eye, but this is between the artist and his or her own soul.

They say when the mind is fully occupied, the levels not under conscious control can come to the fore – our perceptions open wider. I believe this, as in the depths of my concentration I glanced up and he was there.

By the door, standing quietly, watching me work. Fair haired, dark eyed, dressed in wool and flax, a leather jerkin, boots of sheepskin bound with rawhide; a gold-hilted sword hung at his hip. His expression was impassive, but for the eyes, and their intense stare drilled into me. I yelped and almost dropped my brush – but he was gone. Between one heartbeat and the next the man, seemingly tangible, vanished, leaving me with a pounding in the chest and a mind unwilling to accept what I'd seen.

For he was the leader of the riders in the painting I would soon begin, and very familiar to me.

* * *

I couldn't tell Derek – how could I? At this point I didn't want to credit my own thoughts, and when I left the house the afternoon sun helped me sideline the very notion. I was tired, perhaps, a bit overwrought, under pressure to complete work for which I'd lost my enthusiasm. Even to me, as reasons they sounded a bit feeble, and I pressed hard on the way, using exercise to clear my head. A few items at the shops – more an excuse to be out than any real need – and I found myself loath to go home just yet. I took a seat in The Rising Sun pub, on Sun Street, ordered tea and apple pie, and tried to organise my thoughts.

This is an old land. Before the drainage projects began in earnest in the 1600s, the whole region had been mainly lake-land, and Isleham was a genuine island, a low hillock rising above the relief of the waters, thus a village centre from ancient times. 19th and 20th century architecture characterises the village for the most part, though the pub dates from the 17th, and original, refurbished coach houses survive in many places. A converted stable block still stands behind this very pub. Many houses front directly onto the narrow streets, elements of times before the coming of the car. Technology is a thin veneer atop old habits, and in light of this perhaps I should look upon my dreams – my visions – the same way.

Over my initial shock by this point, I could be analytical. Was I frightened by the apparition? *Was* it an apparition? Or a memory latent from my dreams, given substance by my subconscious as I concentrated, and presented momentarily to my waking eyes? I had no answer, but wasn't afraid. Despite his intense stare, I sensed nothing malevolent – more an interest. He had reason to be here, I felt.

Was our home haunted?

I shrugged to myself as I enjoyed the pie. How could a recent housing development be haunted by a man who, by his clothing, dated from Saxon times? This set me wondering, thinking back on the all-too-brief treatment of early England in school history classes, where it's dealt with peremptorily in a junior term, as if the real history of this country only begins with the Norman invasion. I swallowed a flash of annoyance and recalled that in Late Antiquity there had been seven independent kingdoms, and the local area had fallen either in Mercia or East Anglia, depending on the date and the ambitions of the kings involved.

Isleham is just a village and has no public library, so I pulled out my tablet and did a little web surfing, reacquainting myself with the centuries between the Romans departing and the Normans arriving, punctuated by the Vikings in between. It was turbulent, records are scant – they're not called the Dark Ages for nothing – and academic best guesses are only gradually filling in the blanks. I had still not accepted that 'my man' was anything more than a figment of my imagination, but I felt better knowing a little more about his world.

I also knew the painting wouldn't wait. When I packed up, I walked briskly north up Waterside Road to Fen Bank, then across the bridge into the marina, and home to Kingfisher Road. As I opened the front door I let myself feel for anything out of the ordinary – any vibration that might tell me I was unsafe – but only fresh air and quiet greeted me.

Now I set up a new canvas and studied my design sketches. I reworked the dress of the mounted figures a little to accord with my impressions from the momentary vision, and began the laying-out process. At times I would glance over my shoulder at the door, but now that I was primed to expect it, no warrior with wild, fair locks ever greeted my gaze.

* * *

When Derek came home he frowned over the new painting. It's not unusual for me to have two or more underway at once – oils take time to dry, after all – but the new piece was so great a divergence that it warranted a raised eyebrow. I told him I was inspired, and he accepted it; but all evening, as we went out to dinner at The Cutter Inn, by the river up in Ely, he suspected there was more to it. Bless him, he let it be – sure I would tell him in my own time.

Dinner on a mild evening for a couple without kids leads to many things, and we enjoyed our quality hours. But after midnight, as Derek snored softly in our wide bed, I found myself standing at a window, looking north across the river to the farms. The crops were rising with the new season, and the night sky was clear and faintly luminous. It's not the world of olden times; everything here is made by human hands, right down to the very meanders of the river, which has been adjusted many times over the centuries to keep these stretches navigable. 'My man' wouldn't know the fens of today.

For a moment I had the distinct impression I wasn't alone, almost felt the chill touch of a hand at my back, and broke out in a cold sweat. I turned sharply, but there was no one there... With a deep breath, I shook my head and ran my fingers through my black mane. *Was* I imagining things? Part of me was beginning to doubt.

* * *

Doubts were laid to rest in the arms of Morpheus, for my dreams that night went beyond anything I had known before.

I stood on green meadowland, smelled the rain, heard the thunder, sensed that odd, acrid feeling of a storm, and I *saw* the horsemen. Heard the jingle of harness, caught the strong whiff of bodies rarely washed as they cantered by – not seeing me, as though I were the ghost here. But something was familiar about this place; the long sheet of a glimmering lake was new to me, but the general lie of the land whispered something I couldn't quite catch. Rich forest crowded upon the rises of a green sea, and I followed the horsemen as a sense of foreboding closed around me.

He was there, the flaxen-haired warrior, accompanied by a single retainer; they moved intently, their business dire. Swords were slackened in sheaths, round shields were slung at their backs, and as they disappeared into the forest, up a low rise, I panted to keep up. *Too late*, part of me cried out, *I'm too late!* And not long after I entered the wood, I heard a terrible cry that shook me from my sleep, so that I sat up, heart beating wildly.

Derek slept on at my side and I pressed a hand to my mouth, part of me wishing he would wake to comfort me – another part glad he didn't, for explanations would be complex. I steadied my inner trembles with a feat of will and after a while slid out of bed, padded downstairs and poured a whisky. The spirit burned down comfortably and I breathed deeply, hanging onto the dream with every shred of will. What did it mean?

Almost against my better judgement, I went into the studio and switched on the full-frequency lights to work again on the new canvas. I drew a painting smock over my nightgown, tied back my hair and immersed myself in the work, finding solace as the paint flowed, storm clouds taking shape even as I heard a rumble in the distance. What a strange circle in time – a storm then, a storm now.

The clock in the hall softly chimed 4am as I worked, and I knew I must return to bed before long. *Just a little more,* I thought, and painted on. The angry sky was taking shape nicely behind the figures, whose underpainting was now dry, and I began to render the values of the costumes and horses. It seemed to fall together effortlessly, though I'd rarely painted figures in oils. Even the composition had given me no pause.

The storm drew nearer as I worked, and I was growing tired once more. I heard 4.30 on the hall clock and decided enough was enough. I set my brushes aside and hung my smock, turned out the lights and headed for the stairs.

A lightning flash somewhere far across the rolling farmlands illuminated the window on the top landing, and my breath caught in my throat as, just for an instant, I saw him. He stood at the top of the stairs, looking down at me, silhouetted in the purple-white glare, but the next flash moments later revealed nothing. I paused with a hand on the rail and had to force myself to ascend, to pass through the very space the apparition had occupied. I sank into bed with the chill feeling that whatever was happening was far beyond my ability to comprehend, let alone influence.

Yet, for all the strangeness, I found myself not really frightened. I was *privileged* to be made part of something as old as this land.

* * *

Derek could tell I wasn't quite myself. I felt tireder than usual and somewhat withdrawn. We sat over breakfast until he missed his morning call at work, and I admitted no more than being a bit down – too many hours alone, I suggested. A lie, and not fair to Derek – his job occupied him as surely as mine commanded my day. I felt bad about it, but couldn't make myself tell him the truth. The moment he left I was on my tablet, researching the Dark Ages again, looking for academic illustrations of clothing and horse harness, anything that might support or refute the images in my mind.

With a few pictures saved, I returned to the painting, working on it to the exclusion of the panorama, trying not to be impressionistic in my haste, and from time to time I glanced at the doorway. Now I was almost sorry he didn't appear, but as with all things spontaneous, it couldn't be forced. In the spirit of the moment, I spoke to the air around me.

"If there's someone here, you've made yourself obvious. I'm listening.

Can you speak to me?"

At once I felt like a fool, as I received the expected silence, but when I changed to smaller brushes and began to develop the features of the proud rider I could almost feel a shadowy presence. *I'm doing it*, I thought, from my heart to his. *If this builds a bridge, so be it. Can you tell me what it is you want?*

I painted on for a while, stopped for a drink, returned to the job as the morning aged, and concentrated hard. Part of me felt he was here, while the rational part was ready to dismiss it all even now; but I couldn't set aside the piece, and my mind raced ahead to grander scenes, panoramas perhaps, with these tough, free horsemen as their theme and soul.

Maybe I was tired from my broken rest, perhaps it was the warm morning or the paint fumes, but after a while I found myself nodding. Though I fought it the first time, the second I let it take me. I relaxed back in my chair and let my breathing shallow away...

And I was in the wood. He stood at my shoulder, unseen, a ghost of a ghost, guiding me to something it was imperative I see.

I hurried on, not really feeling my steps, aware the horsemen were coming, my companion and his. I heard the drumbeat of hooves behind me as I rushed ahead, and when they passed me I was in time to see them draw rein in a clearing where two strangers waited. They were dressed differently, cloaks of vivid green over metal-studded corselets, and their horse trappings varied subtly. Perhaps different tribal groupings – was I seeing the stylistic differences between Saxons and Angles? I was out of my depth; they were all Dark Ages warriors to me, and I concentrated on what was happening.

My 'friend' dismounted, his companion a moment later, and hands were raised in greeting. I could not follow their speech – the language was close to the root of English, its divergence point from German and Dutch – but it seemed a clandestine meeting was in progress, my man, a minor chieftain, making some surreptitious negotiation with a neighbouring people. I had time to appreciate the strength of his features, a certain Teutonic beauty to the hard jaw and high check bones, and I sensed the nobility with which he confronted his dealings.

Thus my rush of panic and need to scream a warning as his companion drew a dagger and plunged it into his ribs. My hands flew to my mouth in the dream. I wanted to wake, but he wouldn't let me – I felt his hands on my shoulders as he stood behind me, making me watch as his living self was done to death. Blood splashed upon the forest green.

When his cries were no more, the treacherous companion rose from his work, hands red to the wrist, shaking badly. One of the smiling strangers unhitched a purse from his belt and tossed it at the man's feet; then he and his companion took up the body and lugged it between them, the dagger still jutting from its torso.

My attention was directed to the weapon and held there by force. The blade seemed bronze, not the iron common by this time, and the handle was of bone, wrapped with rawhide. The pommel was also carved bone, worked with a crest, and the blood from the murderer's hands had invaded the engraving, showing the design in stark relief: three swans, upon a lake, inside a circle.

Still trembling from shock, I followed the warriors as they carried the dead chieftain and soon emerged on the far side of the islet, where what I intuitively knew was the Lark rolled by. Here, they rolled the body in a hide, weighted it with rocks, bound the package with ample thonging, then hefted the mass and flung it into the green-brown waters.

As the foam faded on the ripples I looked up, teary eyed, across green meadows to the misty outline of a Saxon abbey, touched by late afternoon sun. Then the dream dissipated and I came to wakefulness with no apparent dislocation, my brush still in my hand and the work before me.

* * *

I walked around the house, trembling, sipping a whisky, aware the spirit had left me for a time but knowing intuitively what he wanted.

Justice.

Perhaps I was the first one sensitive enough to hear his call, the first willing to believe it, after he had inhabited this land down the centuries – a terrible thought. 1200 years? Perhaps time passes differently for those on the other side; I certainly hope so. Maybe those he reached out to in the past fled in terror or retreated into prayer and penance to escape what should not be. Had priests attempted *exorcism?*

As soon as my hands would obey me, I took pen and paper and drew out the crest I'd seen, the silhouette of three swimming swans, stacked vertically, seen from the left, necks arched back-over in a sharp S, a circle around them. Next, I photographed it with my phone, scaled and cropped the image, cleaned it up, then went to Google to reverse-image search.

I was amazed when something substantially similar appeared at the first attempt, from a folk archive in Bury St Edmonds. It was an ancient heraldic crest belonging to a family extinct since the 1500s, thought to be descended from antiquity. The Tudor-era version had many other elements; the circle had become a laurel wreath, water was more explicitly suggested under the birds, a Latin inscription curled around the foot on a banner, there were stars above the birds – but the design remained substantially the same.

The family name had been Alden. The name fell from use after the coming of the Normans in 1066, afterward smoothed to *Alder*, more pleasing to the Francophone ear than the Germanic original, perhaps. Thus they remained, until the failure of their line in the time of Henry VIII. They had done well enough, then gone the way of so many – debts, ventures, duties, changing times.

They were long since dust, so there was nothing I could do beyond drawing attention to a curious historical footnote; but that called for something concrete, and I was already thinking ahead. As soon as I matched the crest, I took watercolours and pre-stretched paper and swiftly rendered the view from the riverbank where the murdered chieftain had been disposed of: dark water, reflections, reeds on the far side, the green meadow and trees in the distance, a lowering cloudscape, and evening light striking the half-seen abbey over the woods.

The abbey was the key. Most had gone to ruin after 1539 and the Dissolution. Many crumbled utterly under the storms of centuries; many more were plundered for building stone, much as the ancient monuments of earlier times had been to complete churches. Nothing might survive at all – above ground. I was looking for the site of a ruined ecclesiastical building, just north of an ancient course of the River Lark. If I could find it, my man's bones would lie almost directly south, near a low rise which had once been forested.

I sensed him smile as I reached these conclusions, knowing the dagger, with its telltale crest, would be at least as durable as bone; maybe even his sword remained. If one survived, so would the other, and the mark would tell its tale.

His name was *Eadwulf*, I realised, not knowing where the information came from. I looked it up, found it derived from the Old English for 'fortune' and 'wolf' – strangely fitting, as he seemed every bit the adventurer. "Well, Eadwulf, my friend," I mused as I took lunch on the veranda, "I have a few ideas. All will be revealed."

He seemed more relaxed, hovering unseen at my side, and I was no longer troubled by the thought.

* * *

I returned to the panorama, put in a few solid hours, then a little more on the horsemen, and was cleaned up before Derek came home. He sensed I was in better spirits, though still guarding something. As long as I assured him I was all right, he was willing to let my secret lie.

That night, Eadwulf did not come to my dreams. I slept soundly, woke refreshed, and things seemed to be returning to normal. I painted with a will, though I spent time each day casting my net wider, consulting documents and charts in obscure online databases. At last I found what I was after by combining information from two different archaeological surveys.

Both were based on aerial photography which, when performed in the dawn hour, showed up remarkable details in relief that were lost at all other times. One was a resistivity and ground-penetrating radar survey of the foundations of a vanished complex of early medieval buildings, which, by their extent and layout, suggested an abbey. So far, so good. The other drew on records from the commercial owners of the navigable River Lark in the 17th and 18th centuries, again using aerial imaging to find depressions and elevations in the landscape.

I almost laughed when I saw their charts; lost river courses snaked across farmland as elongate depressions, often in the midst of open grain fields. I overlaid one chart on the other, and found an extinct meander about a hundred metres north of the present course of the river, circling a rise revealed by contour charts, more or less directly south of the abbey foundations. It was about two kilometres east, near the village of West Row.

I thumped back in my chair and thought earnestly, *Eadwulf, my friend, that's the best I can do. Now it's down to luck – what's survived and what hasn't.* Part of me wanted to bring Derek into my adventure, but the chance of his scorn kept me from it. *Not just yet,* I reasoned. If it proved out in any tangible way, then I would share all.

I made further discreet inquiries as summer progressed, took our cabin cruiser on afternoon trips along the Lark to the southeast, had picnics on green river banks and watched the crops stand tall. I became adept at reading maps, and found the closest point to the ancient meander – feeling the place and matching it to the dream burned into my memory. And I was more certain than ever I had found the spot.

For much of this time Eadwulf was my silent companion, unseen but often present, watching. But gradually he became impatient, and I felt his desperation. I calmed him with words of understanding, but felt that, like any good man, he had his temper, and the frustration of the ages was heavy upon him.

I painted while summer blossomed, and green became gold as the crops reached harvest. This was the point I was waiting for: when the fields were reaped, I could walk up from the river without disturbing the wheat and betraying my trespass... I told him this as the year passed the longest day, and was sure he had rearranged brushes on my table in the agony of his waiting.

"Not long," I said to the air of my studio on a bright afternoon when I felt his needs most keenly. "Patience, as I have said, my friend." But my heart raced when, at my side, the jar holding my brushes tipped by itself with a clatter.

Now I rose, looked around and folded my arms. "I'm sorry you're hurting, my friend. But being angry with me will not make it come any sooner. I'm doing my best for you. Don't drive me away." My tone was concerned but firm, and I sensed his presence fade, a sulkiness in his air which disappointed me. I gathered the brushes back into their holder and set it upright. "No mischief," I said firmly into the afternoon warmth, but I felt unsettled for the rest of the day.

Weeks went by and I was untroubled by dreams, but Eadwulf's frustration made him a difficult companion. I was constantly on my guard against the tinkering of a bored ghost, and felt our understanding suffered. His self-interest was insulting after the effort I'd expended on him... I smiled with a shake of my head at that thought. It was almost as if a relationship were going wrong.

But our resolution was not far away now, and I cajoled my friend to endure a little longer. A development convention took Derek down to London, and I manoeuvred things for him to spend an extra night with family, an easy indulgence. This gave me ample chance, and on a clear, warm evening I sent our boat thrumming softly down the Lark as summer stars turned over the reaped grain lands and insects sang in the night.

A metal detector had been difficult to purchase without arousing questions about bank statements, but I'd managed it. I chose a powerful model, and tested it thoroughly in our garden, headset on to deaden the monotonous audio tone. I'd plotted the approximate area of my search and taken GPS coordinates for each corner of a rectangle; all I need do was follow the GPS on my phone to ground zero.

This was the theory, at least. When I reached my mooring point and turned off the engine, the quiet of the night closed around me, and I literally felt Eadwulf at my side. *Courage*, he seemed to whisper hopefully, positively. *It's almost done.* I wanted to believe as much as he – I had actually begun to fear his rage, should he be disappointed. So much depended on what I found.

I threw a line ashore and jumped to the bank. A footpath ran alongside the river, and I dropped the line over a post by the path, then drew the boat snugly into the shore and reached into the well for my equipment. Perhaps I was taking a risk, being out and about in the small hours alone, but I hoped our business wouldn't take long. I shouldered the metal detector and set my phone screen for minimum brightness, brought up the GPS and walked up from the river through bushes and rank grass.

About fifty metres on I crossed a farm access road, and before me the stubble of late summer ran about 250 metres more to the village road. I walked silently, breath bated, all kinds of thoughts filling me. This was the very ground where murder had happened early in the 9th century... Eadwulf had been betrayed by his retainer on the barely-discernible rise I had just crossed, and here – here, his enemies had dumped him into the river.

I reached the coordinates for the southwest corner of the grid and stood very still, heart racing. The hide may have protected Eadwulf's body from fish long enough for him to be covered by mud. If so, perhaps something of him remained, two or three metres below the surface – and both the knife and sword should register, deteriorated though they would be. The golden hilt would not have changed in any way.

With my heart in my mouth, I unslung the detector, drew on the headset and flicked on the power. A little fine tuning, and I held my phone in my left hand to guide me as I walked a transect to the southeast corner of the box, listening for the variations in tone that would tell me one metal or another was under my feet. I concentrated, hearing occasional squeaks and blips – an ancient horseshoe nail maybe, a fragment of fencing wire – but this was well-turned agricultural land, unlikely to accumulate rubbish.

I reached the far corner, turned and spaced the next transect by two metres to make my way back – nothing. Two meters further north, I walked the straight line again, scanning all the way. After half a dozen lengths, I was becoming disheartened and rested my ears from the tone, looked around in the blue night, and listened carefully. But for the lights of the village off to the northeast, I was alone with the stars.

Back and forth, on and on, I hoped for that change in tone that would tell me gold or bronze was down there, but after half an hour I had nothing. I paused again, sighed, let my wide-open pupils take in the night, and was heartsore at the thought I might let Eadwulf down. At the thought of him I glimpsed, just for an instant, his familiar outline standing in the dark farther north, near the far end of the box, and I smiled tightly. *Just maybe...*

When I reached that end I turned at right angles and scanned the area, and in one minute I had a reading. The tone changed acutely into the ranges I was searching for, indicating bronze, iron and gold, and I could have wept, for this was all the tangible evidence I might ever see. It might be nothing at all, was unlikely to be more than long-buried waste, even World War II junk. But I knew I'd reached my limits, and logged the coordinates of the contact before I headed directly back to the boat.

Now it was all about subterfuge, and at least Eadwulf understood *that*.

* * *

The Archaeology Department of Cambridge University received an anonymous tip concerning a metallic contact at certain coordinates coinciding with an ancient river course. While I knew their purview was science on the world stage, there was always the chance some grad students would take the opportunity for field experience to put in a test-pit at the *X* I had given them.

Weeks went by as I painted and held silence about my nocturnal forays, and I sensed Eadwulf growing restless again. I spoke softly to him in the night, asked for his patience – and at last a news story passed across my tablet one morning. An excavation was being performed while the farmlands stood fallow.

In late summer, the news was full of images of an interesting find: a partial skeleton accompanied by a badly corroded iron sword, the gold hilt of which remained pristine, and who seemed to be the victim of murder, as the lethal weapon – a dagger – remained in his thoracic region. A professor was interviewed, describing a heraldic crest, one of the earliest thus far discovered...

I walked down to the riverbank and sat in the sun, feeling my man at my side, and could only close my eyes to the bright day and sense his touch, his thanks, his overwhelming flood of relief, for he understood no more was possible. A 1200-year-old murder had been revealed, the Alden line connected; this was as close to justice as he might ever come, and he relaxed. I almost sensed him lie back on the riverbank, heave a sigh as old as time, and look up at me with silent gratitude.

A moment later, my impression of him was gone.

My dark thoughts lifted; my urge to paint in blacks and reds abated – but I had found a new market for Constable-fanciers and continued to paint the fens of yesteryear under my now-trademark storm clouds. However, up toward Christmas I was approached by the team from Cambridge via my agent, for permission to exhibit my painting of the horsemen under the stormy sky, as a backdrop to their public presentation of the sword and dagger from the excavation, at the town hall in nearby Mildenhall. They were amazed at the similarity in the depicted objects, and felt it was the perfect compliment to 'their' discovery. Perhaps some wondered, putting two and two together regarding the anonymous tip, but none mentioned it, and I fielded questions about inspiration skilfully at the opening of the exhibit. I saw eyes go from the sword in the glass case to my painting, and heads shake in wonder at the fact the painting had appeared on my agent's website months before the sword came to light. Soon after, I was approached to illustrate a historical text, and another new market beckoned.

I've never told Derek about my summer's adventure – there seems no point. We're happy, Eadwulf is at peace, and the secret of the Lark is told at last.

THE SCARLET M

MICHAELE JORDAN

"I really shouldn't have used magic," admitted Kay, looking down at the body. "I knew the price would be high, and I figured there was bound to be some natural means available. I mean, it's not like she was a celebrity with a bodyguard." She shook her head. "But I just couldn't get it together. I never dreamed she would be so hard to kill."

I expected her to turn and go. The morgue was cold and there was no place to sit, not to mention that the body was more than usually unattractive. A real mess, in fact. But Kay just stood there, looking down, as if she was waiting for the body to sit up or something.

Actually I was the one waiting for something. I had thought the body might open its eyes – or rather open the one eye that still had an eyelid to open. That can happen when you bring a body face to face with its murderer, which was the reason I'd brought Kay to see it. That hadn't happened yet. But then, it didn't need to happen. Kay had confessed.

Turned out we were both right, in the end. A moment later the corpse did open its eye. It did sit up. With one hand, it clutched at the shreds of flesh still hanging from the hole where its chest had erupted, like a woman pulling her robe closed. With the other, it reached toward Kay. Maybe it intended to point accusingly. But the wrist bones were damaged so the hand dangled limply and the arm trembled, making the overall effect more beseeching than confrontational. It didn't have enough neck left intact to talk, but it made a mewling sound. I don't like that kind of thing, but I'm used to it. I didn't gag.

Neither did Kay. She looked the corpse right in its glazed eye and said, "Can the crap, Jenny. You had it coming."

The hand fell away and, for a minute, the two faces seemed to hang in the air, staring at each other. They were almost nose to nose, like crazy house mirror images of each other. Then the dead one fell away, back to her cold couch. I swear that even with her face ruined, Jenny managed a sulky pout.

Kay turned away at last and looked up at me. I reminded myself that deep-set brown eyes always looked sad, no matter what the person was really feeling. "So what now, Mr Blake?" she asked. "Are you going to take me to jail?"

I should have done just that, of course. I know that now. Hey, who am I kidding? I knew it then. But I didn't. Instead I said, "No need to rush. They'll send someone to arrest you soon enough." She didn't answer, just went on looking at me, so I said, "You hungry?"

There was a steak joint down the street. It wasn't bad, as steak joints went, and a whole lot better than you'd expect in that neighborhood. Just walking down the street felt like a military operation, with a panhandler stalking us on every corner, while the junkies lay out on the sidewalks, waiting to trip us. I gotta admit, even I get nervous walking Vine Street after dark, and I've got a gun. Kay stayed close – not quite clinging to my arm, but nearly. I didn't hate that.

She ordered a steak. First time in my life I took a woman to this sort of joint and she didn't order lobster. Always order the most expensive thing on the menu, when somebody else is paying, right? But not Kay. That filet mignon wasn't even the most expensive steak they had (that would be the porterhouse). Of course, it might have cost more if it had been big enough to feed a bug.

She took neat, tiny bites, laying her knife and fork down after each cut and occasionally sipping her wine. She glanced over her shoulder a few times, but always looked back to me with a smile – hardly forced at all.

It just didn't make sense. "Why'd you do it?" I asked at last.

She froze, then laid down her fork with a bite of meat still on it. Her eyes slid off to the left while she thought about it. "Do you really want to know? You won't like it." I nodded. She shrugged. "She joined my garden club."

She was right. I didn't like it. So I waited. She retrieved the abandoned bite of steak. But I'm good at waiting. And women like to talk. They don't hold out for long.

When the pause had dragged on too long, she said, "What do you want to hear? I hated her. Surely that's obvious. So I killed her. I know I'm supposed to be sorry. I should be. But I'm not. I'm glad she's dead. God, but I'm glad she's dead." She smiled and reached for her wine. But then she caught a glimpse of something behind her. Her eyes widened and her breath caught. The little smile went away. Interesting. I didn't see anything behind her except the bar, and the same dumpy bartender she'd barely glanced at when we came in.

"But you used to be friends," I pointed out. "College roommates and all that."

She shrugged. "I was fat in college."

That surprised me. She wasn't fat now. Not a slinky knockout like Jenny used to be, but pretty — very pretty, I would have said — solid, but well-proportioned, with broad shoulders and nice curves. She worked out regularly, I happened to know. So maybe college roommates weren't always friends. "She put you down? Because she was hot, and you were fat?"

Kay shook her head. She risked another glance back, and her voice was a little faint when she answered. "No, nothing like that. Jenny always took very good care of all her little lost puppies." I could hardly hear the bitterness in her voice. "She had a whole circle of devoted losers. We were all so grateful to be noticed by one of the popular girls."

Women. I went back to something I understood. "So you used to be fat? Does that mean no dessert?"

Her eyes lit up and she grinned like a ten-year-old. "Of course not! Except... Do you think I should have the chocolate mousse or the crème brulée?"

I don't usually fall for that kind of thing, but I had to smile. "Why don't we have both and split them?" I figured I wouldn't get more than a couple of bites of either one, but that was okay. I ordered another scotch.

Turned out it wasn't just me that didn't get much of the dessert. She took a really big spoonful of the chocolate mousse, sighed, and licked a little taste off the top. It took her a long time to eat the whole spoonful. But when she put the spoon down, she peeked right and sucked in her breath. The chair beside her was pulled far enough back for someone to sit on the edge. I don't know when that happened. I was sure it had been tucked under the table when we sat down.

Kay pushed her dessert away and turned pointedly back to me. "I sort of expected the police to be here by now," she said. "How long do you think I have before they arrest me?"

Despite what I'd told her, I wasn't actually expecting the police. Not now, not later. Magical murders are hard to solve, and even harder to prove. That's where I come in. "You in a hurry?"

She stared at me incredulously. The penny dropped. "You didn't call them." I didn't answer; instead I made a show of reaching for the check and pulling out my glasses, like I was checking the total. Actually I don't need glasses. But the lenses in these were Glass, with a capital G.

I still couldn't see much, just a shimmer in the air, like heat distortion. That was bad news. A minor Malevolence, I should have been able to see plainly. But this thing was Veiled, which took a lot of Power. What had Kay called up? She shouldn't have needed that much Power just to blast someone she didn't like.

41

She was still mulling over how I hadn't called the police. "Then who are you working for?"

"That's confidential," I told her, and signaled the waiter.

"But…" She shrugged and gave up. "Well, if you're not going to call the police, will you help me?" Eyelashes came into play. Beneath them, her eyes were still large and brown. "I'm in trouble," she told me, and that was about as true as true gets. "There's something after me. Can you see it?" She pointed.

"Tell it to go away," I said

She looked at me like I was crazy. "What?"

"You summoned it," I reminded her. "So it's yours. Command it."

Her eyes narrowed and her shoulders stiffened as she turned back to the empty chair. "Back off. Back off now."

I still had my Glasses on. It grew a little more visible as it focused its energy on resisting Kay. There weren't any details, but I could see something that looked like a woman in shadow. I saw it shudder and tremble and melt. Then it drew itself back together, a little further off. "Tell it to stay there," I whispered. The odds were good it couldn't hear me. Kay was the only real thing in its world.

"Stay," she commanded, and there was real Power in her voice.

I'd already thrown some money on the table. I grabbed Kay's hand and ran, and she half ran, half stumbled after me. We bumped into somebody at the bar. They cursed, but I paid no attention, just kept running, and I don't think Kay even noticed. She just went on whispering over and over, "Stay. Stay."

We ran up Fifth, toward bright lights, crowds and expensive entertainment, until I spotted a taxi ahead. As soon as I saw it, I reached – still running – into my pocket for a pinch of the powder I always keep stashed there. I stuck it in my mouth and chewed it up into a wad. When we stopped, I spat it into Kay's face. I hailed the taxi just as she collapsed into my arms.

The cabbie didn't like me hauling an unconscious woman into the back seat, so I muttered something about too many tequila shots, and pinched Kay under the arm. She almost roused and murmured, "We go'n' home?" The cabbie relaxed and started driving. Kay fell back into my arms.

He drove us to Woodburn by DeSales, where I don't live, and we picked up another cab. This time I said my wife was sick. I grabbed a third cab in North College Hill. The fares were adding up but Kay was good for it.

Eventually we ended up at my place – not the one in Blue Ash, that's just for the legal records – the one on Kirby, just behind St Therese Little Flower

Church in Western Hills. It's very respectable, nobody there knows my right name, and on some jobs, it's not a bad idea to be near a church.

I laid her out on the couch and sealed the door. Nothing fancy: just salt, a few chalked hex signs and a carefully placed candle. But solid. When I turned around she was sitting up, rubbing her eyes and blinking. I didn't like that. She shouldn't have woken up until I said so. "You should be safe for now," I told her. "Your Stay Command held it long enough for us to get out of range, and I spun a few circles to confuse it."

She looked groggy, and wiped her face. "God, did you spit on me? Ew!"

I grinned. "I call it Pause Powder. My brother invented it. He was a whiz at Instrumentality. I've got a ton of stuff you don't need Power to use." She glared, sort of halfway between annoyed and disgusted, and wiped at her face again. "Get over it. I had to make you… psychically inaudible. So even if your Stay failed, it wouldn't be able to hear you."

She nodded, a little grudgingly, and thought about what I'd said. "You don't have Power? But you must have Sight?"

"Nope. No Sight, no Voice, no Touch. You said it yourself. 'The price was too high.' "

"But you know."

I shrugged. "My brother had Power."

"Had?"

I didn't want to talk about it. "So what did you Call? And how did you do it?" She turned away with a pout. "I can't protect you if I don't know what it is."

Her eyes went every which way, looking for a way out of answering. She didn't see one. So she reached into her purse and pulled out a book. She kept her face turned away so that she wasn't looking at it when she handed it to me.

Practical Magic was the title. It looked ordinary but, of course, it wasn't. As soon as I touched it, it radiated euphoria. It wanted to be held and used, so it tickled my pleasure centers to lure me into holding it and using it. My fingers itched to curl around it. Instead I got some gloves. By then her fingers had closed so tightly around it, I had to jerk it out of her hand.

It fell open immediately, showing text on the right page and a picture of Jenny on the left. The picture of Jenny was mesmerizing – man, she had been gorgeous. It took me awhile to make myself look at the text.

"Huh?" I looked back at Kay. "This is a love spell."

She sighed. "Yeah. I told you, I didn't want to kill her with magic. I figured if I just made her love me a lot, she'd give me an opening to do it one of the usual ways." I stared at her. It was the craziest thing I'd ever heard. She shrugged and looked away. "I guess I did something wrong."

"You don't actually know how love spells work, do you?"

"Sure I do. It tells you right there." She pointed at the book. "Ten drops of blood – and you can use your own, that was another reason for going with the love spell. Most of the other spells, you had to kill a cat or something. Then you add ..."

"No," I said. "Not how you launch it. How it works. Why do you think you use your own blood in a love spell?" She gaped at me, utterly clueless. "You use your own blood because you're casting the spell on yourself."

She continued to gape. Like she hadn't even heard me and was still waiting for an answer. Finally she shook her head. "No. I told you, I cast the spell on her to make her love me."

"That's not how love spells work. You cast them on yourself to make yourself lovable to your target. And yours did work. Big time."

"No, it didn't!" Kay's fists were clenching and unclenching. "It didn't work at all! She wasn't the least bit sorry for how she treated me. She went right on laughing at me and pushing me out of her way. If anything, she got worse."

"You didn't cast a spell to make her sorry," I answered. "You cast a spell to make her love you, and she did. As much as she was able, anyway, which may not be saying much. You said yourself she didn't put you down in college. She tried to push you aside because you were the center of attention, as far as she was concerned." I could almost see the gears and cogs whirling in Kay's head as the facts fell into place. "What did you do when you thought the spell didn't work?"

"I... I repeated it," she whispered. "And then she dropped dead. I don't know why, but she did."

Ouch. "Because she already loved you as much as she could. When that wasn't enough, her heart burst right out of her body trying to love you more."

There was a slam as the door flung itself open. A cold wind blew through the room, extinguishing the candle and scattering the little heap of salt. That shouldn't have been possible. Nothing could get past that seal unless it was invited. Except...

"I thought you said it couldn't track me!" wailed Kay. She had retreated to the corner, and was huddling behind an armoire.

"It doesn't have to track you." I did the only thing I could think to do. I slapped the book closed and held it up in front of me, while I backed into the corner in front of Kay. "It IS you. Your blood, your love." The cold air took on misty shape, and something vaguely like a woman came toward me, leaning first left, then right, trying to get around me. I shifted the book back and forth to hold it off. The space between the wall and the armoire where Kay had squeezed herself was very small. I blocked it completely.

"What are you talking about?" demanded Kay. "That's not me – it's Jenny. And I don't love her. I hate her."

"Like there's a difference?" The image was solidifying as Kay spoke, her every word summoning it a little more fully into the real world. The more solid it got, the closer it pressed up against me, trying to reach around me. It looked a lot like Jenny. But not exactly. It also looked a lot like Kay. Like two out of focus photographs superimposed on each other. "If you hadn't loved her, the spell wouldn't have worked. It feeds on your love. That's the other reason you have to use your own blood."

"That's insane," she whispered, but without conviction. "Can you kill it?"

"Without killing you?" The thing was pressed gently up against me now, its body unmistakably female. The skin texture was way off, almost fuzzy, but it was warm, and it seemed to breathe on my neck as it reached its arms around me. It was really reaching for Kay, but it still felt like an embrace. The book was pressed against my stomach. I wished I had held it higher, so that it would be between me and her breasts, which were surprisingly firm – more so than any other part of her – with nipples that had grown genuinely hard. It reached a hand down, looking for an opening between my legs, I guess, but it sure felt like personal encouragement.

I had to get it further back from Kay, and I was rapidly losing the will to resist it at all. So I stepped forward into its arms, pretended it was a woman and kissed it, still walking forward. Its lips were inhumanly soft, but that only made it harder to tear free of them.

I didn't drop the book when I wrapped my arms around her, so when we reached the opposite wall the leather cover was pressed into the small of its back as I pushed myself against it. It squirmed as if eager, or maybe the book was burning it. I turned my head to Kay and croaked, "Run!"

But she didn't. Instead she followed us, pressed up against my back so I was sandwiched between them. "Slut," she spat over my shoulder. "Grabby, self-absorbed little teacher's pet. Get your hands off him. You think it's all for you, everything's yours, everybody else is just standing around waiting for a chance to suck up to you? Well, this one's here to help me. Just once, somebody's going to put me first. So why don't you just stay dead?"

It answered. It had grown so solid it could talk. "I put you first. Always."

It tried to push me away, and I let it, but I held my arms out as I backed off a step, still keeping it contained for a moment. I glanced back toward Kay. "I told you to run. I don't know how long I can hold it off."

"Don't bother," said Kay, stepping out from behind me to one side. The Jenny-thing turned toward her, and pressed up against my restraining arm. "There's no point running, is there? It'll always follow me. It'll always find me. Let's get it over with, here and now."

I nearly rolled my eyes. What a time to grow a backbone. "Don't be stupid. What do you expect to do? Just get out." She just stood there. "Really, Kay. You gotta go. Now. You only make it stronger when you engage. We need some time to work up a containment spell."

Kay shook her head. "How can you contain it away from me? Didn't you just say it is me?" Unfortunately, she had a point. "No, I'm just going to do what I should have done in the first place." She dropped into a karate stance and kicked out, under my arm, catching the Jenny-thing right in the stomach. "Kill her with my own hands."

I was pretty sure that wasn't a good idea, maybe not even possible. But the Jenny-thing doubled over, just like a real woman taking a hit. Once it was down, it was able to duck out from under my arm. It lunged at Kay before I could catch it, and then the two were rolling on the ground. "You think you can beat me?" it hissed. "Your karate always sucked. You never even got your belt."

"Yeah?" snarled Kay, gaining her feet and throwing what looked like a perfectly good punch to me. "Well, you only got yours because you were sleeping with the teacher." The Jenny-thing landed on the coffee table, which creaked and split so that the center caved in, and a lot of stuff went sliding onto the carpet. That's how solid it had gotten.

The fight was actually kind of entertaining to watch, but I knew I needed to break it up before the Jenny-thing became wholly real, not to mention what they were doing to my apartment. There wasn't time to chew up Pause Powder – which probably wouldn't work on the Jenny-thing anyway. I made my way past them to the desk and got my Stop-Watch out of the drawer.

It's a nasty, dangerous thing, so I save it for urgent. It feeds on all human energy, not just Power, and it can drain you until you drop. Even if you live, you still feel like you died with a really bad hangover. But it works.

Kay and the Jenny-thing froze in comical postures so unbalanced that they should have fallen over, only they didn't. Unlike what you see in the sci-fi movies, they weren't oblivious to the un-Stopped time passing around them. They could see and hear me. They'd have glared if they could move.

I picked up Kay and carried her to the couch. She was rigid and pale gray, which made her look as unreal as the other. It burned my skin to touch her, but I didn't want her to fall when I un-Stopped her. Then I hauled the Jenny-thing into the back room and drew a circle around it. I was already so exhausted that it seemed to weigh a ton, although it was actually a lot lighter than real flesh. I probably couldn't have lifted it, otherwise. It burned me even worse than Kay. When I had it in place, I set a Hold-box at the head of the circle.

The Hold-box was the last thing my brother invented. If he'd finished it five minutes sooner, he'd be alive today. It could hold anything. I know, because it saved me after he died. It would hold Jenny. By then I was so woozy from feeding the Watch that I had trouble remembering where my desk was, and my hands were so blistered from handling the Stopped that I could barely hit the button to turn the Watch off.

I fell forward over the desk, and lay there. There was a faint thump when Kay's limbs were released to collapse onto the couch, followed by an 'oomph'. I heard scrabbling sounds from the back room. Then thumping. Lots of thumping. Like I cared.

Minutes? Hours? Hell, maybe days later, I heard Kay croak, "Stop that," and after a pause, "Stop that!" again, louder. I made the effort to push myself upright, half expecting to see the Jenny-thing had escaped after all. But no, Kay was lying limply on the sofa with her eyes closed, whispering, "Stop it, stop it, stop it," to the empty air.

I limped to the back room. The Jenny-thing had given up thumping on the barrier, and was tumbled in a disconsolate heap at the head of the circle, its soft non-flesh piled up around the Hold-box, all ready to spill out over the edge first chance it got. And then I heard it. The thing was crying. It wasn't loud, rather a soft, almost subliminal whimper, but once you heard it, you couldn't stop hearing it. It filled the mind, the room, the world with sorrow. It was a song of utter heartbreak, of loss beyond bearing and the futility of life when love is dead. God, I hate it when women cry.

Kay came up behind me and laid her head on my shoulder, and we both looked down. "Can you stop it?" she asked, not sounding hopeful, just curious.

"I'll try." I didn't sound very hopeful either. But I had to try. The neighbors were bound to complain.

I checked my spell books first. I don't have a lot of them, because most spells need Power. So, nada. Kay looked through her book, too, and then got on my laptop and did a search on Silence spells. She got 7,360,000 hits. Meanwhile, I hauled out a trunk of my brother's old gadgets. Two were promising, and one was a maybe. All three required assembly, prep and elaborate calibration. Eventually, it turned out that none of them would do the job. All the time we were working, the crying went on and on.

I paused a little after daybreak. Some creatures hate and fear sunlight. The Jenny-thing wasn't one of them. It huddled up a little more, and a new note of earthy misery crept into its keening, but it didn't flee and it didn't stop crying.

Kay was sitting right next to it, with her shoulder hunched like she had an ear ache. I hadn't noticed when she gave up on the computer search, but it looked like she'd been sitting there a while. "Hey, Kay," I said. "One thing we haven't tried – distance. What say we go grab some breakfast and see if we can still hear it from Rookwood?"

It took her a long time to answer. "Won't work. I'd hear it on the other side of the world." She reached out a hand. It looked like she meant to stroke it.

"Don't!" I grabbed her wrist. "Are you crazy?"

She turned those sad brown eyes up to me, and there were tears on her face. "It's so unhappy," she whispered. "I thought I hated her, I thought I wanted her dead, but this is too much. This is worse than death." She turned back toward the circle. "Isn't it, Jenny? I never dreamed I had the power to cause you this much pain."

It looked up when she spoke to it. It stopped crying and lifted itself halfway up, like a woman who's been beaten up by her boyfriend. "I don't understand," it whined. "You were my BFF. You were supposed to love me forever."

"But you didn't love me!" wailed Kay. "You never cared about me. You just wanted a side-kick. An audience."

Its lip quivered in a heartrending pout. "Did so love you. Gave you homemade cookies."

I pulled Kay up by the arm. "You've got to stop talking to it. Don't you see? You're feeding it. It's already way too close to real. If you let it cross over into the Here, it can't ever go back."

"It already can't go back." She sighed. "It would have to leave me to go back. You said it yourself. She loves me as much as she can." Kay shook her head. "She's a cat. Cats do love their people, you know. As much as they can. That's just not very much. 'Cause they're cats. So they still bite and scratch and care more about licking their butts than they do about you." She shuddered. "And I tortured her to death and beyond because she wasn't capable of better. How much better does that make me?"

I saw it coming a second before it happened, and tightened my grip on her arm. But that didn't stop her. She smiled at me and said, "There's only one way past this." She stepped forward, pulling her arm free of me only after the rest of her was already in the circle.

As soon as she was completely in, the Jenny-thing flung itself into her arms. "Girl! Where you think you get off being so mean to me? Good thing I can't stay mad at you!"

Kay opened her mouth to reply, but nothing came out. By then the two were fusing. First, two women hugging. Then Siamese twins. Then a woman with two heads. Finally just Kay. The look on her face...

I packed up everything I couldn't afford to lose before I called the police, and cleared out before they actually showed. It said in the newspaper she died of a heart attack. Or something.

LEVIATHAN

An Anna and Turk story

JOHN PAUL FITCH

The boy in the bag screamed.

Joe Ramsden turned and kicked the cloth sack until young Paul McGuire stopped his yelping and went quiet. He turned and waded into the knee-deep mud. Joe did not care that the mud slinked its way down the insides of his boots and in between his toes, nor that it would never wash out of his trousers. He did not care that fresh blood had dried onto his scoutmaster's shirt. None of it mattered anymore.

Joe had brought the other nine kids here one by one. Sleeping pills in their soup made it easy. He trudged the journey back and forth from the scout hall to this place all afternoon. McGuire was the last of them. The Great One would be fulfilled and then he would have his reward.

He slung the cloth bag over his muscled shoulder, his thick builder's arms hefting the weight of the ten-year-old with ease and moved towards the rotting trunk of a fallen tree. Joe dropped the bag and clambered over, his breath coming in heavy gasps. Sliding into the bog, he bent double and coughed, blood flecks spattering onto the muddy ground. He gasped as a wave of nausea ran through him. His stomach distended, the things inside of him roiling and rolling over each other. He waited for the sensation to pass. The pain was more intense now. The Great One called. He needed to hurry.

Joe reached back over the log and grabbed the bag once more, his boots squelching in the mud as he pulled it over the trunk. He supposed the night was cold. It was November. Scotland was supposed to be cold in November, but he could not feel the cold upon his skin, nor did the breaths he drew chill him the way they would have done a few days ago. *No.* He was beyond that weakness now. Beyond human sensations like cold and heat and hunger. The Great One had taken all of that away. Tears pricked the corners of Joe's eyes. Tears of gratitude. The Great One had called for Joe to bring it more so that they may be saved from pain also. That's why the boy was in the bag.

By the time they reached the swamp the McGuire boy had begun to moan again. Joe looked up at the trees. They grew in a circle, with only a small crack between the thickest of the two trees for a person to squeeze between. Joe could not believe he'd found the place. Scouts had been camping on these grounds for generations and none of them, not one, had

found the grove of trees and what they protected. It was as if the world had revealed itself to him, lifted its skirts and invited him to savour its secrets.

The pine trees grew in an almost perfect circle and reached up towards the sky almost a hundred feet above. They bent towards each other, their upper branches intertwining, wrapping themselves around each other like lovers, concealing this secret place from the eyes of the sun and moon. This was indeed a secret place. *Occulted,* that was the word. The ground sloped away from Joe sharply, forming a round, muddy bowl. Joe leapt into the mud and sank up to his thighs. He pulled the bag behind him. The water of the bog brought the boy round and he began to moan once more as Joe dragged him into the centre of the grove and to the monument that stood there. The Rune-Stone. The grey, granite monument protruded from the ground and stood twice the height of Joe. The surface was flecked with streaks of silver and something that shimmered even at night. Carved into the surface of the stone was a pattern etched in crimson. It resembled a man encircled by a swirling red pattern that coiled itself around him repeatedly. At the top there was a dragon head: its jaws wide, ready to consume the figure in its grasp. All around the outside edge of the stone were runic markings, some of them worn away by the passage of time, scoured from the surface by hundreds of years of rain and wind. Joe smiled as the tears ran down his jowls.

He lifted the bag to his chest and turned it, shaking the fabric, and the McGuire boy dropped into the mud. The boy curled himself into a foetal position, his moans morphing to sobs. He blinked and looked up at Joe. He whimpered, shivering.

"Joe. Please."

Joe wiped the tears from his face as the smile spread wider and wider.

"He's coming to save you. From the pain. You'll see. He wants to save us all."

"H-help me, Joe."

The smile fled from Joe's face. "Talking only makes it harder."

He turned and waded back through the mud towards the gap in the trees. Joe was a few feet from the gap when he felt the ground shift under him. *He* was coming. Joe laughed and clambered his way up the incline.

"He's coming for you." Joe yelled to the McGuire boy. The boy glanced around, tears upon his own cheeks now. "Fear not. He is here to save you. It only hurts at first."

The boy pushed himself to his knees and tried to stand. He leant on the Rune-Stone for support. A gust of wind spun inside the circle of trees like a centrifuge. The boy fell over once more, landing on his arse. This time he did not get up. The trees shook, the trunks bent as they danced, and a wave rippled through the mud. It started just below Joe's feet and made its way around in an ever-tightening circle towards the Rune-Stone.

The McGuire boy screamed as the ground opened. Joe began to sing, joy filling his heart. He sang as the boy was pulled down into the mud. Then it was over. The trees ceased their dance, the ripples subsided, and Joe was left alone in the grove.

He sank to his knees and awaited his reward. He sank his fingers into the mud, clawing the top layer away, unveiling the fresh ground below it and the prize that was sent to him. Dozens of small white worms wriggled their way to the surface. They rolled over one another blindly as Joe reached for them, his fingers pulling dirt as he snatched them up and pushed the worms into his mouth. He did not even chew them, swallowing the worms whole, his teeth caked with dirt. More worms found their way to him, and Joe filled his fists with their bodies and pushed them into his mouth, smiling, tears streaking his face, singing through the throatfuls of grubs. He slurped the last of them between his lips and waited till the squirming in his belly stopped. Having eaten his fill, Joe stood and regarded the Rune-Stone once more.

"Thank you."

* * *

Anna Barlow rolled over and bumped against the sleeping body beside her. A staccato snoring broke out of the woman. She rolled over and snaked a hand over Anna's waist. Anna waited till the woman settled again before looking at the hand with its painted fingernails, silver bracelet and diamond wedding ring. Anna groaned.

What the hell did I do last night?

A hangover beat a tattoo behind Anna's eyes. She opened them slowly and scanned the room. An unfamiliar wardrobe, a vanity mirror, pictures of a woman and man on their wedding day. Clothes strewn across the floor. She recognised her black jeans and heavy black boots next to a sparkly pair of high heels decked with sequins.

Anna looked back at her bed partner. A mass of blonde waves nestled under the duvet. Warm breath on Anna's shoulder. Anna lifted her side of the duvet and inspected the body that lay beneath it.

Shit.

A flood of memories, initially dammed up by the fog of alcohol, burst forth.

Pub: dank, dingy, sticky floor. Whisky: copious amounts of. Jenny: sexy, older, married. She bought Anna drinks, cried on her shoulder about her bastard husband (Barry: balding, overweight, cheating). Anna showed her some cheap conjurations. None of them *real* magick. Just easy parlour tricks she often used when chatting up. She gave Jenny a tarot reading – *'You'll meet a dark stranger who will change your life'.* They left the pub arm in arm. Grabbed a taxi to the West End and canoodled in the back. Anna took her to *The Colosseum*. The dancefloor heaved with women. They ploughed right on in. More drinks, swirling lights, dancing.

Dancing. Anna shuddered.

Jenny stirred again. She rolled over to face Anna and snaked an arm across her stomach. Anna sighed. She gently lifted Jenny's arm and slid out. Anna scanned the floor for her clothes and, lifting them quietly, made her way out of the bedroom. She crept along the hallway as quietly as she could to the living room. Her stomach lurched in revolt. Too much booze, too many cigarettes, but she swallowed the bile down. Dressing quickly in the living room, she slid her leather jacket across her shoulders. Anna spotted Jenny's handbag on the coffee table.

The heavy purse inside was packed with cash. *She won't miss a couple of quid.* Anna pulled a couple of tens from the purse, enough to pay for a cab home and to buy herself a good breakfast and put it back into the handbag. A set of car keys lay on the coffee table next to an almost full pack of cigarettes and a lighter. Anna shrugged and took the cigarettes, slipping them into her inside jacket pocket. She exited the front door of Jenny's place into the fresh morning and let the door slam behind her. She walked quickly to the corner, scanning the early morning roads for a taxi.

By the time the cab pulled up opposite the *Greasy Egg Café*, the grey clouds that smothered the city had lightened somewhat. It was close to seven. The roads were filling with buses and cars; tradesmen on their way to work, bankers trying to get a start on their day. Anna slid out of the cab as rain pattered the pavement, kicking up the smell of wet, dirty tarmac. She popped the collar of her leather jacket up around her ears. A gust of wind cut through her like a scythe, mussing up her shoulder-length, punk-cut hair as she crossed the road. She splashed through a puddle and stepped up onto the opposite kerb, dodging a bright red sedan before throwing her shoulder into the café door.

The place was at its usual level of emptiness. Anna loved it for its privacy. The only people who came in were tramps with a hatful of spare change, or drunkards on their way home from a day of drinking cheap wine and beer. It was, in her opinion, perfect. Anna spotted Turk occupying their usual back booth seat, his hands folded on the tabletop, a grin spreading across his face. He waved to Anna, in his rumpled white suit and open necked blue shirt and that stupid side parting in his lank hair.

"You look like a real estate agent on holiday in Malta or somewhere shit like that," she said, throwing herself in the seat opposite. She pulled the cigarettes from her pocket and offered one to Turk. He shot her an annoyed look and waited for her to speak. Anna took a long drag, savouring the heat of the smoke as it filed her lungs. Another reason that *The Greasy Egg* was Anna's favourite place to eat was because it was one of the only places left that let her smoke indoors. Everywhere else in the city; the bars, the restaurants (not that she ever frequented anything remotely classy), the clubs, and mostly the cafes, all of them made you go outside every time you needed to spark up. But not this place. She leant back with her eyes closed and exhaled slowly, the smoke billowing in the air. Turk stared at her the whole time, expectantly. Anna gave him the finger.

"Don't even start," she said.

"I wasn't going to, honestly." Turk sniggered.

Anna glanced around for Nancy, who waved over. Nancy was already pouring her a cup of strong milky-sweet tea. Turk grinned like a lunatic.

"Give it up. I'm not biting."

"Okay... but I did tell you so," he said.

Anna gave him the finger again.

"Hi Anna," said Nancy, plonking the mug of piping hot tea on the table. "What can I get you today, love?"

Nancy looked like a stereotypical café waitress. Late 50's, chubby, bingo-wing arms, too much cheap jewellery and several inches of make-up. She often was proceeded by a haze of overpowering hair lacquer and perfume. She wore an old-fashioned beehive haircut dyed platinum with a knitting needle through it. Anna had once seen Nancy take it out and threaten a biker, forcing it against his cheek hard enough to draw blood. All because the guy had slapped her arse as she walked by. Nancy was a force to be reckoned with, but to Anna she as sweet as the tea she served.

"I'm in the mood for a full English today, Nancy."

"Ooh, someone's hungry," said Nancy, scribbling down the order and dropping the notepad into her yellow apron pocket. She pulled out an almost black cloth and quickly wiped the table. "Won't be too long, love." Her plimsolls squeaked on the linoleum floor as she made her way back to the kitchen. Anna wrapped her fingers around the warm mug, the heat spreading through her cold hands.

"So, what's new?" said Anna.

Turk looked at her quizzically.

Anna sighed. "Do we have any work?"

Turk nodded to the seat beside Anna. There was a creased newspaper there, folded, the corners curled up. Anna lifted it and opened it up. It had a coffee cup ring on it and what Anna guessed was baked bean sauce.

"Page twelve," said Turk.

Anna opened the newspaper and rifled it to the page.

"Bottom right corner." Turk gazed out of the window. Rain peppered the glass lightly. Anna ran her eyes down the page, scanning the stories and sub-headlines till she spotted it.

SCOUT TROOP MISSING

Anna mumbled the details as she read.

"Ten kids plus one troop leader... due back two days ago... no contact... camp empty... search underway. Police have no leads at this time."

She folded the paper and placed it back on the seat.

"What's so special about that? They got lost in the woods or they fell down a gorge or eaten by a mad cow or something."

Turk turned back to look at Anna. She knew that look. "You've got a feeling about this.' She ran a hand over her face. "Dammit. Come on."

They stood and Anna zipped her jacket up to the neck. She lifted the newspaper and put it under her arm and they both turned to leave as Nancy came out from the kitchen with a massive plate of food.

"Where are you going, love? I've got your breakfast."

"Sorry, Nancy. I've gotta go."

A look came over Nancy like she had discovered someone had taken a shit in one of her teacups.

"Well at least let me put it in a container for you. You look like you haven't eaten for a week."

She spun and pushed her way back into the kitchen.

"You're a good woman, Nancy." yelled Anna.

* * *

Anna pushed her way into the flat carrying a plastic container packed with a full English. Turk trailed behind her, all the languid poise of a stoned iguana.

The kitchenette held nothing more than a sink at the far end that overflowed with dirty cups and plates and several head-height cabinets that clung to the walls in a haphazard fashion. Soiled clothes lay in piles next to the washing machine and some garments of underwear dangled from a ceiling pulley. Anna slid open a drawer and fished around for a moment before pulling out a dull and not entirely clean looking fork. She popped the food container open and speared a sausage. She shoved the whole thing into her mouth and chewed it twice before swallowing then plucked a piece of crispy bacon and cracked it between her teeth.

"Shouldn't we get down to business?"

Anna spoke between mouthfuls. "Hungry. Must eat. Food good."

"Didn't your mother ever tell you that have to chew your food before you swallow it?"

"Hard to hear her when she was in the nick most of the time... and besides, it's my place and I'll eat how I like."

Turk shook his head.

"Do you miss food?" asked Anna. Turk thought for a moment before answering.

"Not anymore. I did at first, but after a while you see how animalistic it is, the consumption of other things. It's really kind of gross to witness when you no longer have any biological impulses to satisfy."

Anna finished her mouthful of bacon and looked at the greasy egg and fried toast that lay in the bottom of the container. *Dammit, he's right.* She tossed the fork down onto the counter. She moved past him and made her way into the lounge room.

Turk stepped over the threshold of the living room and instantly felt queasy. Anna had secreted a charm in the wall above the door and buried another in the floor where the carpet stopped. She mixed salt with paint and coated the door frame with it, followed by the lounge room window. Magickally speaking, the place was hermetically sealed and crossing into the room always gave Turk a quick bout of vertigo.

The lounge room contained one chair and a two-seater couch set against one wall. A small television stood in the corner on a wooden stand, an old VHS on the floor beneath it, surrounded by a dozen or so tapes. What the room lacked in furnishings it more than made up for in occult knowledge. The other three walls were entirely dedicated to bookshelves. Stuffed with books and pamphlets and leaflets on everything from Chaos Magick to Kabbalah, to Conjuring and Banishing, they varied in authors from Peter J Caroll to Aleister Crowley to John Dee. Turk admired the volumes, some ranging from the time of Queen Victoria, through to the 16th Century, to the modern day. The volumes were interspersed with items of power: daggers and occult fetishes, jewelled mirrors crusted with pearls, and small sealed boxes containing things Turk had never seen because Anna would never open them. The carpet underfoot had a pentagram woven into it, a safe space for Anna to do her workings. The room throbbed with power.

Anna slipped off her leather jacket and stripped down to her skin-tight vest. Turk admired the intricate tattoos and scars that adorned her arms. It was occult craftwork she had spent big money on. Works of art, all of them, but they were more than that. Each tattoo was a powerful symbol of protection, each with a different purpose, carved into her very flesh.

An Ankh on her left arm warned her of the presence of malevolent entities. It would throb when she was near something evil, or in the presence of a human who meant her harm. Similarly, the seven-sided star on her right palm acted as a repellent for smaller pest entities, the kind of spirits that liked to cause mischief and grief. She called them imps but usually they were anything but impish. The woman who had given her the tattoos, L'Angelle, was much sought-after in the occult world, providing protection and charms for exorbitant prices. The rest of her arms were covered with sigils of her own design, working personal spells and intents, the most potent being the large snake that meandered its way up her right bicep and over her shoulder, disappearing down inside her top. Turk knew that it went all the way down over her ribs and circled her waist. It covered the skin over every major organ in her body and had taken almost six months to complete. Her skin was a suit of magickal armour.

Turk settled down on the two-seater couch and crossed his legs, smoothing out the creases in his trousers as Anna searched a large oak chest that sat beneath the window.

Heaving the chest open, she fixed the prop against the heavy lid to stop it crashing down on her. She reached in and lifted a pair of twin wooden panels which opened outwards on brass hinges, bringing with them three small shelves on each side. The shelves were stuffed with small jars and bags of charms, vessels of powders, bottles of oils, and several wooden implements of uncertain origin. Anna rummaged in the chest with both hands, sinking into the box to her armpits. Turk heard clunking and banging as she tossed things around inside.

"Out you come," she said, and with a grunt she hoisted something up and over the edge of the chest. She pulled it free from a tangle of rope and dropped it on the ground with a thump.

Turk sat up straight.

It was a dagger. The blade was a dull brown and was etched with a florid symmetrical design. A ridged centre line ran from the hilt and down the length of the blade to the tip like a tube. The handle itself was bound in leathery hide the origin of which Turk could not ascertain and a red gem shaped like an eye was embedded into the cross guard. Anna picked it up and held it so she could inspect it. The handle was hollow and threaded inside. She peered into it, aiming it towards Turk, who she could see perched on the edge of the couch.

"What is that thing?"

"You'll see."

Anna grabbed a small cloth bag from the fold out shelf and a bottle of inky blue oil. She lifted the dagger and the other items and headed back to the kitchen. Turk's curiosity was piqued. He leapt from the couch and followed behind.

Anna leaned over the sink, the cloth bag lying on the kitchen counter next to the now open bottle of oil. Anna shot Turk a warning glance.

"Get back. This part is tricky. And a little dangerous. For you anyway."

Turk retreated to the relative safety of the hallway. Then he moved behind the door frame, just in case. Anna tugged the drawstring of the cloth bag before she took a teaspoon from the sink and gently slid it inside. She stiffened and held her breath before removing a tiny amount of grey powder on the rim of the spoon. She twisted her body at the waist, desperate not to spill a grain of the powder. She held it above the bottle and slowly began to pour the grains of powder into the oil. The oil immediately began to pop and fizzle. A head of white foam boiled up. Anna tossed the spoon in the sink. She grabbed the lid and screwed it down onto the bottle top as tightly as she could. The bottle began to dance on the kitchen bench, rattling and shaking as the reaction inside its glass walls grew more violent. The oil turned green, then yellow, orange, and red to, finally, black. After a few minutes the shaking stopped, and the kitchen grew quiet.

Anna let out the breath she had been holding for what felt like an eternity. She sat herself down on the linoleum floor, crossing her legs and leaning back against the wall.

"What the hell is that stuff?" said Turk.

Anna turned her head slowly and looked at him.

"Motivation. Right, where's that newspaper gone."

"Living room."

It was on the little coffee table. Anna grabbed the paper and opened it, ruffling through the pages till she found what she was looking for. Turk came around behind her to get a better look.

"Obituaries?" he said.

Anna ran her finger over the obituary notices, she stopped at the third from the bottom.

"Perfect. Let's go."

"But it's raining," protested Turk.

"You're a ghost, what do you care?"

* * *

The Necropolis was a beautiful place. Populated by faux-Roman and Egyptian structures, tombs, and memorials, it was a memory of aeons gone by. Old stone carvings and statues of angels made up the architecture of the place. Anna and Turk wandered among the gravestones. Anna carried a hold-all and a shovel.

"You should see this place at night, Turk. All lit up with spotlighting from below. The statues all look amazing. It's a magical place."

"Answer me this, Burkey O'Hare. Why exactly are we here in a graveyard, on a miserable Thursday, when it's pissing down? You know the kind of beings that hang around these places, right? Living *and* dead. Sometime both at the same time."

"What, like you?"

Turk shot her a look, and they kept walking. "Trust me when I say that you're probably the worst smelling thing in here, Anna Barlow."

Soon enough they came across the headstone they were looking for. Anna double checked the name on the obituary before nodding. It was a freshly laid grave. The headstone was a black marble book on a plinth which had white letters chiselled into its surface. Anna read aloud.

"Here lies Michael Peterson. Loving father, son, brother. Taken too soon."

"Shame," said Turk. "You wanna say something before we start?"

Anna looked at Turk. "Like what?"

"I don't know, a prayer, a eulogy, something respectful."

"We're not laying him to rest, Turk. Quite the opposite, in fact. Right. Keep an eye out for coppers."

"What am I supposed to do if someone comes looking? Shout 'Boo'?"

Anna plunged the shovel into the dirt.

The light was fading, and the sky had taken on a darkened hue by the time she cleared the dirt off the coffin lid. Turk leaned on the gravestone checking his fingernails. Dirty and tired, Anna tossed the shovel out of the hole. She clambered up to the edge of the grave and rummaged in the hold-all, finding the stand-alone spotlight she'd brought with her. She angled it down onto the coffin and climbed back down. The lid was covered in scratches and Anna noticed several burrows around the sides of the grave.

"Look, Turk. A few hours later and the rats would have gotten to him. We made it just in time."

Clearing the last of the dirt off the surface with her hands, Anna traced her fingers around the outside of the lid till she found the edge and, with a tug, wrenched it open.

Michael Peterson lay, suited up, on a bed of white linen. His face was caked in make-up.

Turk scoffed. "Jesus. He looks like a kid that found his mum's make-up drawer. Got enough foundation on there, mate?"

"Shut up, Turk. I bet you looked the same when they buried you."

"No chance. Look at me. I don't need make up to look good."

Peterson had already begun to swell as his insides liquefied and released gas inside his body which, despite the make-up, tinged his skin a greenish tone.

Anna stood over the corpse, feet either side of his inflated, balloon stomach. She reached for her holdall and pulled out the strange, hollow dagger. She sank to her knees and straddled Peterson's belly. She raised the dagger high above her head and muttered an incantation.

"Dead man, cold man, sad man, dead man.

Stiff man, hard man, frozen man.

Raise man, live man, moment, stand,

For a while, dead man, stand."

"That was lovely. You should be a poet," said Turk.

"Shut it."

Anna slammed the dagger down into Michael Peterson's forehead with all the force she could muster. The dagger pierced through the thick bone with a meaty thunk, puncturing its way into the brain.

She pulled the small bottle of black liquid from the bag and popped the lid. Crouching, she screwed the bottle into the top of the dagger and watched as the viscous fluid began to run down the chamber, through the ridge in the blade, and into the Peterson's brain. When the bottle was empty Anna clambered up out of the grave, leaving the dagger embedded in Peterson's forehead.

"This take a while, does it?"

Anna was about to tell Turk to be quiet when Peterson's eyes snapped open. He sucked in a dusty breath and screamed. The dead man raised his arms stiffly and brought them to his head. The joints cracked and popped loudly. His yellow fingers felt around the hilt of the dagger and traced the length of the blade to the new hole in his head. He wailed in anguish.

"Wha-duh-choo-doo-tha-for?" Peterson struggled to sit up. His jellied eyes flicked in their sockets, wobbling as they moved.

"Oh, right..." Anna pulled her penknife from her back pocket and hopped down into the grave again. "Your lips are sewn to your gums. They do that to corpses so that the lips don't sag." She glanced up at Turk and smiled. "Helps with the mourners."

She held Peterson's lips open with the fingers of one hand while she worked at the metal threads that held his lips to his gums.

Peterson looked as shocked as it was possible for a corpse to look. "Ah-dead? Sint's when?"

"Hold still, Peterson." Anna struggled to cut the threads and was relieved when one gave way. Soon after she had cut the other and climbed back out of the grave. She sat with her legs dangling off the edge beside Turk. Peterson looked around at the dirt around him and at the silky white interior of the coffin lid.

"How did I die?" he asked, holding up his hands to the light, studying the colour of them.

Turk coughed before answering him.

"Said in the paper you had a brain aneurysm while having a wank. Your wife and kids were shocked when they found you. Midgets and that."

Peterson looked shocked and began to whimper. Anna rolled her eyes as Turk began to chuckle to himself.

"It's okay. He's only kidding. I think you had a heart attack or something. Look, we don't have much time, Peterson. I'm going to ask you a couple of questions, then you can go back to rest, okay?"

She pointed the penknife at him as she spoke, punctuating her words with a flick of her wrist. "I need info, quick-smart. I need to know if you heard anything about missing kids when you were down there."

"Kids? Hang on, how long was I dead?"

"You're not listening Peterson. Think. Remember. Before you woke up here, where were you?"

Peterson's eyes roamed his surroundings as he struggled to remember. "Yes. I was... it was dark for a bit. Dark and quiet and cold. Then I was in a waiting area. A long, arched room. Chairs. We were all waiting for our names to be called. Loads of us. There were two doors at the far end, at least that's what everyone talked about. I couldn't see them they were so far away. One white and one black door I heard. No one wanted to be called through the black door."

"Good. See? It's not difficult. Now, people gossip, right? Word gets around about things, particularly in the afterlife. What else did people there talk about? Anything about demons? Things that prey on little boys?"

Peterson closed his eyes and furrowed his brow as best as a corpse with a dagger in its forehead could do.

"Maybe. I-I think... there was a lot of whispers going on. They all talked incessantly. About events, about things happening back here in the living world, about their families and friends. About lovers. They're so preoccupied with sex." Peterson laughed. "But some of them were all scared. I heard them talking about something growing, pushing through the boundaries of the world of the dead and the living. Something strong." He paused. "Where is my family? Are they here?"

Anna clicked her fingers in front of his face. "Oy. Focus. Did they mention any names?"

Peterson looked her in the eyes. "Yes. They whispered a name. Began with an L?"

Anna craned her neck. "An L?" She knew what he was going to say before he did.

"L-lev-leviathan."

Anna ran a hand over her face and swore under her breath. "Fuck."

Turk began to grumble behind her. Anna jumped down into the grave again and crouched so she was nearly face to face with Peterson. From here she could smell the putrescence, the sickly-sweet smell of decay that the dead always carried. Anna held her hand up.

"Peterson. I just wanted to say thanks. High five me, my man."

Peterson touched his hand to hers with an air of confusion, like a man lost in a foreign country who has woken up missing one or more of his kidneys.

"Do I go back now?" Peterson looked up into her face like a child. Anna grasped the dagger with one hand and put the other over Peterson's face.

"Yes. I'm afraid so. Bye-bye Peterson." She pulled the dagger from his head. Peterson fell back into the grave, stiff and entirely dead.

* * *

"Who or what is Leviathan, dare I ask?" asked Turk, ensconced on Anna's two-seater couch.

Anna sat on the pentagram rug surrounded by piles of books. Her hair was a mess, she was covered in dirt, and she stank of dead bodies.

"Oh, he's nothing much to worry about. He's only a prince of hell." She paused. "You know, for a ghost, you're pretty clueless."

Anna stood and carried the large leather book she was studying over to the couch and sat down beside Turk. She began to read the description.

"Leviathan: Hebrew, the Serpent of the Abyss, the Great Dragon, representing primal secrecy, the element of water, the direction of the west, and the chalice of ritual."

There was an illustration there of a large serpent with wings and the face of a man breathing fire.

"In Binsfeld's *Classification of Demons*, Leviathan was a creature of the primordial world; monstrous and chaotic, of eternal hunger for the flesh of the innocent"

On the next page was a picture of the large head of a serpent, devouring children whole. Turk recognised it as part of a larger painting he'd seen many years before. It was Rossignolo's *The Last Judgment*. Anna closed the book on her lap and lay back on the couch.

"So. The big question is... what do we do about it?"

Anna sighed. "I don't know. This is way out of my league. I usually deal with smaller, weaker mites and lower caste demons, even the odd poltergeist. This is way too deep."

"But we're going up there. To the campsite, right?"

"It's miles away. We'll have to get a cab, or head to the bus depot." Anna rubbed her face with her hands. Turk thought for a moment before turning to her.

"Know anyone who has a car we could borrow?"

* * *

Jenny answered the door in a dressing gown and slippers. She was two-deep into a bottle of prosecco and pulled her gown about her body when she saw Anna standing before her.

"Hi Jen. It's Anna. Remember? From, you know... last night?"

"Umm. Yeah, how are you? I wasn't expecting visitors." Her face softened and she stared at Anna with large eyes. "You left so suddenly." She cast a glance over her shoulder. A man's voice rumbled from somewhere inside.

"Who is it, love? At this time of night?"

"No-one dear. Just a door-knocker. Charity thing."

"Get rid of them."

Jenny turned back to Anna and spoke quietly. "I'm sorry. I've taken him back."

Anna smiled. "Relax. I'm not here for that."

"Oh. Okay."

Anna sucked in a breath. There was a quiet pause.

"Can I ask a favour?"

* * *

Anna drove quickly. They cleared the city limits in no time at all and soon raced through the narrow country roads, with their waist-high stone walls holding back the crowds of trees and fields. Anna held a map across the steering wheel as she drove. She had marked it with the location of the campsite in a bold red circle.

"We're not far now, Turk."

"How can you tell?"

She looked at her arm — the ink tattooed there under the skin danced and tingled with ripples of light.

"That's how," she said. Electricity singed her skin across her body. It was like a thousand little electrodes were sparking at once. Warding tattoos acted like a magickal compass.

"The sign said we had about a mile or so to go."

"Then what we're dealing with is something powerful, Turk. I don't remember feeling this amount of dark energy in a long time. Feels like razors under my skin."

They came upon the entrance to the scout camp so suddenly that it took Anna by surprise, and they skidded past it, tyres squealing like garrotted piglets. She threw the car into reverse and then took the turn up the driveway. The car left the relative modernity of the paved main road, plunging headlong into the wild surroundings of a pine forest. The car bumped along a gravel track for several hundred feet before they came to the scout hall.

The building was festooned with Police tape. It criss-crossed the doorways. A perimeter had been set up with cones, tape binding them into a large square meant to block the entrance of any vehicles that may come by. Anna parked the car and got out. The scout hall, a concrete building with a flat roof and long, tall windows, stood dark. Anna marched up to the front double doors, ducking the police tape that spiderwebbed the entrance. She jiggled the heavy-duty padlock that hung on the front door before thumping her fist on its steel surface.

"Hello? Anyone home?"

"Looks like the police have come and gone," said Turk.

"Strange. They couldn't have found anything. They'd still be here if they had."

She placed her ear against the door, straining to hear any signs of movement. She pulled away and shook her head.

"Silence."

They moved around the side of the squat building, passing a pair of large freshwater tanks. The back of the building was identical to the front. A set of large windows looked out onto a clearing where makeshift football goals had been erected. Beyond the clearing stood the tree-lined darkness of the woods. Anna turned back to the building. She scratched at her tattoos unconsciously.

Turk broke the silence. "This feels... wrong, Anna. This whole place."

"I know. That hall looks deserted, and it smells like cow shite."

"Does it?" said Turk.

Anna moved back to the car and opened the back seat. She removed her hold-all and the torch she had packed. She hefted the torch in her hand. It was police issue: strong and heavy enough to be used as a baton if the need arose. Flicking it on, the beam cut through the night like a white-hot laser. She then went to the front passenger seat and popped open the glove box. Fishing around inside she pulled a small leather wallet and slipped it into her jeans pocket. Anna made her way back up towards the scout hut. She moved around the other side of the building, tearing the police tape that barred her way, and found a door beside a stack of milk-crates. This one had no padlock on it. Anna propped the flash-light against the milk crates, angling it up towards the lock on the door. She pulled the leather wallet from her pocket and opened it, revealing a set of small, thin tools. A lock-picking kit.

"Look at you, you're like Inspector Clouseau."

Anna stopped picking the lock and stared up at him quizzically. "Clouseau?"

"Yeah, the guy from The Pink Panther."

"He was the detective."

"Really? Who was the burglar then?"

"I dunno, some old guy. If you're quite finished, I'm trying to work." She twisted the picks back and forth, jiggling them to get them into position, then she turned both of her hands to the right sharply. There was a click. Anna stood and turned the handle.

"Voila," she said, before lifting the torch and entering the scout hall.

They were in a large room that doubled as a kitchen and storage room. On one side it was filled with tents and plastic chairs and on the other, a chrome-plated kitchen. Anna placed a hand over her mouth and nose as the stench of rotting food assailed her.

She coughed. "Jesus. That's rank."

"What is it?"

"Smells like off meat, eggs and that."

She pushed through the kitchen to a short hallway. A door to the right opened into a bathroom with half a dozen shower stalls and three cubicle toilets. The hallway led through to a larger hall that was empty except for a dozen or so sleeping bags sprawled out on the floor, and knots of muddy boot prints on the ground. Soft drink cans and empty crisp packets littered the ground here and there. The police had placed yellow numbered cones near places they thought were notable. The green glow of a fire-exit sign sat above a door in the corner. Anna spotted a bank of light switches to her left. She flicked the switches and one by one the overhead strip lights flickered, illuminating the hall. There was no sign of the missing boys. The place was empty.

"There's no-one here. Not one kid. There's no signs of blood, nothing. It's like they just *left*." said Turk.

"They've got to be somewhere nearby, Turk. I can *feel* it."

"If they're not here, then somewhere nearby, somewhere else. Follow your tattoos." They slipped out of the door and began to wander the perimeter. Anna kept looking out over the clearing towards the bank of trees there. *Follow your instincts, Anna. They haven't let you down yet.* She marched off across the clearing. By the time she reached the first of those tall trees, her body told her she was heading in the right direction.

"Turk. This way."

The trees pressed against Anna as she pushed her way through. The ground quickly became thick and spongy. Anna's boots sank into it up to the ankles. Low branches barred her way and ducking under them Anna felt twigs scrape at her face and pull at her hair. She kept her torch on the ground just ahead of her in case any potholes or logs threatened to trip her; a broken leg out here with an unimaginable evil lurking and nothing but a useless ghost to help would certainly mean death.

"Come on. Where did you take them?" she puffed, her breath coming in small white clouds. The cold bit at her fingers and toes.

Her tattoos screamed. She could feel their magick searing its way down

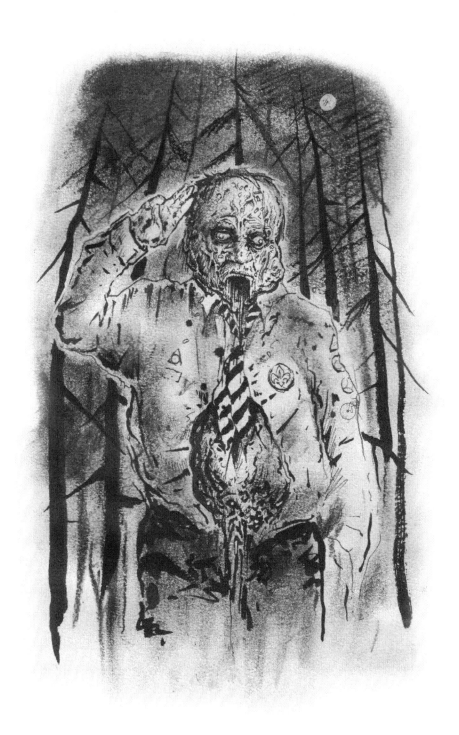

to her bones. She came upon a large log and started to clamber over it when her light beam fell on the bulk of a man standing with his back to her. He leaned back and craned his neck to the canopy of trees above him. At first, she thought he was laughing quietly as his body was jiggling back and forth, but the man clutched at his sides and stomach. He bent double and cried out in agony. Anna took a breath to compose herself and looked around for Turk. He was nowhere to be seen, but there was no time to wait. Anna stepped off the log and approached the man.

"Hey mate. You seen any kids around here?"

The man stopped shaking, becoming eerily still.

Anna went on. "Scouts. They're missing." She stopped a few feet from the man. "Along with their scoutmaster."

The man turned slowly, like a plate of jelly on a lazy Susan. Anna, a veteran of the occult, still wasn't prepared for what she saw.

The scoutmaster's face was alive with crawling vermin just under the surface of the skin, which was marbled with dark purple and red lines. Flies had lain eggs in his face at some point over the past several days which were now beginning to hatch. The man's flesh was like cheese, soft and rubbery. His eyes sagged in their sockets, barely keeping their consistency, like egg yolks gone bad. He tried to turn his bloated, gas-filled body towards her, and his scout shirt burst open at the effort and fell off his shoulders, baring his black mottled chest and stomach to Anna. She retched. The man's stomach undulated with things inside him, long things that burrowed through him. Anna couldn't believe he was still standing and in one piece. She guessed it wouldn't be too long before he ran to jelly. His trousers were soddened at the crotch as his innards liquefied and poured from his orifices. Anna could smell his stench from where she stood.

The man attempted to speak. A voice of catarrh and phlegm escaped his mouth along with a gurgle of black slime.

"You know, I don't think you're a well man. You should probably have a lie down."

Joe took a shaky step towards her, his legs like rope, and he tumbled to the ground. Anna heard bones snapping softly as he fell. Joe hit the ground hard. His skin split in multiple places and the last of his juices began to seep from the fresh openings. Joe's skin lolled to one side as he tried to turn to look up at her.

"You don't have long left. Do yourself a favour. Tell me where the kids are. If you believe in any kind of God or afterlife, you're gonna want to get some good karma on your side."

Joe closed his eyes for a moment and then looked up at her with a look of regret and pain. He forced himself up onto his elbows and raised one jellied hand and pointed to a circular grove of trees up ahead.

"They're there?"

Joe nodded.

"Did you bring them here for *Leviathan*?"

Joe closed his eyes, and a low whimper came from somewhere inside his chest.

"How do I get to them?"

Joe curled his flabby forefinger into a hook and motioned *down*.

Anna nodded. "Okay. I understand."

Joe sagged. Anna crouched down and gazed into his putrid eyes. Anna gritted her teeth.

"I want you to know something before I go, maggot-face. Where you are going there is no light and there is no God. It is not the afterlife; it is *anti*-life. And it is filled with little hungry things... and not so little things... in fact I've heard they're massive."

The strength went out of Joe's body, and he collapsed back onto the ground. A split opened in his side, the gash ran from his armpit to his hip and the fermented slop that was his insides spilled out onto the mud. The veneer holding his eyes together gave out and they too ran out of his skull. At last, he gave up all vestiges of life.

"Bloody hell. You've made a right mess here." Turk stood atop the fallen tree trunk.

"Where the hell were you? I'm here on my own dealing with a ghoul of some kind and you're nowhere to be seen."

"Are you sure he's a ghoul? He looks undead to me."

"Dead, undead, whatever. He was alive now he isn't. Screw him. You didn't answer my question."

A sheepish look came over Turk's face. "This place... it's weird. There are energy trails all over the place. I had to find a way through without—"

"Without what?"

"We'd be best not to draw attention, if you get my meaning."

Anna stopped herself from scolding Turk again. She'd never seen him this way before. He looked scared.

"What's wrong, Turk?"

He glanced around at the woods before fixing her with a stare. "We've seen plenty of weird shit. This, though," he gestured to the gloopy mess of Joe's body, "This is infernal. The power here is like nothing we've encountered before. It's dangerous, for both of us."

"I can't leave these kids, Turk. I won't."

He smiled. "I understand, but I can't come in there with you," he nodded to the circle of trees, "I'm not sure I'll make it back out."

"Okay."

Anna stood and headed for the trees. She pushed through the only gap she could find. It was just big enough to get herself through. She wondered if Joe had tried once more to get in here, but his size and condition had made it impossible. In the centre of the circle stood a Rune-Stone. Anna had seen them before, mostly in books. They indicated places of power, of worship. Most people these days thought that standing stones were the kind of things those weirdy beardy Druids used to erect to scare the Christians, but Anna knew better. She waded through thigh-high mud towards it. She gasped when she got close enough to make out the pattern etched into the stone's surface. A scarlet serpent consuming a man. Leviathan.

Anna thumped her hand onto the Rune-Stone and set her jaw. She turned back to the tree-line and spotted Turk standing over Maggot-face's body.

He pointed at the remains and mouthed 'Oh My God'.

"I have to do something stupid now, Turk." she yelled to him. A look of genuine concern crossed his face. Anna's tattoos were burning so hard they brought tears to her eyes. She stuffed the big police torch in the back of her jeans.

"How stupid?" he yelled back.

"Don't know yet." Anna smiled weakly. She couldn't hide her apprehension. At first nothing happened.

They both heard it at the same time. The rattle of the trees as the wind picked up. It grew intense quickly. She sensed the snaking movement before she saw it. All around her the swamp seemed to be writhing. It took only a second. Before she could cry out, a black wave of mud raised up like a lip and swallowed her. Anna managed to suck in a quick breath before it fell over her and she was smothered.

It was wet and cold, and Anna began to panic as the mud pushed its way up her nostrils and down the back of her throat. She clamped her hands over her mouth and nose, but it didn't help. The sheer volume of metallic muck was too great. It slid between her fingers, seeped between her palms and her lips, and found its way into her mouth. She could taste metal and the dirt. Her body wracked with convulsions as she could no longer hold her breath. She opened her mouth, her lungs desperate for air. Spots flashed behind her closed eyelids. *You're about to die. You're about to drown in a fetid swamp looking for a flippin' Prince of Hell.* Anger flushed in her chest. How stupid could she be to step into an evil swamp and let the mud take her without even thinking about it first? *She should have hired a digger, a JCB, and bloody excavated the whole place till she either found the lost Scouts, or the lost 9th Legion of Rome, or the bloody gateway to Hell itself.* Her chest began to convulse, and she could no longer hold her breath. Anna opened her mouth and sucked in a throatful of mud. Then she felt herself let go of the anger and she slipped into that place that people go between waking and dreaming.

Anna's arse hit solid ground. Her mouth opened and air shot down her throat like nitrous oxide. She gasped and immediately began to cough, heaving in lungful of air after lungful of air and was sure that she breathed in at least one beetle and probably a few worms, but right now she did not give a shit. Her body pulsed with every heartbeat, the blood in every vein moved in unison. It was ecstasy. She was alive and she was the happiest she'd ever been just to be breathing, even if her tattoos stung worse than that one time she got vindaloo sauce on her lady bits. Anna couldn't tell if her eyes were open. It was pitch black.

She sat up slowly. Pain raked her left hip where she had landed on the metal torch. Her thumb found the big rubber button and she pushed it. The beam cut through the dark.

"Thank Christ."

Anna shone the torch around. She was in a hollow underneath the swamp. Above her hung a mass of wet mud, held in a canopy of tree roots and a membrane of vegetation. The dry dirt walls were veined with knots of thick tree roots. *They look like tentacles.*

"Turk? You here?" No answer. "Dammit."

She expected her voice to echo in the tunnel, but the soft earth swallowed it like it was soundproofed. Anna's legs wobbled as she stood. Pain shot through her back. She hobbled down the tunnel, following the torch beam. Tree roots jutted from the walls, and she dodged them as she stepped around boulders that littered the floor.

She stopped. Movement to her right on the wall beside her head. She pressed herself against the opposite wall and held the torch steady. A white tree root unfurled itself and snaked its way out of the wall. It waved in the air, as if searching for her. Anna ventured a step towards it and held the torch close to the fumbling appendage. It was covered with minute hairs like black needles. The skin of the root pulsed and undulated with an alien intelligence.

Anna felt that deep revulsion that one feels when faced with something completely at odds with nature. She made to move away when she walked directly into a pair of legs hanging from the compacted mud above her head. Anna tripped on a rock and sprawled. The torch spun from her fingers and the light pitched up, illuminating the sunken face of a dead boy in a green uniform.

The boy was embedded in the dirt. Roots speared him from every angle and plunged into his abdomen. They had penetrated every orifice in his face, two spearing his eyes and one thick root pulsing as it drew the boy's innards out of his mouth. They pulsed and undulated, sucking the nutrients from the boy's body. *They're feeding on him.*

Anna scooped up the torch and ran the light over the cavern ceiling. The scouts were here. Suspended in clutches of roots were the bodies of the ten missing scouts. Kids sacrificed by a real-life monster, and here they hung in an exhibition of death.

Anna stumbled down the morbid gallery, checking the boys' bodies for signs of life. She couldn't bring herself to raise the light to their faces, the faint outline of ruined features was enough for her. Her eyes blurred as anger spread through her. Anger at the scoutmaster for what he did, anger at the evil in the world, and anger at herself for letting herself feel something. She did her best to blot out the world every day to avoid feeling things. Not because she didn't care for anything at all but because she cared too much. She couldn't take the nightmares anymore and she was damn sure that she'd be dreaming of this for a long time if she was lucky enough to get out of this situation. She wished Turk was here with her now.

"Damn you Turk," she whispered, "you coward."

Anna turned her light on the last scout. The boy's pale face stirred. He had some colour to his cheeks still. His features were untouched by the trees for now. A single root poked from his neck, thin, worm-like. Anna slipped her fingers onto his thin wrist. There, beneath the skin, was the tickle of a pulse.

"Christ, he's alive!"

Anna quickly turned the light up to the roof of the tunnel. Other roots snaked their way towards the boy blindly, waving back and forward like worms. Anna whacked the root in the boy's face with the torch, breaking it off up near the ceiling. It took three good strikes before it came away clean and thick red goo began to seep from the stump. She pulled at the boy's clothes. Dirt rained down on her, filling her mouth and eyes. Anna spat it out and blinked as she worked to free the boy from the ceiling. Just as he began to shift, a thick root found him and wrapped itself around his neck, searching for the trickle of blood that oozed from the open wound. The boy became the prize in a perverse game of tug-of-war. Anna let go of the boy's body and launched herself at the root. Gripping it with both hands, she pulled herself up and worked to unwrap it from the child, the hand holding her weight white-knuckled with effort. She felt those fine needle hairs press into the flesh of her hand. It was like gripping barbed wire. She wrenched the noose free from the boy's neck and as he slipped, she let go of the root and they both tumbled to the dirt floor. The boy was a dead weight in her arms, pale and weak, but clinging to life.

"I'm gonna get you out of here, little man. Can you hear me?"

She put the boy over her shoulder and shone her light back along the passageway. There was nothing back there but dirt and mud and roots. Anna heard a strange chattering sound and the tattoo that covered her from shoulder to hip seared into her flesh. She spun and shone the light down the tunnel. At the edge of the light was a shape much like a man. *No, wait, two men. No, more.* A long-segmented body shifted. It had too many legs and arms to be a man. It lifted its front end clear of the tunnel floor and floated backwards, away from the light. A warm air current blew in the tunnel.

Leviathan.

Anna saw two fleshy appendages waver in the air before it moved suddenly towards her. The thing moved with insectile speed. Anna's tattoos began to glow white hot. She screamed. Leviathan stopped for a moment, pinpointing the sound of her scream, and then it lunged at her. Anna dived out of the way, but the enormous fingers on one of its many hands found her chest. It was like an electric current passed through her. The world, the tunnel, the boy, it was all gone in a flash. Anna saw the place Leviathan occupied. She saw Leviathan's domain, the hell world it occupied. A place of rotting flesh, walls of bone, rivers of dark, venal blood, all leading towards a black vortex. She knew it instinctively: the Jaws of Hell. Anna's mind began to fragment, she felt the corners of her consciousness begin to collapse. She did not know if she was screaming or not. Then the vision was broken. Anna collapsed to the floor, the body of the child landing heavily beside her. Anna sobbed and put her hands to her head. She wanted to tear the visions from her mind, using her fingers if necessary. She heard Leviathan's voice, thin as a reed, yet echoing in air around her.

"Partake of me. Live forever."

Anna saw herself there, in the realm of the Leviathan. She felt it touch her and strip every remnant of her humanity, changing her into something… else, something unique.

"I will make you my queen. You will rule my dominion. Be my bride. I will take away the pain. You will have power. Be my bride, Anna Barlow."

For a moment she almost gave in. She saw that place again. She saw Leviathan and saw what it would do to her. *Transfiguration.* And she *wanted it*. Anna felt her groin flush with blood. Her breasts ached. Her heart thumped in its bone cage. The Leviathan waited for her acceptance. She had to choose to let him in. *Seduction.*

The moment stretched into eternity. Anna knew what it wanted to do.

"Fuck off!" she screamed.

Leviathan moved backwards slowly. It was still wreathed in shadows, but Anna could see the shape of its head. It raised itself above her and Anna closed her eyes, waiting for it to bring its horrendous weight down upon her and crush the life from her body. In a flurry of movement, Leviathan's trunk contracted, and then it exploded into the darkness and the dirt.

Anna realised she hadn't breathed for a while. She let the air in and filled her lungs from bottom to top, and when her chest ached from holding in the air, and it felt like her lungs might pop, she let it out in a primal scream. Crumbs of dirt fell on her head. She lifted the torch to the ceiling in time to see a crack open in the dirt, and the ceiling begin to crumble. Leviathan's fevered tunnelling had loosened the soil. It was caving in.

Hefting the boy, Anna ran back the way she had come, through the dangling legs of dead boys, stumbling over rocks and stones. Tree roots tore at her clothes and skin. She reached the place where she had fallen through. The mud slid down the walls as the place began to collapse. Leviathan was gone. Her tattoos ached no more. It had presumably taken whatever power had held this place intact with it. Muck slopped around Anna's knees and thighs and then a hole opened above her as the ceiling collapsed completely. Anna dug her heels into the ground as the swamp fell into the tunnel, sliding past her, reaching up to her chest. It took all her might to fight the current of mud and rocks that swilled around her in the tunnel. She lifted the boy up as high as she could, keeping him above the landslide. A rush of air billowed past her as it was pushed out and up by the collapsing dirt. Then, silence. Just as quickly as it started it was over. Anna stood chest deep in a sunken mud pool. The boy began to stir as the cool night air settled on them. Anna pulled him close. She fumbled at the back of his shirt, pulling the label out so she could read his name – Paul McGuire.

The ring of trees had given way, collapsing like dominoes as the ground had pitched under them. They no longer formed a living vaulted roof. She stared up at the clear night sky as a wave of exhaustion hit her. A thin face came into view above.

"Need a hand?" Turk smiled sheepishly.

"Where the fuck were you?"

"Let's get you out of there and I'll tell you."

* * *

Anna slumped in the booth as Nancy plonked a rather large bowl of lentil soup and a cup of tea down onto the table.

"Thanks Nance."

"Eat up, love. You look like you've been dragged through a hedge backwards."

Anna couldn't stomach food, not yet. She reached for the tea and slurped it, savouring the sweet, warm liquid as it made its way down her gullet.

She turned and stared out at the street. Ordinary people hustled by, going about their ordinary people business. Women with kids in tow. Cars and buses honking and revving. Nancy ran her eyes from Anna's head down over her mud-stuck clothes.

"You uh… been up in the countryside then? Hiking or summit? You've got… dirt… on you."

Anna dragged her gaze from the window to Nancy's friendly face and almost burst into tears.

"Something like that, Nancy."

The waitress looked at Anna's clothes, caked in grime, and at the trail of footprints from the door to the booth, then at Anna's mud-caked boots curled up underneath her legs on the leather seat. Nancy made to say something but thought better of it and moved off to clean a table nearby. Anna slurped the tea once more. It was piping hot. It burned her mouth, but she didn't mind. She hoped the scalding tea would burn away the memories of the previous night. She'd probably burn her clothes when she went back to the flat too.

Turk fidgeted in seat opposite. Anna was ignoring him. He hadn't said anything at all to her yet. He just sat there shaking. When she drained the last of her tea, she turned to him. Turk looked strange. *Thin.* No, not thin, *see through.*

"Anna. I'm sorry."

Anna sighed. The sweet tea had given her some energy back and she felt her mood brighten a little.

"I can't stay mad at you, you tart."

"I know. I'm still sorry, Anna."

She looked at him wearily. "What for?"

Turk gulped visibly, which was a strange thing to see a ghost do. Anna felt a tingle of concern. Turk never acted like this. He was usually so nonchalant, what with being dead and all.

When he spoke, his voice was like a child's voice. "I'm sorry I couldn't help you. Under there."

Anna sighed. "Look, Turk. There was some powerful magic at play. It's not your fault you couldn't—"

"It wasn't magic that stopped me coming to you. I was afraid."

She did a double take. "Say that again? I couldn't hear you coz my ears are full of mud."

"I was terrified. Whatever that thing was—" He shook his head and looked out the window before going on. "I think I have to go away from a while, Anna."

Anna felt a chill run through her again. She leant towards him, searching his face for clues. *Go away? Go where?* Turk had been with her for as long as she could remember. Even when she was a kid, he was there. He was her brother and her father rolled into one.

"Turk. You're starting to freak me out."

"I wanted to tell you before, but you were busy with the boy and then the police came, and then the parents. You were so busy, and I couldn't interrupt you."

He paused. "I can't stay here. That thing. It left a part of itself in you, or on you." He looked at her in a way that shook Anna. "It won't leave you alone now. Don't you see? It'll find you wherever you go."

Anna felt a cold realisation in the pit of her stomach. "Turk."

"It'll hunt you, Anna. I-I have to go. There's something I must do." He began to fade out of reality, his outline blurring, the weight of his body becoming transparent.

"Don't you fucking dare, Turk. Don't leave me here alone!"

"I'm sorry."

He was gone. Anna glanced around in a daze at the café. Nancy was nowhere to be seen. The tables stood empty. The counter, deserted. Anna heard the buzz of the halogen lights above her. She spun and looked out of the window. The streets were deserted.

The window was a black mirror. Her pale reflection stared back at her like a ghost.

COLD CASES

AVOIDING SATANIC PANIC WITH THE SATAN SLEUTH

"M.J."

Hello, my name is M.J., and I love reading fiction. Not just any fiction, I especially love vintage horror fiction, including books deep within the *Paperbacks From Hell* vein. As I enter my fifties, I find myself rediscovering media from my youth including the various paperback books that were typically found in the checkout aisles at the local grocery store around the time of the 1970s and 1980s.

My discovery of *Paperbacks from Hell*, by Grady Hendrix, in collaboration with the massive physical paperback collection of Will Ericksson, has only fueled this fire within me and many others around the world.

Now enter, THE SATAN SLEUTH series. This series consists of three books: *The Satan Sleuth #1: Fallen Angel, The Satan Sleuth #2: The Werewolf Walks Tonight*, and *The Satan Sleuth #3: Devil, Devil*. The Satan Sleuth is an occult detective book series written by the late Michael Avallone and first published in 1974. The author is best known for writing media novelizations as well as pulp, mystery, and crime fiction. What drew me in at first were the covers that were reproduced in *Paperbacks from Hell*. It's not simply one element of the cover, but everything all at once: the font, the color story, the artistry, and the imagery. They simply delight and overstimulate the senses. Everything about each cover screams and oozes vintage vibes. Of course, the next thing that captured my attention was the fact that all of the storylines contained occult and supernatural elements. Throw in a vigilante occult fighter and I was all in to find this series and start my hunt. I simply could not resist the urge to read them all.

Physical copies of the series available on auction sites sell for around $50 a piece in the United States. To my delight, all three books in the series are available on Amazon's Kindle Unlimited service and well worth the price of admission. What an affordable and accessible way to enjoy trendy and rare vintage books!

I read all three books earlier this summer and enjoyed each for different reasons.

The first book, *The Satan Sleuth #1: Fallen Angel,* is the set up and gives in full detail the origin story of our protagonist, Phillip St George III, a wealthy world class adventurer who endures the severest of family traumas and transforms a side of himself into an occult detective the like of which the world has never seen. His wife is brutally murdered in their home. This is a revenge novel of the purest form. After the tragic event, Phillip St George III dedicates his life's mission to shedding truth and light on criminal acts hiding behind the magic and mystery of the occult and supernatural. Phillip St George III is everything an occult detective aspires to be – handsome, athletic, smart, and obnoxiously rich. Key

words: obviously rich. The Satan Sleuth also has loyal friends on the payroll to help him organize and meet his needs for a disguise, tactical supplies, exotic weaponry and other similar demands. Our protagonist utilizes his wealth to the fullest extent in order to get the job done, yachts, scuba gear, helicopters, hand grenades, etc. He conceals his identity so as to avoid attention from the public eye and paparazzi. The first book in the series combines revenge with physicality. This is my favorite of the trio specifically because of the origin story. I noted that this tragic event has a slight familiarity to the Manson murder which had occurred a few years prior, and Avallone's son, David, confirmed this in an email, which I have quoted below. The villains in this book are pretty much obsessed with Satan and are a transient bunch. Another facet to reading vintage books is the reflection of current culture – fashion, language, cultural events, social norms and mores.

The second book, *The Satan Sleuth #2: The Werewolf Walks Tonight,* carries a different tone and plot. Instead of seeking out revenge, our protagonist is looking to expose the truth behind events categorized as supernatural. Phillip St George III, specifically seeks out supernatural crimes by scouring newspaper headlines nationwide for the Devil's signature. In

rural America, a number of mysterious murders are happening, and rumors circulate that it may be a werewolf! Phillip St George III, obligated by his life's mission, sets off for this small town in rural America to sniff out the underlying and deadly truth. Remember, he isn't interested in werewolves, but the truth behind the rumors. Our protagonist does not believe in anything supernatural or otherworldly, including cryptids. In this book, Phillip St George III creates and assumes a different identity to infiltrate and assimilate with the townsfolk to find answers. His goal is to find the murderers, to educate the townsfolk, and to proclaim that the supernatural does not exist. This was my least favorite of the series as, while the first book contained so many shocking and impactful moments, this book had a more typical case-file feel to it. Don't get me wrong, I still enjoyed the story, just not as much as the first.

It seems that while Warner Paperback Library in the US published all three books in the series, the UK publisher, Mews (an imprint of New English Library), only bothered with two of them, skipping book two and renumbering book three as book two.

The third book in the series, *The Satan Sleuth #3: Devil, Devil,* has, in my opinion, the most interesting and entertaining storyline. This is the ultimate battle between good and evil. In this installment, our Satan Sleuth is keen on solving a series of murdered females and searching for the answers. Rumors of witches covens, cults, Black Masses, and the Devil himself abound. Phillip St George III is fueled to take on yet another well-crafted alias identity and infiltrate this Satanic cult that operates in high society New York City. And now enters Phillip St. George's toughest opponent yet – a drop dead gorgeous and sexy Satanic cult leader. This book adds back the darkness the second book was missing. *Devil, Devil* has a cat and mouse storyline that works very well between our gallant hero and the evil seductress. Their tension is palpable. In this installment, there are plenty of occult references, bits, and bobs within the prose that gives it an extra evil edge. *Devil, Devil* reflects back the cultural notes of the times including the hint that new age culture and Satanic Panic is on the rise! This is the third book in the series and absolutely left me wanting for more.

All three books in the series are entertaining. I personally find there to be a positive sleuthing element to each ending, and they are always wrapped up neatly with a bow. These books were published after the Charles Manson murders, post counterculture movement, the takeover of the new age movement, and the beginnings of Satanic Panic.

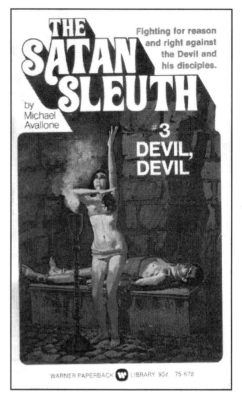

Add in style and fashion references, cringy sexual language of the era, relationship trends, and an insanely dashing and massively rich protagonist, and you have the formula for a very cool and entertaining retro occult detective series. Highly recommended for anyone wanting to read occult detective fiction with a 1970's flair or starting out on an occult detective journey, like me.

As reflected in *Paperbacks from Hell*, there are two more Satan Sleuth books that have never been published. Which leads me to some fantastic news! When I posted a video review of The first book, Michael Avallone's son, David, contacted to let me know that he has in his possession manuscripts for both, and they will hopefully be published later this year! David Avallone also said that these are the best two books of the series in his opinion, and I honestly cannot wait to read them.

I later emailed David to check details, and ask a couple of questions. Here's what he told me...

MJ: How did the Satan Sleuth series come about? What was your father's inspiration for series?

DA: My memory is that Warner Books asked dad to pitch a series. He was at the height of his career. Curtis books had recently published a bunch of novels from the *Ed Noon* series, his *Partridge Family* tie-ins had sold millions of copies, he had written the novelization of *Beneath The Planet Of The Apes*. He had dozens of books in print in the early seventies. Dad was a huge fan of the pulp adventure heroes of the 1930s, and The Satan Sleuth is his tribute to *The Spider* and *The Shadow*: dark vigilantes who strike fear into evil-doers and who are merciless to those who prey on the weak and the innocent. The Manson murders were a few years in the past, but they were still very much in the public imagination: The Satan Sleuth is published the same year as *Helter Skelter*, and a year before the popular TV movie about it. I have always explained the character to people by saying, "What if Charles Manson had killed the fiance of the adult Bruce Wayne?" He becomes a very different kind of Batman. One dedicated specifically to catching the maniacs who killed his beloved, and who becomes obsessed with satanists and cultists.

MJ: Can you give our readers a teaser of the two upcoming releases in the series?

DA: The paperback market imploded somewhat around that time, and the series didn't sell as well as Warners hoped, so the final two novels were never published. I'll have them out hopefully in the next year.

The Satan Sleuth #4: Vampires Wild: Young starlets are turning up dead, all the blood drained from their bodies. The Satan Sleuth travels to Hollywood and to find out if miraculously well-kept movie star Lola Vane is using something other than plastic surgery to maintain her eternal youth.

The Satan Sleuth #5: Zombie Depot: Fear stalks the streets of Haiti and the country is in chaos, as a revolutionary leader raises an unstoppable army to seize power. The Satan Sleuth heads to the island nation to destroy the Zombie Depot and the designer drug that turns men into slaves.

Stay tuned!

THE BUTCHER OF HEMMING STREET

Naching T. Kassa

"You come highly recommended, Mr Whitney," said Lady Dahlia Battleroost She looked up from the yellow writing pad on her mahogany desk and stared into my face. If not for her strange violet eyes, I would have said that she resembled the actress Margaret Rutherford. Her face seemed capable of the same comedic expressions.

She tapped the pad with her pen. "Tell me, when did you first become a ghost?"

"I was involved in a plane crash, ma'am. The same one which killed my employer, Lord Lucas Brackenstall."

"Ah yes. I remember. Lucky Brackenstall never was much of a pilot." She scribbled something on the pad. "You seem no worse for wear. Spirits involved in accidents usually show signs of... injury."

"I've learned to control that, ma'am. I was a butler for most of my life and I've always appeared appropriately."

"Why haven't you moved on? Do you have some unfinished business here?"

"To be honest, ma'am, I have no clue why I'm here. As far as I know, my business was concluded upon my demise. I've been wandering for a few months now. By happy accident, I happened upon the *Occult Times* and read your advertisement. I assure you, I am a most competent butler."

The lady frowned. Her pen scratched the pad, then she glanced up once more.

"Are you familiar with the works of Sir Arthur Conan Doyle?

"I am. Most of my reading has included Sherlock Holmes."

"Then you've read the three novels and fifty-seven short stories?"

I smiled. The lady seemed to be testing me.

"Beg your pardon, ma'am. But there are *four* novels and *fifty-six* short stories."

The lady smiled. "So there are. What of the works of Sir Stephen? Do you know those?"

"Sir Stephen?"

"Sir Stephen King, of course. The gentleman who wrote *The Shining* and *Salem's Lot*."

"I don't believe he's been knighted, ma'am."

Lady Dahlia scowled. "With the exception of Sir Arthur Conan Doyle, a greater writer has never existed. He should have been knighted ages ago. If you wish to work for me, Whitney, you will keep that fact in mind."

"Yes, ma'am."

"Now, what of Dame Agatha Christie. What do you think of her work?"

I paused. The lady regarded me with her strange eyes and the expression of a curious St Bernard.

Another test.

"Dame Agatha is overrated," I said at last.

The lady dropped her pen on the pad. Beaming, she rose from her chair. She reached out, and to my surprise, shook my ectoplasmic hand.

"You have the position, Mr Whitney. You may assume your duties at once."

"Thank you, ma'am."

"Please, address me as Lady Dahlia or milady. No more of this 'ma'am' rubbish."

"As you wish, milady."

She rounded the desk and led me to the study door.

"My housekeeper, Mrs Farnsworth, will show you your room and acquaint you with your duties. I shall expect you in the drawing room at midnight."

"Midnight?"

"Mrs Farnsworth will explain. Please, don't be late. I should like to brief you before my client arrives."

"Yes, milady."

She opened the door. A tall woman, dressed in black, waited outside. Her gaunt and pale face held no smile.

"Mrs Farnsworth, this is Mr Whitney. He'll be taking Mr Shelley's place. Will you show him about?"

The woman nodded. "This way, please."

I followed her into the hall.

The afternoon sun filtered through the stained-glass windows in the western wall, casting fragments of multi-colored light across the stone floor. Mrs Farnsworth seemed untouched by their luminescence. Her dark garb absorbed the light, rendering her an impervious shadow as she traversed the hall.

She didn't speak until we reached the grand stairway at the northern end.

"Your room is on the second floor, in the west wing," she said as we climbed. "Please, do not enter the eastern part of the house. Her ladyship does not allow staff or visitors there."

"Understood."

Dim lamps lit the second-floor hallway, and dark portraits with dour subjects lined the walls. The scent of furniture polish permeated the air, rich carpeting muffling our footsteps as we approached the first door on the left.

"This is your room," Mrs Farnsworth said, opening the door.

A large and sumptuous room met my gaze. Bookshelves, filled with tomes, lined the walls. Finding myself speechless, I entered.

"Is it satisfactory?" Mrs Farnsworth asked.

"Indeed," I replied. "These volumes – some are first editions."

"Most are Lady Dahlia's. Others belonged to Mr Shelley. He wrote most of his new poetry at that very desk. Oh – I would not open it if I were you. It once belonged to his deceased wife and she kept some rather odd things within the drawers."

I paused before the desk.

"Her name... was it Mary?"

A smile formed upon her lips for the first time. "It was."

"The ghost of Shelley? Serving here as a butler?"

"Yes and Lady Dahlia is well rid of him. He used to march about the house in his big shirt spouting verse at all hours of the night. We were all glad when he finally put his affairs in order."

"Amazing. I cannot imagine him performing any type of duty in this house."

Mrs Farnsworth's reserve returned. "I have spoken too hastily. He was accomplished at his duties, and diligent. As you must be."

"What are my duties?"

"You must look after the kitchen, pantry, and wine cellar. And supervise the staff, myself included. You'll also assist in Lady Dahlia's investigations, serving her in whatever manner she sees fit."

I raised an eyebrow. "Her investigations?"

"Lady Dahlia is a private detective."

* * *

Midnight crept in on the chimes of an old clock and the velvet gloom of a moonless sky. Ever prompt, even in death, I materialized in the drawing room as the bell tolled twelve.

The spacious room was filled with large, overstuffed chairs, bookshelves, and curious artwork. Many of the books on the shelves bore the name Stephen King, while the paintings had been created by the Spanish artist, Goya. One such piece, *Saturn Devouring His Children*, occupied a place of honor above the fireplace. Lady Dahlia, now clad in a tweed jacket and skirt, sat beneath it and to the left, with a book in her hands. She wore a pair of silver-framed spectacles and when I approached, she lowered them.

"Sir Stephen is in rare form tonight," she said, displaying the book's cover.

"*Bag of Bones*? I'm afraid I'm unfamiliar with that one."

"It's an interesting book. A story of a writer and a vengeful ghost I'm not sure why I picked it out, but it must have some bearing on tonight's events. Sir Stephen's books have always possessed a prophetic quality where my clients are concerned."

An end table stood to the right of her chair. On it sat a small, squat lamp with a green shade, and a pile of correspondence. She extracted an envelope from the pile and held it out to me.

"Tell me what you think of this."

"Do you wish me to touch it, Lady Dahlia?"

"Yes, yes, go ahead. Your ectoplasm won't damage it."

I accepted the missive and studied the return address.

"Mr August Cortney, 20A Cheshire Street, London."

"Read the letter."

I opened the envelope and the folded sheet inside. The message had been hastily scrawled.

"Aloud," she said.

"My Dear Dahlia, I must speak with you regarding a highly urgent matter concerning my most recent haunting. May I call upon you at fifteen past midnight this coming Friday? Yours, August Cortney." I glanced up at the lady. "He refers to this haunting as 'his most recent' and yet, his wording seems rather familiar for a client. He is a friend?"

"He is," she said, a smile on her lips.

"The appointment is a late one."

"Spirits are most active at this time of night. Especially at the witching hour."

"I see. He chose this time to avoid the spirit."

"Exactly. Unfortunately, this is also the best time to catch them. They are closest to the mortal veil within these few hours. What else have you learned from the letter?"

"This paper... if I'm not much mistaken, is kraft paper. The type used by butchers to wrap their wares. Judging by this unusual stain in the corner, and the unmistakable scent of blood, I would say Mr Cortney is a butcher."

"Bravo, Whitney. Your observations and conclusions are quite correct."

A knock came upon the front door. It echoed through the hall outside the drawing room.

"There is Mr Cortney now. Let him in, will you, Whitney?"

I nodded and quickly dissipated. Seconds later, I appeared at the front door where I admitted a large man dressed in a tight-fitting dark suit. Balding with a well-trimmed black beard, he entered without giving me a second look.

"May I take your coat, Mr Cortney?" I said.

At the sound of my voice, Cortney jumped nearly a foot in the air. He turned to me, his eyes wide and hands raised.

"Who the devil are you?" he cried.

"I'm the new butler, sir."

"New one? What's happened to the old one?"

"I'm afraid he's moved on."

"Shelley has moved on? Where?"

"I couldn't say, sir."

The gentleman lowered his hands. "You really shouldn't creep up on a fellow like that. My body has been trained as a deadly weapon. I could've killed you with my karate reflexes."

"That would be an amazing feat indeed, sir."

"You doubt I could do it?"

"Oh, I have no doubt you are capable, sir. I only meant it is quite impossible."

"Why?"

"I am already dead."

Cortney grew white as the proverbial sheet. He gibbered at me for a full minute before issuing forth the loudest squeak I'd ever heard.

"D-D-Dahlia!"

"Oh, Gusty. Do calm down," Lady Dahlia said, peeking out from the drawing room doorway. "He won't harm you."

"Another ghost!" he shouted. "You've brought another ghost into this house?"

"All my servants are ghosts. You should know that. Now, come in here at once. We've only 'til the witching hour to solve your little problem."

Cortney sidled past me, never taking his piggish stare from my face. I considered transforming into my true appearance, complete with ragged flesh and oozing wounds, but reconsidered. I had no wish to make an unprofessional impression on my first day.

Cortney rushed into the drawing room, and I followed.

"You and your ghosts," Cortney said as he entered. "Why can't you bring someone living in for a change?"

"Spirits are more reliable."

"But you know how I feel about them. They're so frightfully... dead."

Lady Dahlia frowned. "I don't hire my servants based on your comfort level, Gusty." She waved him toward the chair opposite her own. "Sit down and tell me what's happened this time."

Mr Cortney settled into the seat across from Lady Dahlia and trembling, glanced at me. "Does he have to be here? Couldn't he go haunt some other part of the house?"

The urge to change into a mutilated corpse filled my mind once again.

"He stays," Lady Dahlia said. Her violet eyes bored into Cortney's and he shrank beneath her gaze.

"All right, then," he said, tugging at his collar. "If you insist"

"I do. Now, tell me your story before it's too late to help. I'm sure you don't wish to wait until tomorrow night in order to be rid of it."

Cortney shifted in his chair. "As you've no doubt gathered from my note, my new house is haunted. I did everything you told me to do. I smudged, I salted, I had the place blessed before I moved in, and the damn thing still got inside. How can I end this curse?"

"You know, there is but one way to end these hauntings for good. You should reconsider that option."

"What you suggest is out of the question. I cannot move my business to another part of town. It's taken me twenty years to establish it. And, I cannot abandon my profession. I know nothing else."

"Then you must remain the Butcher of Whitechapel," Lady Dahlia said. "And simply deal with the ghosts who believe you to be their killer. Am I correct in assuming this is yet another case of mistaken identity?"

"You are. Though I have been tempted, I've not taken a cleaver to any of my customers. At least, not yet."

Lady Dahlia smiled and picked up her pen. "All right then. Please, tell me about this ghost"

"It is a male this time. Appeared out of nowhere about two days ago. He started off violent, shrieking and shouting, accusing me of being the Butcher of Whitechapel. And today, he threw everything but the kitchen sink at me.

Why, I had to flee for my very life." He buried his face in his hands. "Help me, Dahlia. I am at my wit's end."

"Have you tried showing him a business card?" I asked.

Both Lady Dahlia and Cortney turned to stare at me.

"A calling card might convince him you are a simple butcher. After all, how many murderers carry cards announcing their business?"

"You'd be surprised," Lady Dahlia replied. She turned back to Cortney. "What does the spirit look like?"

"Rather like a barrister. One of the expensive kind. Three-piece suit, very fashionable and modern. Styles his hair like a hedgehog. You know the type."

"Hmmm..." Lady Dahlia said. She rose from the chair and hurried over to the corner of the room. I had not noticed it before, but two file cabinets stood there, covered by a tablecloth. Lady Dahlia tossed the cloth aside and opened one of the cabinets.

"Is he blonde?" she called.

"No. He has dark hair – and a dimple in his chin."

Lady Dahlia withdrew a folder from the cabinet and rejoined us.

"Is this him?" she asked, taking a newspaper clipping from the folder. She passed it to Cortney.

"That's the fellow alright. Stabbed in the chest, he was. Every time I see him, he's oozing on the carpets."

"I've heard of this case," the lady said, handing the folder to me. "They never found his murderer."

I perused the contents and found another photograph, accompanied by a brief paragraph. The fellow appeared just as Cortney had described.

"Read that aloud, will you, Whitney," Lady Dahlia said, resuming her seat.

"The body of one Benjamin Smith, 34, was found on Hemming Street near Whitechapel early Sunday evening," I read. "The young man had suffered several stab wounds in the chest but neither the assailant nor the weapon could be found. Scotland Yard offered no comment and would neither confirm nor deny whether the young man was yet another victim of the Butcher of Whitechapel."

"What's the date on that, Whitney?" Lady Dahlia asked.

"3rd November 2003," I replied.

"Are there any other articles?"

"Several on the Butcher."

"I want one about Smith."

"There's an obituary dated 17th November 2003."

"Read it, please."

"Benjamin Smith, security consultant for Red Eye Security, and former Lieutenant in the American Army, was killed Sunday, 2 November. He is survived by his mother, Anna, and his wife, Marjorie, both of Tallahassee, Florida, USA. Smith was described as a brave and conscientious employee by Mark Hopkins, his former employer."

"The anniversary of his death was two days ago," Lady Dahlia said. "Tell me, Gusty, did you take anything home with you that day? Anything unusual?"

"I don't think so."

"No, strange jewelry or coins?"

Cortney's small and beady eyes narrowed. "I did find a few coins in the street, about three of them, all stacked in a neat little pile. I believe they were American."

"Did you take them home?"

"Yes. I dropped them in a jar near the door."

Lady Dahlia shook her head.

"Gusty, sometimes I think you've goose-down for brains. You, of all people, should know not to remove items from a memorial."

Cortney's face grew white. "Memorial? I saw no memorial."

"Americans, especially soldiers, tend to leave coins on the graves of their comrades," I said. "Each denomination has a different meaning and significance."

"This was not a grave," Cortney cried. "Just a pile of coins."

"Perhaps, the visitor was unaware of the location of Smith's grave. He would, no doubt, have heard of the murder, and decided to memorialize his friend at the scene." I said.

"Oh dear," Cortney said, eyes bulging. "What have I done?"

"You've brought the spirit home with you," Lady Dahlia said. "And now we must help him move on. Whitney, fetch the purple carpetbag from the closet in my room. Then, meet us outside in the drive. Did you come by car, Gusty?"

"I did. I've hardly enough for cab fare and your fee."

"Fibber. Last I heard, you had enough money to cover cab fare from here to the Isle of Wight. Never mind. You'll have to leave your car here and come with us. If you follow, it will take too long." She turned to me. "On your way, Whitney. Time is growing short."

I bowed and vanished from the room. When I opened my eyes, I'd reached my destination. The interior of Lady Dahlia's bedroom was not what I had expected.

I'd thought Lady Dahlia might favor something dignified, perhaps even Victorian in this most private of rooms What I found was a large waterbed with two nightstands on either side. Both were painted black. An azure-hued lava lamp stood on each of the nightstands, and blue light filled the room. Strange shadows climbed the walls and the song, '*Green Tambourine*' blared from an unknown source.

I found the large walk-in closet on the opposite side of the room. The purple carpetbag lay inside. I picked it up and traveled as only a spirit can, to the front door and the driveway beyond.

A 1928 Rolls Royce Phantom, blacker than the night about it, waited on the white gravel. Its engine purred like a voracious cat. Lady Dahlia stood beside it.

"Ah, thank you, Whitney," she said. "Will you hold on to it until we reach London?"

"You wish me to accompany you?"

"Yes. You've a clever mind and I wish to make use of it."

"Very well."

The lady slipped into the back seat of the Rolls. Cortney barred my way.

"I insist he sit upfront with the driver," he said. "My nerves are on edge as it is."

"Gusty—"

"I don't mind, milady," I said.

"All right then. As long as you don't mind." She tapped the driver's seat before her. "20A Cheshire Street, Rodolpho." The spirit behind the wheel nodded and pulled out of the drive.

The journey to London took no time at all, for the Rolls traveled under the same power as myself. Within twenty minutes, we'd left the countryside behind. Within ten more, we'd entered Cheshire Street.

I had studied the folder since leaving Battleroost Manor, and closed it just as we stopped before 20A. Cortney quickly alighted and hurried up the steps to unlock the door.

"Be ready when we get inside," Lady Dahlia said to me. "The emotions in vengeful ghosts tend to escalate whenever their target is near. I've no doubt this one has gone full-on poltergeist"

"You can count on me, Lady Dahlia," I replied.

Cortney stood outside the door as we climbed the steps. He allowed us entrance and took up the rear.

A dark hall lay before us, its gloom so deep, even my enhanced vision could not penetrate it. We moved inside and the door slammed behind us.

Cortney wheezed.

I strained my eyes against the dark. Something lurked in the room to the far left, emitting a mélange of rage and fiendish glee. I stepped close to Lady Dahlia as Cortney fumbled at the light switch.

"He's in the second room to the left, milady," I whispered.

She nodded.

"Damn," Cortney said. "The switch isn't working."

"Hand me my bag, Whitney."

I passed the carpetbag to Lady Dahlia and she dug into it, producing a small torch. She switched it on. Cortney used the function on his cell phone. Both swept the hall, piercing the gloom with illumination.

"Where is your coin collection, Gusty?" the lady asked.

"Here, on the table near the door."

"Pick it up, please, and make for the sitting room. We shall face the spirit there. Whitney, let me know if he decides to show himself."

"Yes, milady."

Cortney led us to the sitting room across the hall while I monitored our quarry. He remained in his room, his rage growing. We reached the doorway without incident.

Lady Dahlia set to work the moment we entered the room. She pulled several long tapers and a box of matches from the bag.

"Keep an eye on our ghost, Whitney," she said, as she lit the first candle. She set it in a holder on the mantle. "If he comes rushing in, let me know. Gusty, find those coins. I've a feeling they'll be quite important to your ghost"

I stood at the door and concentrated my efforts. The spirit remained as unmoving and as dangerous as a coiled snake. Cortney settled himself on the floor and poured the coins onto the carpet.

Once the candles were lit, Lady Dahlia retrieved a box of salt from her bag. She approached Cortney, who grimaced.

"I hate this part," he said.

"It's this or the spray bottle of seawater, Gusty."

Cortney sighed and shut his eyes. She poured salt over his head and then turned the box on herself.

"It'll keep the ghost out of our bodies," she said to me. "And give him a nasty burn if he tries to throttle us."

She tossed the box into the unlit fireplace and turned her attention to the armchair beside it. Pushing it aside, she revealed a patch of carpet covered in dust.

"Perfect," she said under her breath. She reached into the bag a final time and withdrew a small primer.

"*Miss Pulsar's Occult Magic for Young Ladies*," I said, reading the cover.

"I've had this book since my school days," she replied. "The magic is somewhat juvenile, but useful in a pinch."

Lady Dahlia opened the book to the fifth page, and muttering to herself, raised her left hand in the air. She gestured in a semi-circular motion, as though she were the Queen waving outside Windsor.

The dust on the carpet stirred.

Particles rose into the air to form four small, funnel-like clouds. They churned, rising higher and higher. When they reached the ceiling, the lady dropped her hand to her side.

"What's our angry spirit up to now, Whitney?"

"I believe he's gathering energy for an attack. His rage is growing by the minute."

"Have you found the coins yet, Gusty?"

"I have." He held them up on his palm.

"You're sure there were only three?"

"Yes. A nickel, a dime, and a quarter."

Lady Dahlia took them from his hand and inspected them beneath the beam of the torch.

"Invaluable," she said.

A sudden rush of violent emotion assaulted my psyche. It radiated from the room down the hall.

"Mr Cortney," I said. "What do you keep in the room two doors down?"

"Several collections of sentimental value."

"Would a selection of medieval weapons count among them?"

"Yes. Why do you ask?"

"Our friend has discovered them and he's on the move."

My warning came not a moment too soon. A second later, a morning-star mace smashed through the sitting room door and flew across the room. It lodged itself in the flat-screen television.

"Gusty, come over here!" Lady Dahlia shouted. "And for heaven's sake, get down!"

The doors of the sitting room were blasted off their hinges as various weapons crashed through. The spirit entered.

A slew of different weapons floated in mid-air. They bristled about him, much like the hair on his head. He glowed pale light from head to toe.

The former security officer focused on Cortney, who cowered on the floor.

"Murderer!" he howled.

"Please, calm down, Mr Smith," Lady Dahlia said.

The spirit glanced up. He stared at the lady with opaque eyes. "This is not your affair, woman. Step away from that cringing coward."

Lady Dahlia's mouth formed a grim line. "I'll ask you once again. Please, calm yourself or I shall have to use force."

The spirit laughed.

"And, how will you do this, woman? You cannot contain me! I am as inevitable as time, as immutable as a storm!"

"And as detestable as Limburger cheese. Tell me. Are you always filled with this much hot air?"

The ghost wavered and, eyes blazing, surged forward three steps. The tiny funnel clouds roiled above his head.

"I take no joy in harming innocents," the ghost intoned. "But you try my patience, woman."

"My name is Lady Dahlia Battleroost. You'd do best to remember it." She snapped her fingers.

The funnel clouds ceased their turning. As they touched the ceiling, they spread and billowed, becoming dark clouds. Thunder filled the room and lightning forked. It flashed out, striking the spirit in the center of his spiky head.

"Ouch!" the spirit cried. "That hurt!"

The medieval weapons fell to the floor with a soft *thump*. The spirit rubbed his head with one hand.

"Are you prepared to listen?" Lady Dahlia asked. "Or must I zap you again?"

"I'll listen," the ghost replied.

"This man is not your murderer."

"Yes, he is. He's the Butcher of Whitechapel. He stabbed me in the chest"

"Mr Cortney is a butcher from Whitechapel. He deals in retail meats, not murder."

"I don't believe you."

"Show him your card, Mr Cortney," I said.

Cortney rose to his knees, dug into the inner pocket of his suit coat, and pulled out a card. He held it out with a trembling hand and the lady took it. She handed it over to the spirit.

"August Cortney. Fine meats and sausages, 12 Hemming Street, London," the spirit said. All the anger drained from his face. "I've made a dreadful mistake."

"Indeed, you have," Cortney said, rising to his feet.

"I am so, so sorry. I do hope you'll accept my apology."

"I should have you exorcised. Coming in here, smashing and breaking things. Why I could sue your family for damages."

"Oh, hush up, Gusty," Lady Dahlia said. "You brought him here when you took his memorial money. I'd say you're both even."

"But—"

"If you don't close your mouth, I shall increase my fee."

Cortney fell silent.

"What am I to do now?" the ghost cried. "I was sure I'd found my murderer."

"I would be more than willing to help you," Lady Dahlia said. "If you'll let me."

"How can you help?"

She took his ectoplasmic hand and placed the three coins on his palm.

"Someone left these for you. The dime means the visitor served with you; the nickel means you were in boot camp together. The quarter—"

"Means the visitor was there when I was killed." He looked up into Lady Dahlia's face. "There is a witness to my murder."

"Precisely. We need only find the witness."

"Perhaps, we could speak with a Miss Peggy Jones, of 223 Pinchin Lane," I said. "She was a colleague of Mr Smith. They both worked at Red Eye Security and she served in the American Army with him."

Lady Dahlia blinked. "However, did you discover that?"

I held up the file. "I read it here, milady. She wrote you a letter a month ago, saying she'd like to speak with you about her friend Ben and the Butcher of Whitechapel. Her address is on the envelope. She has a house on Batty Street."

"Mr Whitney, you are a treasure."

"I'm glad you think so, milady. I had large shoes to fill."

"I think you mean a 'large shirt.'"

"Indeed. A very large shirt."

A hint of a smile appeared at the corner of Lady Dahlia's mouth. She turned away.

"I'm afraid you're on your own now, Gusty. Mr Smith, Whitney, and I must pursue another adventure. Should you be haunted by another ghost while I'm gone, I suggest you have your calling cards ready."

She crossed the floor and vanished through the door with Mr Smith on her heels. I would have followed her, but Mr Cortney blocked my way.

"You there, Whitney, are you going to leave me here like this?" he said. "Couldn't you help me clean this up? After all, you are Dahlia's butler and—"

I faced Cortney and he stepped aside. His face grew pale and wan as I grinned through my torn visage.

"You are correct, Mr Cortney," I said. "I am Lady Dahlia's butler. I serve no other."

He gibbered away as I stepped through the door.

NIGHTLINGER: SINS OF THE WEREWOLF

STEVEN PHILIP JONES

I

There's no such thing as a werewolf.

Feril Nightlinger couldn't get the cliché out of his head.

There's no such thing as a werewolf.

He groped, searching for a breach in the ice. Either the one he and the beast made when they fell into the lake, or something like a drill hole left by a careless fisherman through which he could suck air.

There's no such thing as a werewolf.

Nightlinger had been submerged for seventeen seconds. Normally he could hold his breath well over five minutes, but the impact pounded most of the oxygen out of his lungs, and in frigid forty-degree water, he knew there were thirty seconds between him and dissolution.

There's no such thing as a werewolf.

The fingers and knuckles of his left hand were shredded from the ice's ragged underside, and he prayed he was still clutching his last hope in his numb right hand.

There's no such thing as a werewolf.

Nightlinger had been firing his revolver, a long-barreled .44 Magnum Ruger Redhawk, when the beast slipped under his spread and drove them over a bluff into the lake. After regaining his senses, Nightlinger had used his left hand to search for a way out, unwilling to let go of his big bore, though it was probably useless underwater. Circumstances now dictated he reconsider that opinion.

There's no such thing as a werewolf.

Even if he was still holding his revolver, there were problems with the bullets. Instead of Winchester brass jackets, his were cast in silver. He had water quenched the cases to heat-treat them for maximum hardness and minimum brittleness, but even so the soft metal would probably flatten out when it hit the thick ice. The one thing in his favor was the flat point design of the bullets, especially the wide nose, engineered to maintain good penetration in any animal as large as a Cape buffalo.

There's no such thing as a werewolf.

A frightening red film glazed over Nightlinger's restricted vision as he imagined himself lifting his right hand above his head, bringing the Redhawk's barrel close to the jagged ice, and squeezing the trigger.

* * *

Mike Segretto waited on the shoreline, shaking from the February wind and fear, searching for signs of life.

Almost a half-minute had passed since she saw Nightlinger and the beast fall through the ice. Mike had not taken her eyes off the breach since, even while she parked her Silverado, climbed out and ran to the edge of the lake, calling her employer's name. At the same time she ejected the fuzzy-tipped tranquilizer darts from her shotgun and replaced them with 20 gauge shells loaded with silver pellets.

After that, the only sound the young woman could hear besides the wind was her breathing. Stars speckled the infinite purple sky and the western horizon was awash in additive colors. A thicket lined the southern horizon, an uninhabited poacher's cabin tucked a few yards inside the wood line. Farms and pastures monopolized the world to the north, while bluffs stood sentry along the east. Minneapolis was an eternity and nearly a half hour away, ten miles west on county road M-43 and then almost twenty miles north on I-35.

"When a tree falls in a forest when no one is around, does it make a sound?"

Unable to think of anything else to do, and unwilling to give up, Mike took a step onto the ice and then jerked her foot back when thunder issued beneath the lake.

Thunder echoed again, followed by a violent cracking, and one hundred black birds took to the sky, a fluid swarm madly cawing, a kaleidoscope of noise made even more resonant by the isolation.

After a third sound of thunder, Mike spotted a fairy dust trail of ice geysering from the center of the lake and filter downwind.

"Feril!"

A lump of ice, about two feet square, flew into the air, ejected by a leather-gloved fist. Another hand, clutching a monstrous steel revolver with telescopic sight, breached next. Wrists and elbows followed like the whips of a squid, securing a perch, and with an exhausted heave Nightlinger hauled himself out of the water.

Mike cheered and dashed towards Nightlinger, lying motionless on his back. Maybe sixty yards separated them, too great a distance for him to hear her shouting, the winds carrying her cries away from him, but she hadn't run ten feet before her elation was guillotined.

A shape rose out of the initial breach made by Nightlinger and the beast on the east side of the lake, and in spite of the terminal daylight and a distance of over two hundred yards, Mike recognized the unique physique. Anthropomorphic, covered with copses of hair, with broad shoulders and a deep chest that tapered to a svelte waist and a pair of graceful hind-limbs between which hung a dense and length tail. From this distance the figure resembled the shadow of Pan.

The winds that had carried Mike's voice away from Nightlinger now wafted his scent towards the beast. Just like in a nightmare, Mike watched the shape pivot with a purpose and sprint for the prostrate man with the speed and grace of a jaguar.

* * *

Feril Nightlinger was unaware he could hear anything, too amazed that he was still breathing to notice anything except that he was alive.

The first sensation to distract him from his revelry was pain. His lungs felt bruised as he gulped air, and his right ear ached as if branded. He removed the thermoset mask from his face and saw its right side was smeared with blood. Without a second thought he tossed away the headpiece, figuring if the wound, whatever it was, hadn't killed him yet, it probably wouldn't any time soon.

The second sensation was that he must be cold. His skin and shoulder-length blonde hair were soaked. So were his sheepskin trench coat, slacks, sweater, and the protective chain mail he wore underneath, none of which were designed to insulate him against sub-zero temperatures. A weaker swimmer would have been dragged down by the weight, but the fact that he was shivering was further proof that he was alive, which made Nightlinger smile.

His chattering teeth called his attention to the sensation of sound, which alerted him to the rhythmic hum of the winds, then the insistent cawing of dozens of birds, and finally a familiar voice.

"Mike?"

Nightlinger coaxed his head off the ice to look, and sure enough, he spied the insufferably comely and effervescent Mike Segretto running towards him. He could tell she was shouting, but he could only recognize the frantic music of her voice, none of the words. Then Mike dropped to her knees, slid to a halt a little less than thirty yards from him, snapped the butt of her Deerslayer against her shoulder and aimed at something behind him.

Common sense was the final sensation Nightlinger regained.

There's no such thing as a werewolf.

Adrenalin pumped and he hopped to his feet, whirled, brought up the Redhawk and sighted the lycanthrope in his crosshairs, the beast less than half a football field away and closing fast.

"Hey!"

Nightlinger could not hear Mike's frantic pleas and he did not need to. He knew he had stepped between her and the charging creature and blocked her shot. Nightlinger had every confidence that Mike would have already switched the chlorpromazine tranks in the Deerslayer with sterling shotgun shells suitable for Tiffany's, in case the beast had managed to free itself from under the ice without him. Even so, by the time she re-positioned and aimed again it would be too late.

But Nightlinger had made his choice. It looked like there was no alternative now but to kill the monster and if so, he wanted the blood on his hands, not hers. In the long run, it was best for all involved.

Nightlinger paused one moment before firing. The werewolf was near enough that Nightlinger could make out one of Mike's fuzzy-tipped darts embedded in its right jugular, as well as the blood-encrusted mat of hair near its left shoulder, where one of Nightlinger's silver loads had pierced the creature earlier. Nightlinger also noticed a lack of the exhilaration he typically felt at the climax of a hunt. He was facing a monster, but under the surface, where it counted, this was a man.

"I'm sorry."

The beast leaped, forcing Nightlinger to adjust his aim, the werewolf nearly on top of him.

II

It was not so much like waking up from a sound sleep as being jolted out of a nightmare.

At the same instant that John Dalton realized he was conscious he also felt that he must have been awake for a while. His brain just had not been receiving incoming data in a rational manner. For some reason Dalton had not been thinking and reacting cognitively, much like an infant using its senses but being unaware it possessed them.

All systems were percolating now, however, and Dalton had no trouble recognizing – much less appreciating – the towhead, blue-eyed angel with a slightly innocent tomboy's face coming into focus in front of him. The angel concentrated on him for a few seconds, her expression perplexed, then turned to talk over her shoulder.

"I think he's going to stay awake this time," she said. "But at least the chlorpromazine worked out there."

"Eventually." A man's voice, wry.

Sounds of boot-shod feet crossing a planked floor, approaching, and the seraph stepped aside for a Gallic giant with cautious emerald eyes.

He's wary of me, Dalton thought. *What's so scary about me?*

Two years had passed since Dalton turned fifty, and he had never been one to skimp on the red meat, potatoes, or gravy. A brisk jog of one block made him gasp for a solid minute. Besides that, Dalton was eight inches over five feet tall and one and half stone shy of two hundred pounds, while the stranger looked fifteen years younger and had eight inches and seventy pounds on him.

Dalton asked: "What's going on?"

The stranger cocked his head, which let Dalton see a wound blemishing the big man's right ear. The injury must have been painful, but the stranger appeared not to notice as he contemplated Dalton.

The giant asked: "Don't you remember anything?"

"Like what?"

"How about last night? You were trying to find me. My name is Feril Nightlinger."

The name kindled a spark in Dalton's memory. "Nightlinger." He was not parroting, but feeling the word move his lips and tongue, realizing he had said this name before, over and over, like a mantra.

"There's a store in Minneapolis called The Haunted Bookshop," Nightlinger said. "You visited it yesterday and talked to the man who works there. His name is Stick. You gave him a business card. This card."

Nightlinger held up a black business card with embossed gold lettering. The card looked crumpled and limp, as if it had been washed and tumble-dried. Nightlinger handed it to Dalton. "Turn it over."

Dalton did, and gasped as everything he needed to remember ripped to the forefront of his thoughts.

Scribbled with silver metallic ink in his handwriting was: *CED-REL MOTEL ROOM B.* Underneath this was an archaic token, one Dalton had seen recently, once each the previous two evenings.

"You instructed Stick to tell me to meet you…"

"…before moonrise or innocent people will die. Were you too late?"

Dalton forced himself to watch Nightlinger nod, then bowed his head to pray, but not for himself.

"Good Christ, bless and receive their souls."

With his head down and eyes closed, Dalton never noticed the big man praying along with him, or that after he crossed himself and said, "Amen," Nightlinger silently mouthed the word with him.

Keeping his eyes closed, Dalton rewound and played back his final sensible moments from last night. The mental block gone, he had no problems re-experiencing the torturous pain that had attacked him like a ravenous, pouncing animal, an arthritic cramp that threatened to bow his fingers backwards. He could remember squeezing his right hand around the wrist and trying to stem the agony the way a tourniquet dams the body's circulation. Blood was already spreading out from his left palm, welling up from five straight grooves that intersected at right angles to form a star enclosed by a circular trench that touched each point of the star. A pentagram, just like the one he had sketched on the black business card. After that, everything rational evaporated, drowned out by the sensation of drinking molten coke and dancing with the dryads of a primeval forest who stripped the flesh from his body with bone burins.

Nightlinger said, "Maybe you should start by telling us how you became a werewolf."

* * *

Of course, one doesn't just become a werewolf. There are always unique circumstances. In Dalton's case, lycanthropy could have fallen under workman's comp.

"You see, I'm a sin-eater," he started. "It's been a family tradition for as far back as anyone in the Black Mountains of Wales can remember." Dalton had been born in Llanthony in County Gwent, his folks moving to America when he was a child.

Mike was confused. "What the heck is a sin-eater?"

"Some Celtic Christians will lay the body of a recently deceased family member in state and spread food and drink around it. I come and recite a sacrament while consuming the offerings, transubstantiating the food and drink into the deceased's sins. In this way I assume those sins, allowing the deceased's soul to ascend to Heaven."

Mike's face shriveled. "Pardon my French, but that sounds like a pagan loophole."

Nightlinger asked Dalton to forgive Mike's frankness and continue.

"I also own my own small business. I manage parking ramps and such in Kingston, Iowa. But I'm proud of my family's heritage, and when word-of-mouth spreads that I can help people, and they call to ask for my service as a sin-eater, I accept. After checking references. You have to be careful when dealing with the public. I'm sorry to say I wasn't careful enough on my last call."

Three weeks earlier, Dalton had been contacted by a Chicago advertising executive, Ed Gorman, whose son Moe had committed suicide. Reportedly the Gormans were long-standing Catholics and the father had a genuine concern for his boy's soul; nevertheless, Dalton had a priest, Father Connie Morrow, check on the Gormans through the archbishop at St Bartholomew's in Chicago, where the family attended mass.

"Everything checked out. Cook County coroners ruled Moe died of a self-inflicted gunshot wound to the head. All of the authorities seemed satisfied there was no foul play, although a suicide note was never found, so the boy's motive was a mystery. Moe was performing well at Northwestern, where he was a sophomore, although his grade point average did slip some during the second half of the fall semester."

Dalton had not sensed anything wrong during or after his service. Gorman did keep Dalton's presence a secret from the rest of the family, including his wife, but that was not unusual. "Suicides are hard enough on families without the additional stigma of a sin-eater. If anything struck me odd at the time it was Gorman's attitude."

"Which was?" Nightlinger asked.

"Indifferent. He was the most nonchalant client I've ever had. Or maybe relieved is a better word. In any case, Gorman is tough and not the kind of man who wears his heart on his sleeve."

After the service, Dalton drove back to Kingston, and a few days later he began to feel odd. "Ill, I thought at the time." He was warm, but not feverish, and sore, as if he had overtaxed his muscles. An itch was also driving him nuts, and his clothes felt tight. His shirt bit into his armpits, its collar scraped his throat, and the inseam of his pants pinched his crotch.

"I went to my G.P., Pat Krejci. Pat was also a friend and a patron at St. Wenceslaus, where I'm sort of Father Morrow's unofficial deacon."

"'Was'?" Mike asked.

"Yes." Dalton's eyes grew whiter and his shoulders slumped. "He agreed to squeeze me in for a visit two nights ago after he closed up at four o'clock. The first full moon of the month... rose... while he was examining me."

Dalton coughed. Cleared his throat. Blinked back tears. Finally could continue.

"When I recovered my senses the next morning, it didn't take me long to figure out what happened. Moe Gorman was a werewolf. He killed himself, but even with a silver bullet, suicide won't expunge lycanthropy. Such sins can't abolish curses, so when the next full moon rises, the werewolf rises from the dead. Gorman must have known that, so he hired me to consume both Moe's sins and the curse."

Dalton collected himself again.

"I have had occasion in my line of work to hear about you, Mr. Nightlinger. How you help people. Well, I need help. Maybe more than anyone you've ever tried to help before. Tonight's the second full moon for the month, and I have to die before dusk. But I can't kill myself. I'll just rise again, which would be an abomination against my Savior. You can kill me, though."

Mike shook her head and looked at Nightlinger, positive he would be as flabbergasted by the request as her. Instead, he appeared sympathetic, as if he had expected this crazy plea. Before Mike could appreciate what Nightlinger was saying, he answered, "Yes. I will. But only after you have tended your obligations here on Earth."

III

In Chicago that afternoon, no one at Davis & Hester Advertising gave it a second thought when Ed Gorman canceled the day's remaining appointments, dismissing it as grief, his son and only child buried one month ago today.

In truth, John Dalton had called to say it was time for them to square their account.

A few minutes after two o'clock Gorman parked his 1953 Mark IV in one of two empty stalls inside the garage of his country estate in Benchurch. The garage was connected to a rambling Jacobean-style house with unusually small heavy gables and windows set higher than is customary, the secluded home and acreage surrounded by a massive brick wall. Gorman's wife, Marie, was using the Aerostar while in Sarasota, staying with her parents for the winter, mourning Moe's suicide.

Gorman would have given his right arm to be with Marie and comfort her, but it was his job to attend to these loose ends. After all, he had been the one to stumble across Moe's frozen body in a ravine on the estate, a Remington 870 Winchester still clutched in the boy's hands. Gorman had suspected Moe's problem, and when the suicide note confirmed the impossible he tore it up and burned the pieces. After that, he surreptitiously began searching for a sin-eater and soon heard about Dalton living less than six hours away in Iowa.

Inside his home, Gorman required very little time to arrange things for his guest. He had expected Dalton would come back and had prepared for direct and indirect confrontations. By three o'clock there was nothing left to do but wait, so Gorman puttered in his den, half-reading correspondence until 4:16, when the doorbell rang.

Gorman opened the center drawer of his desk for the hundred and sixth time. Peeked inside. Shut it. Then got up to answer the door.

A gracious host, he ushered Dalton into the den, where Dalton sat in a chair in front of the desk. Gorman sat back down behind the desk.

With a trifle encouragement, Dalton was more than happy to vent his hostilities. Gorman listened while keeping track of the time in his mind's eye. When the time felt right, Gorman casually opened the center drawer for the hundredth and seventh time, removed a Glock 19 9.mm, looked at his watch, and interrupted Dalton.

"Three minutes before sunset. Close but no cigar, pal."

Gorman had figured Dalton would stare at the Glock, not at him, but Dalton never took his eyes off Gorman. It made this chore harder, but Gorman pressed ahead.

"Don't worry, it's loaded with silver bullets. Let's not either of us pretend you didn't come here for this. And after what you did for my boy, I figure I owe you. So thanks."

Gorman wasn't sure, but it looked like Dalton was getting ready to say something as he fired. Once. Then again. The first bullet in the heart and the second in the head, the combination knocking the dead man almost out of the chair. Instead the body started to slump and would have fallen to the floor if Dalton's armpits had not hooked over the armrests.

As if on cue, a stranger wearing a long black coat and a mask that covered the top half of his face stepped through the entrance to the den, aiming a chrome-plated Redhawk at Gorman's chest.

"Nice piece," Gorman said, placing the Glock on the desk and raising his hands.

No reply. The stranger stepped coolly, quietly, towards Dalton. In a heartbeat he surveyed the damage, his attitude clinical, then looked back at Gorman.

"So who are you supposed to be? The Green Hornet?"

"I'm John Dalton's friend."

"Oh. I guess you know what's really been going on, then. Well, what now? Gonna kill me?"

Dalton's friend cocked the Redhawk's hammer.

Gorman imitated Dalton and stared at the stranger instead of the gun. "But that wouldn't make sense. Dalton coming here, *that* makes sense. He wasn't after vengeance. Where would it get him? His waiting to come here until moon rise was only a couple of minutes off forced my hand. I had to kill him or end up dog meat. He figured I'd be prepared for it, which I was. Now he's free from that damned curse, just like my boy. Everybody's happy. Except you. But you killing me? That doesn't cut the mustard, so I'm betting you've got something else up your sleeve."

The masked man waited and listened.

"Let's say I kill Dalton," Gorman continued, "which I have, and then you show up and call the cops? That makes sense. I'm arrested and do hard time. Everything's wrapped up with a bow. Dalton's free from the curse and I'm paying for what I did."

"Sounds feasible. Maybe we should try it."

"Too bad it won't work."

Dalton's friend cocked his head as if curious to hear why not.

Gorman smiled. "Say you call the cops. I'm a respected citizen with public sentiment on my side. I'll just say Dalton got into my house and I plugged myself a burglar. Who's to say different? You? A guy wearing a mask with a story about werewolves and sin-eaters? This is Chicago!"

The masked man said nothing.

"No, that plan won't fly, nice as it might have sounded on paper. So either you kill me, which I think you would have done by now if you were going to do it, or take a walk and let me get busy feeding Dalton's body into a wood-chipper."

Gorman waited. The stranger seemed to mull for nearly a minute, then, finally, backed up towards the open door.

"I'm glad we could talk this through," said Gorman. "You can show yourself out?"

The masked man paused at the entrance. "By the way," he said, "when you left to let Dalton in, I switched the bullets in your gun."

And he left.

The sound of the door locking from the outside clacked in Gorman's ears. Snatching the Glock, he slid the clip out. He had loaded it with silver-jacketed Hallowpoints, but these were steel-jacketed.

Ragged, furious breathing stole Gorman's attention. He looked to where Dalton had fallen, but the sin-eater's corpse was gone.

Sitting in the chair was a tawny devil with tattered fur. Bones were popping and breaking inside the awful creature's body even as its nose and mouth elongated, metamorphing into a lupine snout, fangs sprouting through tar-colored gums. The only thing worse than those hungry jaws was the fingers and nails of the monster's hands, tapered like claws, its bleeding palms resembling the pad of an animal's paw.

An effortless pounce, and the werewolf was on him.

* * *

Nightlinger listened until he was sure Gorman was dead and the werewolf was busy feeding. His right ear hurt as he pressed it against the door, the wound still fresh from where one of his bullets ricocheted off the ice and sliced the lobe. He only wished this was the worst pain he would have to deal with tonight. Rather than give himself time to think, Nightlinger unlocked the door and re-entered the den.

The werewolf turned and snarled, ready to charge. Nightlinger raised the Ruger, and unlike the night before, he aimed and fired in one smooth motion. If he missed now, there would be no delayed reaction from Mike's tranquilizers to subdue the monster.

In its last moment of existence, the werewolf's expression changed from rage to cheerless resolution.

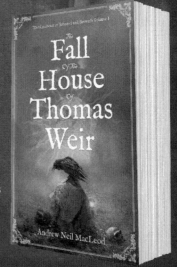

INN GOOD SPIRITS

NANCY HANSEN

It was Labor Day weekend, time off for most Americans, yet there was still work to do for the self-employed. Chandra Smoake and her young understudy and faithful companion, Emma Gilbraith, had been informed of another potential client desperately in need of their services. It wasn't a long drive away, so they decided to check it out. They had just entered the charming Berkshire Hills area of Massachusetts when the gas gauge indicator was touching 'E'.

"Oh drat, we're going to need petrol soon," Chandra said with a bit of a frown, "and more concise directions would be useful as well. Emma dear, keep your eyes open for a refueling business."

"You mean a service station?" the blond college student with the big blue eyes said as she shut her text book and sat up properly in her seat. She already had a term paper due in a couple of weeks, and had been trying to get in some studying.

"Whatever they call them here, yes," Chandra said with a sigh.

An hour later, gas tank filled, tires aired, with a clean windshield and sipping the last dregs of two thick green glass bottles of icy cold cola, they pulled up in the charming old village center of Webster Falls. Most of the homes around the area were well-kept Colonial era farmhouses or Victorian buildings with multiple gables and turrets. The few people out in yards or walking dogs stared at the newcomers rather curiously, for it was unusual to see two women driving alone. Chandra was used to that sort of thing; the short, plump woman's somewhat darker skin as well as her well-tailored, though understated, clothing always seemed to confound people about her heritage. Of course the New York license plates on the Buick might also generate some interest. They probably looked like tourists out leaf-peeping.

The small, square, three story Webster Inn stood before them. Built in the late 1700s, it had once been a stagecoach stop and then a hotel, but now served as a rooming house for college students and young professionals. The current owner was Henry Windham, a short prematurely balding man in a sport shirt and slacks with dark horn-rimmed glasses. He had been informed that Chandra was coming to speak with him today, so when her vehicle pulled up, he met them out at the curb.

After introductions, Chandra got right down to business while Emma pulled out a notebook and a ballpoint pen to scribble the details in shorthand.

"What seems to be the problem here, Mr Windham?" Chandra asked. She couldn't sense very much about the building from the exterior, but it certainly was old enough to have garnered some leftover psychic phenomena.

He gave her a sheepish look. "I feel foolish admitting this, but I think the place is haunted. I've owned it for almost five years now – got it for a bargain because it was unoccupied and badly in need of renovations. I had two different work crews in because the first one couldn't deal with all the strange things going on."

"Really?" Chandra interjected with an encouraging look.

He began to explain. "Believe me, it was beyond explanation! Tools would disappear and then were found somewhere else. Properly installed fixtures came crashing down unexpectedly. Doors would slam shut or reopen themselves behind you, and one man said something came up and tugged his cap off."

That was fairly typical in poltergeist activity, but she had to ask the usual question. "You're positive this wasn't just a case of shoddy work habits and wild imaginations?"

He sighed. "Well yeah, at first I figured it might be something like that, but even the second crew had similar experiences. And these fellas were from a different area, so as far as I can tell, they didn't know each other. We eventually got through it and the work was finished. Once I had rented some rooms things settled down for a bit, but then my tenants began to have problems. It's been an uphill battle all along."

"I'm sure it has been quite trying," Chandra said in a soothing tone. "So now you're having trouble keeping tenants?"

"I sure am," he admitted with candor, running his fingers through his thinning hair. "Things have escalated recently, and I can't keep apartments rented. So I'm losing my shirt on this place. You see, as it gets into fall like it is now, the... um... *activities* seem to increase."

"Interesting," Chandra said, and she nodded to Emma to make a note of that. "Can you describe what is currently going on? Is there any particular malevolence in it?"

The man had to think that over. "Well, people have told me that doors slam shut even when the windows are closed, and books and personal items come flying off of shelves to land on the floor. There's been the sounds of footsteps on the stairs at night or in the early mornings, and sometimes someone rapping on the doors, or where doors used to be but we bricked over the openings. Yet there's never anyone there! One elderly woman was livid because she came home to find pictures of her family had been tossed about. I thought at first maybe we had a problem boarder, but even with the new locks on the apartments, someone or something keeps getting in. Out of eight apartments, I only have two rented now and I've gotten notice from one of those tenants that she's moving out."

"That is really unfortunate, though I'm sure it has been quite trying for the tenants. I'd like to speak to them if that can be arranged," Chandra said as Emma was furiously scribbling notes.

"I can ask," he said uncertainly. "People really don't like to talk about it, we all feel rather foolish." He looked somewhat forlorn.

"It's not as uncommon as you would think," Chandra said kindly as she looked around the area. "This is a very old building in what was once likely the village center of a small and tightly knit community. A classic setting for a persistent spirit, but what we need to find out is *why* the essence of that being insists on lingering here. They do usually have a reason; generally some sort of unfinished business. What time of day do these events seem to take place?"

Henry Windham shrugged, his hands in the pockets of his slacks. "There's no real specific time. Nothing I could put a pattern to, except for there's more incidents at night. But then again, tenants are home more at night, and people get jumpier in the dark."

"Indeed they do," Chandra said, and then she had a thought. "It occurs to me that we have the rest of the weekend to ourselves, and I was going to secure a hotel room somewhere anyway. If my assistant is willing, would you be able to accommodate us to stay here? It would give us a chance to get a proper reading on the place."

Windham didn't completely understand what she meant by 'reading' but he saw an opportunity in cooperating, because he could deduct the rent for a couple of days from Chandra's fee.

"Of course! I do have a small two bedroom apartment on the second floor that is currently vacant, though you'll have to share a bathroom with another tenant. There's only one gal upstairs now, and she's a nice young woman who always pays on time, so I'd hate to lose her. The fellow downstairs is a Fuller Brush salesman, so he isn't home often, and we have facilities for him on the first floor. He's supposed to be back tomorrow if you're staying."

"If we decide you have an actual problem here, and we sign a contract, we will stay as long as it takes to get the job done," Chandra reassured him.

"Well, we'll see how it goes then. You'll have to find your meals elsewhere of course because we don't allow cooking inside, but if you take a short drive into the city, there are some nice diners."

"What do you think, Emma?" Chandra asked the girl.

"I have a few days off, so I could totally dig that," she said without thinking, but at Chandra's frown, Emma corrected herself and said, "I mean, that would be fine, thank you."

"All right then," Windham said in a relieved tone. "Parking is in the rear, just drive around. I'll get you a key now, in case I'm not here when you get back. In the meantime I'll make sure the rooms get aired out, and I'll scrounge up some clean bedding. I'll see you ladies possibly tomorrow afternoon, after church."

* * *

They did find a small restaurant to eat in not too far down the country highway, for the Berkshire hills in fall were a popular tourist area. While they waited for their meals, Emma and Chandra went over their notes and talked in low voices of what might be happening at the Webster Inn. Once the meal was finished they headed back to the inn. While unloading their bags they were delighted to find a youngster by the name of Tommy, who had been told to wait nearby and help two ladies with their suitcases.

"Mister Windham said I might get a dime for carrying your bags upstairs," he said hopefully as Chandra handed them over.

"I should think we could manage a dime for each bag," Chandra told him, and got a big toothy smile.

"Are you really a ghost hunter?" Tommy asked as he hefted her suitcase and took Emma's as well. Chandra insisted on carrying her purse and her tote bag of occult supplies. You didn't trust such things to children.

"You could term it that way," Chandra answered with her own smile as she climbed the stairs behind him. She did like children, even when they were inquisitive. This one seemed ambitious as well.

"Well, ghosts don't scare me! Besides, my dad says they're just make-believe."

"Many people seem to think so," Chandra answered in a noncommittal tone, though her psychic senses were already tingling. There was no spirit chatter but a couple of presences stood out, and one of them was quite reticent in nature. It could prove to be an interesting night.

Tommy was paid his two dimes and encouraged to run along. Chandra made sure the downstairs door was securely locked behind him. The young gentleman who lived on the ground floor didn't seem to be in – presumably he had his own key. She headed back up the central staircase, which was well-worn but polished wood, and heard Emma talking to another woman.

"Miss Chandra, this is Lucy Parker, and she's been telling me some pretty interesting stories," Emma said with her usual aplomb. Emma was an amiable young woman who made friends readily and set people at ease, which was another reason Chandra had taken her on as a protégé. Chandra greeted the other young woman and asked her if she'd like to come into their apartment to talk while they unpacked and got settled in.

"Oh heavens, no!" Lucy said with unmistakable distaste. "That room has the most problems in the building right now, and I can't abide it." She was a dainty little slip of a thing with dark hair and big eyes in an oval face, and she continually wrung her hands. "I suppose we could talk in my room, if you don't mind the mess."

"Whatever makes you comfortable Dear. We're not here to judge your housekeeping," Chandra told her in a soothing tone. Lucy Parker appeared to be high-strung, and that sort seemed to witness more poltergeist activity. There was something about nervous energy vibrations that restless spirits were drawn to, though they also responded to certain personality traits. Chandra had made a great study of such things, and now she wondered which of the entities had latched onto the young woman.

The little efficiency apartment they entered was actually relatively neat except for piles of folded fabric, a sewing machine, and an ironing board that took up almost a quarter of the space. Lucy moved some of the fabric off of chairs and asked them to sit down. "I wish I could offer you some coffee or tea, but we're not supposed to cook in here. It's a fire code thing."

"Thank you, but we just had dinner," Chandra said as she crossed one leg over the other while Emma laid her usual notebook out on her lap and clicked a pen to add the time and date to the new page. When all was ready Chandra said, "Now please, tell us everything you've experienced, from the beginning."

As usual, it was quite a tale. Lucy Parker was working her way through college by doing some sewing and tailoring, which she appeared quite good at. She needed a low cost rent that would allow her to sew at odd hours when she didn't have classes. She'd been a tenant for a year and a half, and was close to getting her first degree, but might have to leave before the final term because the problems with the building had become too hard to handle.

"I don't get enough sleep, and because of that I can't concentrate in class," she told them. Emma nodded sympathetically, some of the instructors did tend to drone on.

"I'm so sorry, I wish your landlord had contacted us sooner. Tell me what keeps you awake."

She related that there were knocks on the doors and rapping in the walls at night that woke her up. Sometimes the inner doors in the building – including even the unoccupied rooms – would slam shut or open of their own accord. She'd heard a girl sobbing in the night and heavy footsteps on the attic stairs when there should have been no one around. Most frightening were the repeated creaking noises and groans from the attic above them. It was a chilling account, even without any overt malevolence involved.

"Do you know your downstairs neighbor at all?" Chandra asked pointedly. There were some men who delighted in frightening women, and she had to make sure that he wasn't adding to the reputation of the building for his own purposes.

"Not very well," Lucy admitted, "but Mr Owens seems like a nice enough fellow. He's friendly for the most part, though he's not here very often. He always says hello if he sees me. You don't think he's doing this, do you?"

"We're going to speak with him if he comes in at some point," Chandra remarked as Emma jotted that down.

A bell in the local Congregational Church tower rang eight times, and Emma glanced up in surprise. Looking out the small window, it was already dark. She gave Chandra a sideways glance through her blond bangs. They still needed to get settled in, and it had been a long day with a very early start.

"I think we should be going," Chandra said, and got to her feet. "You've been quite a bit of help Miss Parker, and we're going to do our best to resolve this issue while we're here."

"Thank you both," the young woman said with relief as she saw them out, and then locked, bolted, and chained the door shut behind them.

* * *

Back in their own apartment, Chandra and Emma unpacked and made ready for bed. Because traveling was such an ingrained part of what they did, they always brought along enough clothing and toiletries for a couple days of a stay somewhere.

The bedrooms were small, no bigger than a large closet, which they did not have, though there was a small chest in each and some pegs on the wall. The was a central parlor with a small sofa and chairs. The bathroom was communal in the hallway outside.

They sat together for a bit and went over the notes.

"Do you think this is legit, or is Lucy giving us a snow job?" Emma asked around a yawn.

Chandra was also tired, and so didn't bother correcting her language. "There's definitely something here because I can sense it. Whether Miss Parker also senses it or is simply spooked and imagining things, I've no idea. If I have understood your question correctly," she added with a hint of disapproval for Emma's slip back into Beatnik slang, "she does not strike me as someone to make things up just to gain attention. She genuinely seems frightened."

"I thought so too, because when I first started talking to her, Lucy had a bad case of the zorros." At the look Chandra gave her, she rephrased it. "I meant," Emma yawned again, "she was a nervous wreck. She seemed to calm down once we sat with her."

"I'm not surprised. This sort of thing is disconcerting and yet no one likes to feel like an odd duck." Chandra smiled at her own use of slang. "You appear quite tired, Emma. Why don't we call it a night?" The younger woman had her text book open on her lap but hadn't turned a page.

"Maybe you're right. I mean, I've really got to get on the stick with this term paper, but I'm bushed right now and I've got to catch some Zs." She got to her feet, and gathering her things, headed for the bedroom that was hers. "Nite!"

"Sleep well. I'll be turning in soon myself," Chandra said as she shut off the nearby lamp. She sat in the dark for quite a while after Emma's door closed, reaching out with her occult senses, trying to get a better read on the place. It was easier to do that in the dark, with less visual distractions.

There was a lot of spiritual residue, but again only two main opposing entities were present. She decided that whatever issues they had were not with the tenants as much as each other. Chandra got the impression that they were locked in some sort of perpetual battle of wills. While trying to sort through it, she stretched out on the sofa and put her feet up. Tired from the day's drive, she fell fast asleep.

She had the most vivid and disturbing dream...

* * *

It was darkening and spitting snow, a cold that seeped through her hooded cloak and the dress beneath. She was trying to run, but the big belly hampered her as she dodged through the trees and brush, trying to leave the horseman behind. He was relentless in pursuit, his steed plodding noisily over the crusty ground. She didn't dare take the time to turn around and see how close he was but just kept blindly hurrying on, knowing that if he caught her, he'd beat her because she hadn't complied with something that he wanted her to do after he left for Boston.

She stumbled into a hollow, and had trouble getting up. The horse passed by with her unseen. She lay there on her belly, breathless and quivering in fear. Then the knifing pains began, and she cried out in agony as spasms grew intense.

He heard her and came back. He waited while the small life passed from her, too soon, and took it away, saying things would be well now after all.

The scene changed.

They asked her lots of questions that she couldn't answer, because she couldn't recall much that happened on that cold night. Neither could she remember how she found her way back, nor where the babe was. But they eventually found it – dead. Murdered. Drowned like an unwanted kitten or puppy.

She screamed for mercy beneath the hood when the floor fell from the gallows, but that scream was cut off by the choking sensation of the rope. She was kicking and struggling to breathe and they had to pull on her legs to make it end.

* * *

"Miss Chandra, are you all right?"

Emma stood above her in the darkened room, a penlight in her hands. Chandra started at the sight, not realizing where or even who she was, and then relaxed.

"I'm fine, dear," Chandra said with a groan, sitting up wearily and running her hands down her face. "Put the lamp on please." She reached for the notebook, which had landed on the floor. Emma handed her the pen, which had fallen with it and rolled away, and then sat down beside her mentor while the older woman jotted down notes and read through them, making corrections where necessary before shutting it with a sigh.

"You cried out in your sleep," Emma told her in a concerned voice. "Was it a bad dream? Or... something else?"

"An unpleasant dream and perhaps a message of sorts," Chandra said in a low tone. "Something dreadful has taken place in this vicinity." She handed the notebook to Emma, who read it with interest and growing alarm.

"So she's the source of the problems they've been having here?" Emma asked, handing the notebook back.

"I would say that's a good wager. What time is it, dear?"

Emma glanced at her wristwatch, which she wore most of the time when they were out on a case. "It's 2:31 a.m. You must have fallen asleep here after I left the room."

"Yes I did, and I'm now going to finish my night's sleep in a bed," Chandra told her, heaving herself to her feet and collecting her things. "In the daylight hours, we're going to have a look at that attic, we'll inform Mr Windham when he comes by after church. I need to understand why this girl's spirit lingers here, when it seems to me her baby was stillborn elsewhere."

* * *

When they went out to a late breakfast on Sunday morning, Chandra and Emma could hear the sewing machine running in Lucy Parker's room. Hopefully she at least had a peaceful night. Once back at the Webster Inn, not only was Henry Windham's dark blue Hudson Hornet out front, but a two-tone red and black Nash Rambler convertible was parked behind it. Young Tommy, likely angling for another dime or two, was helping carry some bags indoors. Since one of them was the standard black samples case bulging with items, this had to be Mr Owens, the Fuller Brush salesman. Chandra parked her Buick out back and then she and Emma walked around to the front to meet him.

Henry Windham was standing on the wide doorstep talking to Owens, a tall and broad-shouldered, red-haired man in a stylish suit and hat. Following his landlord's glance, he turned to peer at Chandra and Emma with a wide and toothy smile.

"Here they are," Windham said as he quickly introduced them. "Larry Owens, I'd like you to meet Mrs Smoake and—"

"It's *Miss* Smoake," Chandra said primly, and extended a gloved hand. "Chandra Smoake to be precise, of the New York/New England Regional Paranormal Society. This is my assistant, Miss Emma Gilbraith. We're here at Mr Windham's request, for he seems to be having some problems with otherworldly activity, which we are investigating."

"You mean," Larry Owens' face lit up with a big grin, "You're looking for

Casper The Friendly Ghost?" He laughed at his own joke, obviously not taking any of it too seriously.

Chandra did not find that amusing, and it showed in her frown. Henry Windham looked from one to the other, already tense. This was not how he hoped things would go.

"Yes, that's generally the idea," she said with sarcasm dripping from her voice. "though they're not all friendly. I take it you've had no problems during your stay here Mr Owens?"

"Not really," he said with aplomb. "I'm in and out a lot anyway." He tended to gesture with his hands quite a bit. "Old places like this make lots of strange noises, but there's been nothing that bothers me. I'm a heavy sleeper – I have to be, I'm on the road so much. Most of the other tenants have been women, and well... you ladies tend to get awfully excitable about noises in the night. I figured it was just a case of contagious hysteria."

Contagious hysteria indeed! Chandra restrained herself from sighing aloud. If this man could have witnessed the things she had dealt with, he wouldn't be so glib. Henry Windham seemed embarrassed, for he had hired Chandra Smoake's services and now felt foolish for having done so.

"I have a small office downstairs in the rear, Miss Smoake. If you'd care to meet with me there we can go over terms."

"Yes, let's do that," she said, nodding briefly at Larry Owens as they moved past. Owens never noticed for his eyes had been riveted on blond and slender Emma, who had worn a dress rather than her usual dungarees, because it was Sunday. Emma completely ignored him.

"Wowza – I should get myself an assistant like that," Owens quipped as he headed toward his own rooms.

It was a cramped and airless little office area that had two mismatched kitchen chairs placed before a small desk backed by a rolling stenographer's seat. A shelf ran the length of one wall over a filing cabinet and a small safe. Chandra brought out the standard contract along with carbon paper and an extra copy from her folder, and they went over it.

"Jeepers, this'll be rather costly," Windham said unhappily, running his fingers through his thinning hair.

"I understand your concern," Chandra answered. "Yet this is how I make my living, and I assure you Mr Windham that I am competent at my work. I can provide references. You must make the difficult decision whether it is worth the expense to be able to rent rooms without further problems, or to forego it if you feel that my fee is too high. That is strictly non-negotiable," she explained.

In the end he signed it, and paid the customary one third in cash up front to cover their expenditures. Chandra signed and dated it, and gave him his copy.

"I will give you a detailed accounting of whatever our incidentals are, and be assured that having a place to stay will significantly reduce that. Now perhaps we can get to the business of what I intend to do here. How many apartments does this building have presently, on which floors, and what are their capacity?"

"Eight all told. I have three one bedroom and one two bedroom downstairs, each has a sitting room. They are served by a full bathroom right next to this office," he said, indicating the door they had seen on the way in. "Upstairs is the only other two bedroom apartment, which you ladies have, and three single room efficiencies of various sizes. Miss Parker has the smallest one, the other two are vacant. I assume you've seen the bath up there?"

"Yes," Chandra admitted. It was cramped with a small tub, commode, and tiny sink with a little mirror above. Towels and washcloths had been a problem, but they'd been able to borrow some from Lucy Parker. "What about your attic? I noted outside it has three dormers and some end gable windows."

"Right now that is stuffed with leftover renovation supplies along with some furniture and fixtures, but it's accessible through a door in the middle of your hallway that opens on a stairwell. I keep that locked, though the lock seems faulty because we've found it open at times."

"I see," Chandra said, nodding at Emma, who was taking notes, to jot that down. "We should like to have a look around the attic today if you could arrange it."

He shook his head. "I don't know if that's a good idea. It's a big mess, and there's no lights up there right now."

"It is important," Chandra insisted. "We've brought along torches, after all."

At Windham's confused and somewhat concerned look Emma spoke up. "Battery operated flashlights," she reassured him.

"I suppose we could let you take a peek, but you must be careful. The stairs are old and very steep, and the flooring while solid, is buckled in places. This is an old building after all."

"We've explored our share of those," Chandra reassured him as she tucked away her copy of the contract in her briefcase. "Is there a cellar?"

He shook his head. "No, just a shallow crawlspace. We had a devil of a time running new plumbing because of that. There used to be an attached pantry and buttery out back when this was an inn, but there was a fire out there some years back and the last owners tore it down. They took down part of the top floor of this building too, that's where the servant's quarters were. It was unstable because back in the day they had expanded some of it over the rear building, which was a wooden addition, not brick like this part. It was beginning to lean and pull apart, or so I was told. So the roof is newer and those dormers let in some light, which is good since it's not wired yet."

"All very interesting," Chandra said, thinking about the area of the servant's quarters being eliminated in relation to the reported disturbances in the attic and her very vivid dream. She got to her feet. "If you don't mind, we're going back to our rooms to change now, but we'll meet you in half an hour for our chance to view that attic."

"I'll be upstairs by then," he promised. "But I can't stay much longer. The wife is cooking a pork roast and if I'm late to dinner, she'll skin me alive."

* * *

The attic door was in a recessed area next to the second floor bathroom. The rickety stairwell it opened onto went up at an extreme pitch with no handrails. Yet it was so narrow the two women were able to brace themselves against the side walls while going up. Henry Windham stood at the bottom holding the door open, watching them climb until he was certain they were up there safely. Then with one last reminder to please be careful, he propped the door open with a wooden chair and left for the day.

Lucy Parker was out, which was a relief, since she was terribly nervous about them stirring things up. They had left behind the faint sound of Larry Owens singing off-key to a jazz number on his record player, so he at least was occupied.

It was stuffy, dusty, and rather hot up there. The attic was very cluttered, but Chandra and Emma split up and each took an end to explore. Chandra had with her some holy water in an atomizer bottle and her archangel cards as well as a pictorial icon of her patroness Diana in one pocket of her dungarees. She hated wearing what she referred to as 'cowgirl pants', but the fabric was tough and didn't stain easily. One just could not clamber about in a skirt or dress while exploring the neglected areas of old buildings and expect to come out unscathed.

In the back part of the attic, an unseen stack of objects tumbled down.

Chandra called out, "Emma, was that you?" fearful that her assistant might have stumbled and been injured.

"Nope, I'm nowhere near there," Emma answered immediately. "Though I thought I saw something dart past me just before it happened." She sounded uneasy.

Chandra began making her way over to where Emma's voice had come from. "Perhaps it was just some animal frightened of the light and our presence," she suggested in a soothing tone.

"Too big for that, it was almost as tall as I am. And there was a smell, like... cooking grease and smoke mixed with something outdoorsy or maybe herbal. I don't know how to describe it." No matter how rattled she might get, Emma dutifully observed and reported whatever she had experienced.

Chandra reached her side and swept her own flashlight around. There were windows in each end gable, but they had been blocked with dusty old shades of a dark color, so very little light came from them. There were no windows or dormers in the back of the attic at all, where the noise had come from. Just a modern brick chimney that came up through the roof, likely to accommodate the boiler in the crawlspace below that heated the building.

Chandra shone her light around the cluttered space and there was absolutely no sign that anything had been disturbed.

"I don't get it," Emma said with a frown. "I mean, that noise was loud! It sounded like a whole stack of lumber or something slid down."

"Yes it was. We both heard the sound of something falling, yet there's nothing here that has been disturbed in quite some time. I'd wager someone wants our attention. If you are sufficiently recovered, I'm going to try to summon our hidden guest. I think we should make our way toward the stairwell first though, just in case things become a bit volatile."

Chandra couldn't sense anything outwardly malevolent, but there was a definite restiveness to the attic environs that she didn't care for. As near as she could read it, it was the accumulation of some great residual fear and angst that had lingered throughout the ages. Whatever spirit had tenaciously remained resident felt distinctly timeworn and intensely distressed. That concurred with the dream she'd awakened from, which had a Colonial era feel to it. What exactly had occurred here so long ago to prompt this kind of persistent haunting?

"All right Emma, if you are ready," Chandra said in a resolute tone as they stood on either side of the opening to the narrow attic stairwell. "let's see if anyone wants to communicate with us."

After handing off her blessed Michael Archangel card to Emma for her protection, Chandra sprayed the area around them both with the Holy

Water. Then holding up the card for Uriel, the angelic representative of spiritual comfort and wisdom, she took several deep, calming breaths before calling out in a moderately loud and persuasive voice.

"If there are spirits nearby who wish to contact us, let them make their presence known."

She counted to twenty-two, which her study of ecclesiastical texts said was a significant number, and then called out again. This time there was a reaction, for both their flashlights dimmed as if the batteries were dying.

Chandra knew that meant something was drawing down on the batteries stored energy in order to manifest. The answer as to whom or what came not from where she expected though.

The chair at the bottom of the stairs fell over as the door it had been propping open suddenly slammed shut. There was the faint but distinctive clomp and creaking of heavy footfalls coming up the stairs. That elicited the rather muffled sounds of a young girl weeping while she prayed, which seemed to originate from a greater distance than the back of attic afforded them. There was a whiff of old wood smoke, whiskey, and wet woolen clothing as an unseen presence, slow moving but resolute and purposeful, passed between the two women in the darkness. It moved by them impatiently, ignoring their presence as if they weren't even there.

There were quiet spoken, garbled words in a rough and low pitched man's voice, which had an accent and phrasing not readily understood. That contrasted with the repeated protests and pleas from the girl – whilst incoherent, her fear and hopelessness were palpable. A sudden snarled command followed by the unmistakable sound of a hard clout silenced the girl briefly, though she continued to weep. Then came the rustling of cloth, the rhythmic creaking of an unseen bedframe under weight, and the heavy breathing and grunting of the man while flesh slapped flesh repeatedly with growing urgency. It ended abruptly with a low-voiced, triumphant groan. The girl's faint sobbing faded into an echoing silence.

In moments it was all over. Now it needed to be interpreted to understand what it would take to ease the spiritual tension in the building.

Chandra turned her flashlight off and then back on. It lit up again and seemed to work fine.

Emma, who generally had good nerves, was quaking like a sapling in a gale. "W-what was that all about?" she asked in a low and frightened voice as she fumbled with her own flashlight, almost dropping it and the card of Michael Archangel. Chandra took both gently from her trembling hands before tucking the card away.

"We were allowed to listen in on something private but extremely disturbing from the past of this building," Chandra told her, handing back to Emma her now working flashlight. "It must have taken an incredible amount of energy to replay that scenario from a discarnate state. Let's head downstairs and sit quietly for a bit. Then we'll go have an early dinner before everything closes down."

* * *

When they went out for the evening meal, neither Chandra nor Emma spoke much. They found a small restaurant with a quiet corner table they could sit alone at and sip tea while waiting for their meals. Chandra had learned to take things in stride, for she'd experienced far worse situations that this. Yet Emma seemed particularly affected by the encounter, and that made her mentor wonder why.

"I take it that you found this afternoon's experience especially troubling?" Chandra asked her after spending most of the meal coaxing Emma to eat something or talk about their attic adventure. Hadn't Emma understood the significance of that ghostly encounter in relation to the dream? Chandra had no idea how worldly her assistant was, though she was in college so presumably she had some knowledge of such things.

The younger woman looked up briefly, her blue eyes troubled. She stopped playing with her food long enough to answer.

"Yeah, it really bothered me because it reminded me of something that happened when I was a kid." At Chandra's slight gasp, Emma shook her head. "No, not to me. I had a friend who always came begging for a sleepover whenever one of her uncles visited. She told me that he... that he um..." she leaned in and lowered her voice further. "He *did* things to her that no uncle should ever do." Emma looked back down and her blond hair hung over her face. "I felt sorry for her, but I honestly had no idea at the time what she was talking about! So it really creeped me out and I wouldn't let her tell me any more. Then one day her family just up and moved away and I never saw her again. I hadn't thought about her in ever so long – until today."

Chandra reached across the table and clasped her hand. "And now that you can comprehend the heartbreak and terror she went through, you wish you had done more to help. Don't be so hard on yourself Emma, you were too young to understand back then. While we're unable to help your childhood friend find her peace, there's a good chance that we can do that for this lost soul."

Emma looked up. "I thought we were there to help Mr Windham keep his tenants?"

"Indirectly, yes that is our purpose." Chandra had made up her mind what needed to be done. "But those in that building with the biggest issues to be resolved are no longer amongst the living. So tonight we will be having a séance, and Miss Parker and Mr Owens will be invited to attend if they so wish. We now know there are two opposing spirits residing there, one male and one female, and they are causing all the turmoil. I believe it is time they had their final confrontation – before an audience. So that the truth can be known."

"That sounds like a pretty scary thing to do," Emma commented as the waitress came over to clear the table, clucking her tongue in displeasure as she took away Emma's barely eaten meal to bag up for 'the dog'.

"Well," Chandra said as the waitress bustled away with their plates, "scary things are what we get paid to handle, after all."

* * *

Larry Owens was rather interested in attending his first séance, especially once he was offered Emma's leftovers. He was a frugal man used to eating on the road, so not at all averse to picking his dinner cold out of a bag rather than having to pay for it somewhere.

"Sounds like fun. What time and where is this taking place?" he asked Chandra, already munching on a fried chicken leg.

"By eight this evening it will be dark enough, and we'll hold it in our apartment," Chandra told him. He agreed to join them, giving Emma another ogling as she was climbing the stairs to their floor.

Lucy Parker took a lot more convincing, for she was both tired and rather petrified of the entire idea. "I didn't even like scary stories when I was a Camp Fire Girl!" she protested. Yet it was the thought of sitting alone while someone else tried to raise the spirits of the place that changed her mind. What if a wayward ghost came to her apartment instead?

Eight p.m. saw them gathered in the sitting room of the apartment that Emma and Chandra had been staying in. A small folding card table had been appropriated from one of the downstairs apartments along with three different wooden chairs and a stool. Chandra had centered some candles inside a small ring of coarse salt in the middle of the table, and because the tabletop was square, she had placed an archangel card as a ward at all four corners. Her Diana the Huntress icon was within reach in the pocket of the sweater she had donned, for the room felt drafty. Once everyone else was seated, Chandra lit the candles while Emma shut the drapes and turned off the lamps. Then they took their seats.

"Let me be perfectly clear about what we need to do here," Chandra instructed the small assembly. "The purpose of a séance is to give whatever lost souls might be trying to interact with us a chance to have their say. That doesn't mean they will actually speak, but they generally make their presence known. Whether you believe or not is irrelevant, but you must remain quiet, seated, and respectful. This building is very old and it has a long and storied past. Spirits of the deceased do sometimes linger where they either experienced some sort of trauma or left our world abruptly with unfinished personal business. They tend to be very strong or quite troubled personalities and so will act out to gain our attention. That is what has been happening here."

There were some murmurs of ascent from Lucy Parker, who appeared uneasy, while Larry Owens shook his head in disbelief with a scoffing expression on his face. Chandra kept her expression neutral while she waited until they settled down before continuing.

"I know from speaking with your landlord that many people – tenants, workmen, and even former owners – have complained of poltergeist activity. Miss Gilbraith and I have experienced some interesting incidents and rather disturbing situations while investigating. Someone or something remaining in residence has a story to tell us. So tonight we would like to give any unseen entities a chance to open up. I've asked you here as witnesses, so please attempt to keep an open mind and take this seriously. I will guide you in what we must do." Owens looked like he wanted to make some some kind of sarcastic remark but Chandra cut him off.

"Now I will reassure you all that if at any time I or one of you feels unsafe, we will terminate this séance and I'll find some other means of making these presences leave," she added, gazing around the group but lingering long on a still smirking Larry Owens. "Is everyone in agreement with that?"

There were nods and mumbled affirmations. "Good. Now join hands please and do exactly as I instruct."

Everyone linked a hand with the person nearest on either side.

"We need to calm and center ourselves. The best way to do that is to breathe deeply in and out, in a slow, measured manner." Chandra demonstrated and Emma complied immediately, for they had done breathing exercises before. Larry Owens was rather loud about it, almost wheezing like a bellows, and he grinned like an idiot throughout because he was clutching both Lucy Parker and Emma's hands. Lucy had a tough time not hyperventilating, but she did eventually get the breathing pattern down. Chandra let it go on for a few minutes longer than necessary just to make sure everyone was settled. Then she began the call in her projecting voice, her ethereal senses open.

"If there are any lingering souls here who wish to speak with us, let them come forward now and know they are amongst friends. We are not here to judge but to listen and learn." Those lines she repeated over and over like a mantra, matching their cadence to the breathing of the other three people at the table.

Unfortunately nothing happened for quite some time. Eventually Larry Owens broke the silence.

"I figured this was just a bunch of hooey," he said with a shake of his head.

Chandra glared across at him.

"Mr Owens, the one thing we don't need right now is your negative attitude!" she chastised him in a low and commanding tone. He let go of Emma and Lucy Parker's hands and got to his feet.

"Yeah well, I've got better ways to spend a Sunday evening than sitting around playing 'Where's the spook?' with you ladies. So unless somebody floating around out there wants to buy something from me, I'll be downstairs."

He strode to the apartment's outer door and grabbed the doorknob, which refused to budge. No matter how he yanked and twisted it, it seemed immobile. "What the hell – why'd you lock us in?"

"Watch your language young man! I did no such thing," Chandra snapped as she bustled over to the door to check it for herself. The knob refused to turn and the entire door seemed stuck. She was about to say something when Lucy Parker gave a yelp as the candles on the table flared up over a foot high and then abruptly snuffed themselves out. Immediately afterward, they could hear doors all over the building slamming shut.

"I think we'd better go sit down," Chandra told Larry Owens, who was more than a little rattled by then. All four knew they were alone in the building. He scuttled back over to perch gingerly on the stool.

"W-what do we do now?" he asked in an abashed tone that actually did sound rather frightened.

"Join hands again and just calm yourself down. You need to pay attention to what I say. Raised voices and tempers add to any negative energy involved and we don't want to fuel that. What we do want are answers and some way to guide these spirits to a peaceful solution."

"None of the lamps are working. Should I light the candles again?" Emma asked in a quiet tone. There was a pervasive sense of gloom in the building now that was more than just the sudden darkness.

"Don't bother," Chandra answered. "Oftentimes they won't cooperate after they've been extinguished because their potential energy has been drawn off for a manifestation."

"You mean... something is in here using up the electricity and putting out the candles?" Larry Owens asked in a shocked tone. "How can that happen?"

"It's part of how these lost souls manage to break through to our time," Chandra explained. "You see—"

"So very cold," Lucy Parker interrupted in a childlike voice. "There's snow in the air."

They all turned in her direction. With no light in the room, they could barely make out her small form, except for her eyes. They glowed in the dark; not their normal soft, doe-like brown, but pale blue; staring without blinking. Lucy's hands had become icy where they were gripped by both Chandra on the right, and Larry Owens on the left.

Larry's hands were sweaty and he was breathing hard for real this time. He wanted to slink away, but Chandra immediately warned everyone at the table again, "Do not under any circumstances let go of each other. I did not foresee this, but we have with us one of the spirits of this building who's chosen to speak through Miss Parker. We mustn't let Lucy lose touch with who she is or it could be detrimental to her mental and emotional state. Your hand holding hers keeps her mind tethered to this group."

She turned to Lucy, who was now mumbling to herself in a young girl's prattle with a thick accent. It sounded like a prayer. Chandra gently squeezed her hand. "Who are you child? Why have you come forth to speak with us?"

Lucy turned those glowing blue eyes her way, and for a moment there was some sort of luminous fog that surrounded her face, forming briefly into the faint features of a girl with blond hair beneath a mob cap. "I be Brianna Rooney. Me Da runs the inn for Master Webster. I work in the scullery." She had a slightly lilting brogue.

"Brianna," Chandra questioned her, "your time has long passed. Why do you linger here?"

Lucy's body went rigid and she yanked her hands free. She stood up and glared at Larry Owens. "I stay behind until justice be served before God. I didna kill the child I bore, it arrived too soon and wouldnae live long. 'Twas malformed, an abomination! He come and took it away and said he'd bury

the poor bairn, but he din't. He threw it in the pond, with rocks to its feet, but it floated free and they found it. 'Twas I took the blame; 'twas I who hanged, all for what he done to me."

"I had nothing to do with this stuff, I hardly ever speak to her!" Owens protested, leaping to his feet.

"Be seated, both of you," Chandra ordered in a commanding tone, and she took Lucy by the arms and made her sit once more. The young woman's head lolled onto her chest and her dark hair hung over her face. "Emma, change places with Mr Owens and take Lucy's hand. We've got to keep her grounded right now."

Once they were both in place, the questioning by Chandra continued. "Brianna, we want to help you, but we have to know who it was who violated your trust. Who took your baby and tried to hide it?"

Lucy's head snapped up and she went rigid again, eyes glowing feral. "Himself; me Da. He said 'twas a shame on the family, and I should rid meself of it before it showed. But I couldna do that, I couldna!"

"Of course not," Chandra said in a comforting tone. "Why would he ask you to?" she prodded.

"He insisted I was disgraced for what been done to me. I waited 'cause I loved another well, and I din't know had it been one's bairn or t'other. So I waited overlong until it showed. I couldna answer the herbwife when she asked me about the father 'cause I didna know for certain. She wouldn't sell to me the simple to end it without knowin' iffen we might marry instead; for fear of being charged in murder."

"Who was the baby's father?" Chandra insisted on knowing, but Brianna's ghost broke down into racking sobs, yanking Lucy's hands out of their grip and clawing at her face. Chandra pulled Lucy's hands away and held them tightly while the girl struggled and fought to be free.

"We need an answer Brianna, for the truth should be told to ease your way."

It was Larry Owens who answered, but not in his own voice. He sounded like a much older man with a brogue similar to Brianna's.

"Tell them naught daughter," he demanded. "None of yer lies now." It was only a voice, no other manifestation, but there was great power in it, and more than a little menace. When Brianna began to cry harder and covered Lucy's face, rocking and muttering to herself, Larry Owens leapt to his feet and lunged across the table at her. It took both Emma and Chandra to hold him back, he was now completely possessed by the spirit of Brianna's father, who was wild with fury.

"I'll wring your neck like I did that stable boy who rutted on you. You brought shame to us, you filthy little harlot! The gallows was best for you, said I."

It was Lucy's turn to leap to her feet with Brianna's fury and indignation. "Dare you say that in front of these people, Father Mine, when you wouldna tell the judge before he passed sentence on me? Then the whole truth shall be known at long last!" She was quaking in agitation as she gripped the table edge and leaning forward to confront him, began to shout. " 'Twas you that came unto me night after night, once you were well into your cups. Poor Jack in the stable, he did naught but court me with a chaste kiss, and me none the wiser for what might happen because I had no Mam to guide me. But you grew jealous of him, so you killed me poor Jack in a rage, telling me he run off, and saying to Master Webster he'd been sent packing because he deflowered me. I believed you then Father for I knew no better. When you kept coming to me with your vile lust, I didna dare say no and find meself tossed out with nowhere to go. Soon I grew round with child, and I was confused; though now I understand 'twas not me own fault. Only one man could be *that* bairn's father – 'twas you!

" 'TWAS YOU!" she screeched so loudly that the windows shook and the very air seemed to vibrate with the ferocity of her long held wrath. "You made yer own daughter's belly swell. You let her hang for the murder of the misshapen babe that you smothered the feeble life from to keep the truth from being known. 'Twas you all along Father, who bore the shame and not I. NOT I!"

With an inhuman howl, Larry Owens under the influence of Brianna's long dead father lurched again at Lucy Parker hosting Brianna, upsetting the table in his haste to get to her. Surprisingly, the young woman stood her ground amid the wreckage with both her hands held high in a warding gesture, as if her slight form alone could hold him off.

"Ye'll not silence this innocent colleen with threats and beatings, like ye did to me Father. 'Tis too late for that now anyway; for your foul deeds be known by more than you and me at last, and so our time here is at an end. My bones lay in the dust of me cold pauper's grave unshriven; yours falsely sanctified elsewhere; but no matter. Since the truth is out now, I'll go on to whatever awaits, and you can plead your sins to the God you so pretended to worship. Begone from this place and find yer own damnation awaiting!"

There was an oppressive feeling in the still air of the room, with the heaviness of an incoming storm. The doors around the building that had previously shut suddenly slapped open again, including the one to the room they occupied. A cold swirl of musty wind bearing the faint stench of old death passed through the room and out into the hallway, slamming shut the attic door behind it. A lamp that Emma had previously tried to turn on pulsed dimly for a few moments before the bulb brightened to a higher incandescence than anyone had ever seen before; gradually fading to its normal glow.

Chandra caught Lucy Parker as the young woman began to slump and eased her into her chair. Emma wasn't quite as quick with Larry Owens and he fell forward onto the edge of the tumbled card table, bruising his ribs and further crumpling it. She did manage to help sit him up on the floor, and he stayed there for a few moments, catching his breath.

"What happened? he asked, clambering to his feet awkwardly with Emma's help while holding his aching midsection.

"You don't recall any of it?" Chandra asked him.

Larry Owens shook his head. "Something like a dream yeah, but all I heard were voices in a distance. I couldn't make sense of what they were saying, but it sounded like an argument."

Lucy Parker was pasty and shaking, but she was struggling to compose herself. "She... that girl was inside me. Around me. She smelled of something old and moldy. But she was so kind. She was upset and worried about me. How can this be?"

"It's a long story, dear," Chandra said in a soothing tone. "But I believe you will have no further issues here."

After reassuring the women that he was fine, a still shaky and confused Larry Owens left almost immediately, far quieter than he had previously been. Emma saw Lucy back to her room and sat with her for a bit until she was sure the young woman was all right. Then she came back to help Chandra clean up the mess.

"We did something important here this evening," Chandra told her understudy, and Emma nodded with a smile.

"For all of us," Emma agreed as they said their goodnights and each retired to her own bed.

* * *

When they returned after breakfast on Monday morning, Henry Windham had been waiting to thank them and pay the rest of their expenses. He refused to allow Chandra to deduct the cost of the card table and any other damages.

"Look, I've spoken to both Miss Parker and Mr Owens already and they said that you did a great job in getting to the source of the... um... haunting here. Even I can tell that the place has a far better feel to it. That's worth every penny you charged, as far as I'm concerned. Plus neither one of them plans on moving out now. So I have a better chance at securing new tenants."

Chandra accepted the check he wrote her gratefully, for she never knew when her next case would come. "I doubt you will have any additional problems, but if you come across someone else who could use my assistance, here's my card," she said, opening the fancy Stratton case with the celestial symbols on the cover and handing one over.

"I'll gladly do that," he said, glancing at the card before tucking it into his sport shirt's front pocket.

Later on the road, Emma asked her, "Were you expecting him to balk at the price?"

Chandra replied while she navigated the Roadster onto a country highway that was rather scenic. "Some do, but I think Mr Windham knows we saved him a lot more money than I charged. He now can rent the place out completely. If he had been forced to sell, who would pay well for a haunted inn with two disgruntled spirits?"

"Nobody I guess," Emma said, her nose already back in a textbook. The scenery was lovely but she had plenty of catching up to do before she returned to class on Tuesday.

Chandra smiled in satisfaction. It had been a great Labor Day weekend getaway, even with the dramatic events of the séance. Even Emma herself now seemed in good spirits. Chandra wished all her dealings with the occult world were so uplifting.

THE OCCULT DETECTIVE GENRE'S POTENTIAL FOR RADICAL REPRESENTATION & SOCIAL JUSTICE

MARIA DeBLASSIE

The occult detective archetype is one that has gone through a remarkable transformation since its inception in the Victorian era. Preliminary incarnations often featured detectives that epitomized mainstream English or American values and were firmly in the social center: the typical white, able-bodied, hetero, cisgender male with enough money to live comfortably, enough education to have a home library, and sometimes even call himself a doctor. The monsters he confronted were from the nightmares of respectable society – specters from a colonial past, artifacts brought back from faraway lands, or evil *othered* bodies.

At their best, these stories explore our relationship with the otherworldly and our curiosity about things outside ourselves. They show how we grapple with the mysterious, unseen forces in this world (and beyond); how we understand the spectral things that often reach out and touch us; and how we explain away or struggle to logically process such occurrences. At their worst, we get ugly things like sexism, ableism, xenophobia, and racism, to name a few. The supernatural becomes a catch-all term for anyone that doesn't fit nicely in the constraints of polite society and, thus, must be feared. Don't get me wrong – I love the original occult detectives. I've even named my familiar after John Silence's cat, Smoke. Silence was my introduction to the genre and, as such, will always be loved, even as I see the potential problems with some of his investigations. My appreciation of the genre, however, doesn't mean I can ignore perhaps the scariest part of these supernatural tales, the dark side of a genre committed to exploring the unknown which is the complete and utter fear of the other. This fear leads to hatred and a deep need to subjugate or eradicate the seemingly unknowable.

For as much as the genre is about the chills and thrills of confronting the supernatural, its underbelly is far more terrifying. It reveals a shocking desire to normalize privilege and villainize otherness. In other words, anything that isn't a white, middle or upper-class, cishet, able, neurotypical, male body. As a mestiza, it is impossible to ignore the horrors of how non-white, non-male bodies are treated in many of these narratives under the thin guise of stopping a supernatural threat.

We see this in the vampire-ghost-mummy of E. Heron's 'The Story of Baelbrow' (1898). Flaxman Low deduces that a vampire seed, from the ancient burial ground the mansion is built on, impregnates a mummy on display in the house's museum of curiosities gathered from 'excursions abroad.' The only way to get rid of the monster is to shoot it in the head multiple times, club it repeatedly, and set it on fire. (This method of eradicating supernatural evil feels like Supernatural's Sam and Dean Winchester before there was a Sam and Dean Winchester.) The mystery is solved. Everyone is happy.

At no point do they consider that the mummy was not their cultural property and that building a home on a cultural landmark like a barrow is never a good idea. I mean, any B horror movie could tell you that! Even my beloved John Silence faces off with supernatural forces that are often decidedly non-English at times. In Sheridan Le Fanu's 'Green Tea', Dr. Hesselius discovers that drinking too much imported green tea collapses the boundaries between the seen and the unseen world with devastating consequences. In each case, the message is clear: Exposure to foreign people and things is dangerous.

Rudyard Kipling's 'The Mark of the Beast' (1890) features a drunk English soldier who desecrates a sacred temple in India; a priest-leper in the temple touches him, and he becomes something altogether strange. His comrades – the amateur occult detectives who must figure out how to save their friend – capture and torture the leper until the poor soul returns the soldier to his natural state. The emphasis of the story is not in empathizing with the priest (although no doubt some readers did at the time), but in relief that the soldier is restored to his natural vitality. His drunkenness and disregard for sacred cultural spaces are never addressed. He is English, so must be saved, regardless of his lack of reparations for the damage he caused. I could go on, but these primary examples are enough to showcase the xenophobic underbelly of this genre, especially during its golden age.

This dark side of the genre is brilliantly deconstructed and subverted in Tricia Owen's 'White Ghost in the City' (Occult Detective Quarterly #2, 2017). Modern readers flinch at Ash's racism and xenophobia that infest his investigation of the disappearance of an American soldier in Hong Kong. His use of the term 'Orientals' is particularly painful, even though the story is technically set in 1967 when the term might have felt less dated and racist than it does today – but not by much. A careful reading of this story shows he merely vocalizes some early occult detective assumptions about the other, the unknown. His perspective as an unreliable narrator uncomfortably mirrors how easy it is to conflate supernatural evil – if indeed the supernatural must always be evil – with otherness. The beauty of this piece is in the fact that the real evil is the detective's white male supremacy and that of the other soldiers who have been devoured by the dragon. Owen satisfyingly flips the xenophobia and racism of the Victorian occult detective on its head, literally making it the thing that leads the protagonist to his well-deserved doom. The reader is not at all upset about it. This story is the antidote to the Kiplingesque ones of white colonizers doing bad things in foreign places. It reminds us that no one is above the laws – natural or supernatural – of justice.

'*White Ghost in the City*' is just one example of contemporary writers' addressing and rectifying the underbelly of the genre's inception. Before I continue, however, it must be said that progress, especially in genre fiction, is not a linear thing. It would be easy to draw a line showing the transformation of this genre from xenophobic and racist to all-inclusive in the present day. But social justice is rarely that clean cut. For all the problems I outlined in '*The Story of Baelbrow*', it is remarkably progressive in its treatment of women. Flaxman Low is only able to solve the mystery by listening to the women whom the other men have deemed 'hysterical'.

Then we have characters like Diana Marburg, the unmarried lady palmist who earns her own living telling fortunes and solves crimes on the side, starting with the short story '*The Dead Hand*' (1902). She can do this, however, because she was raised a gentlewoman and has the support of her brother. She is also white, even if her supernatural powers are racialized by her 'Oriental' garb. Even John Silence becomes othered through his otherworldliness when he not only acquires but vigorously cultivates his psychic powers, often framed as a more feminine ability. It is only his affluent white male privilege that prevents him from being treated like a social anomaly. In essence, the social respectability of Diana Marburg and John Silence inevitably normalize their paranormal eccentricities in ways that more visible othered bodies can't be normalized.

Tim Prasil offers a compelling take on intersectional feminism with his creation of Vera Van Slyke, a woman with black ancestry who debunks fake-spiritualists and solves ghostly mysteries at the turn of the twentieth century. Many of her adventures include strong social justice angles, including 'A Burden that Burns' (1902), a story centered on the guilt of soldiers disobeying the orders to give blankets infected with smallpox to Native American tribes as an act of genocide; and 'King Midas Exhumed' (1907) about a haunting of a bar that celebrated a man who was thought to be an abolitionist. In reality, he offered to harbor fugitive slaves so that he could get the reward for returning them. The haunting only ceased when that history was revealed. Vera Van Slyke's other adventures document the plight of immigrants, laborers, and other underrepresented voices.

Although Vera Van Slyke is a 20th century fictional character written in the 21st century, she serves as an important reminder that inclusivity and social justice isn't a linear clean-cut thing. There are, and always have been, people from a variety of backgrounds, advocating for equity and inclusion throughout history. Most significantly, her paranormal studies indicate that strong emotions, especially guilt, trigger hauntings, which flips the script of otherness as evil. Instead, the evil, or more aptly, the supernatural phenomenon, is not the other, but the buried histories of violence, oppression, and exploitation of othered bodies. Van Slyke can only resolve a haunting once those stories are brought out into the open.

Still, it is reasonable to argue that much of the contemporary additions to the genre are tools for social justice more regularly than their processors during the era of Victorian Spiritualism (and, by the same token, able to easily reproduce the xenophobia of previous generations). My favorite part about this genre is its transformation over the centuries from a genre of xenophobia (its dark-side anyway) to one with the potential for empowering explorations of otherness. Women, people of color, LGTBQ+ communities, people with disabilities, and, yes, supernatural beings are front and center in contemporary additions to the genre. While the stories I outline here are by no means comprehensive, it points to some of the more significant changes in the genre – most notably the fact that much of the genre now falls under urban fantasy, not just horror or the gothic, with narratives that center on leather-clad women monster hunters.

Women writers and readers have found a feminist home in stories about exploring difference. The modern-day foundation for this was laid by writers like Mercedes Lackey. Her character Diana Tregarde, a romance novelist and witch who had been known to solve otherworldly crimes, first made her appearance in 1989 with Burning Water. Tanya Huff introduces the world to Vicki Nelson in 1991's Blood Price, a police detective turned private investigator as she steadily loses her sight to a degenerative eye condition, even as she begins to see that there is more to this world than most can see. She also is perhaps one of the first examples of an occult detective with a disability. Laurell K. Hamilton's Anita Blake is one of the most well-known vampire hunters in the genre since the 1993 debut of *Guilty Pleasures*. As this series developed, we see Anita exploring her sexuality, ultimately realizing she is bisexual, polyamorous, and kink positive. Hamilton is one of the few writers, even today, who actually researched BDSM culture before she became part of this community, so her work is grounded in real experiences, not just problematic unsafe fantasies made popular by books like *50 Shades of Grey*. Likewise, the author's own experience as a bisexual and polyamorous woman lend a realism to Anita's own journey in the series.

Equally groundbreaking, though for different reasons, is L.A. Banks, who wrote the *Vampire Huntress Legend* series starting with *Minion* (2003) that featured a black vampire huntress and a more inclusive cast of characters. Her work as a black author writing about black and other POC communities in a predominantly white genre in the early aughts is an important reminder that, even twenty years ago, the genre was still not as inclusive as it could be, as she is often held up as one of the few (if not only) authors of color in the genre at the time.

These foundational writers spawned many a story of a leather-clad, wise-cracking female monster hunter. Shows like *Buffy the Vampire Slayer* (1998) continued to popularize the figure of the woman occult detective whose femininity empowers her, rather than takes away from her ability to be the slayer. She builds relationships, empathizes with those around her, and shows us that not all supernatural beings are evil. In fact, to systematically eradicate otherness is an act of evil. We see this in the characters of Angel, a vampire with a soul, and Willow, a practicing witch who uses her powers to fight darkness. Willow later coming out as gay in the series is another example where the show emphasizes that difference shouldn't be equated with wrong, dangerous, or in need of policing, even if the show fell short in how it handled race. From these late-twentieth-century stories, the whole genre explodes into a safe haven for witches, shifters, greywalkers, and other female human and paranormal characters that tackle things that go bump in the night.

At the same time that the feminization of the occult detective genre was taking off in fiction, we have characters like John Constantine in comic books, shifting the narrative away from upper-class detectives and their privileges. Constantine, who first appeared in *Swamp Thing* (1988) is solidly working-class, if cheating and conning for a living can be called 'working'. Along with the fact that Constantine is canonically bisexual and kink-positive, each story he is featured in is inherently political. In *Hellblazer: Vol. 1 Original Sins*[1] (1992) alone, he tackles everything from the gentrification and corporate greed in the shape of yuppy demon investors to the British Boy's racism, homophobia, and xenophobia. He dismantles pyramid schemes designed to prey on the weak and most at risk, and literally bears witness to the horrific violence of PTSD experienced by soldiers coming home from the Vietnam War. And that's just barely cracking the surface of the social justice issues Constantine addresses in his explorations of the supernatural world. He may be the iconic trickster, the undependable anti-hero, the magical practitioner who isn't afraid to get his hands dirty. But he is always on the side of good, in his own way.

We can't mention contemporary incarnations of the occult detective archetype without mentioning Harry Dresden. Like Buffy, his world goes a long way toward looking at magic and the supernatural as a metaphor for race relations. Thomas, Harry's half-brother and a vampire, should be a bad guy because of his othered status, but he isn't. So many other magical creatures are judged not by what they are, but by what they do. Still, the characters are mostly white, with the exception of Susan Rodriguez and Carlos Ramirez, so it is difficult to take these discussion of inclusion too seriously. Shows like *iZombie* and *Wynonna Earp* work in much the same way – an emphasis on inclusion and strong social justice narratives, but still a primarily white cast. It is a rare story that puts characters of color and their lives front and center, like the late TV series *Sleepy Hollow* (2013-2017) or Seressia Glass's *Shadowchasers* series starting with *Shadow Blade* (2010), to name a few.

Still, *iZombie*, compared to other urban fantasy series, does a more thoughtful job of using anti-zombie sentiments in the later season as an allegory for racism and silence on the topic as complicity in prejudice (although the co-opting of the history of the Underground Railroad in later seasons is cringy at best). And yet with a primarily white cast, the gesture can be read as performative, or at least being complicit in the same issues that plague many an urban fantasy or super hero franchise: celebrating difference while also centering whiteness. It must be said, however, that while there are only two main characters of color, the fact that they are both empowered characters is essential to changing the narrative of people of

[1] This is the first trade paperback edition, which collects the first nine issues of the *Hellblazer* comic book (January-September 1988).

color as oppressed bodies in the genre. Clive Babineaux is the black detective and one of the first to learn about the zombie virus. As a result, he becomes one of the experts on how to deal with the outbreak and zombie-human relations. He is also the only human main character that never becomes a zombie, which makes a great case of separating difference from the supernatural, complicating all the ways in which people can be othered bodies. He is othered because he is one of the few black people in the police department, but Liv is othered because she is a zombie.

Still others, like Dr Ravi Chakrabarti, occupy intersectional identities – he is both a person of color and later, a partial zombie. Ravi shines as a smart, successful, competent person of color. He not only predicted this kind of a pandemic, but is instrumental in developing a cure for the virus. In other words, he is not treated as an oppressed body, but a vibrant, fulfilled person – not how many minorities are depicted in popular media, making this representation all the more radical. He is likewise the first person to discover that Liv has been turned into a zombie; he doesn't panic or try to kill her. He doesn't blame her for being assaulted or treat her differently because of her trauma (a clear allegory for sexual assault and the narrative is all the more powerful for showing how a person can heal and thrive after life-altering trauma). He offers her support and begins researching to find a cure – a classic example of how the knee-jerk reaction of fear and violence when confronted with otherness doesn't need to be the norm.

Similarly, *Wynonna Earp* (2016-2021), the TV show based on a comic book series, shines in its depiction of LGTBQ+ romance. Unlike Buffy (a trailblazer in its own right), *Wynonna Earp* normalizes gay romance by eschewing the coming out narrative. Officer Haught doesn't hide her sexuality, despite living in a small town. Waverly Earp's own sexual awakening lacks the fanfare of traditional coming out narratives, and that's the point. She likes Haught, Haught likes her, and that's that. Even their fan group, which has dubbed the couple WayHaught, is a celebratory reminder of how few happy low-angst LGTBQ+ narratives there are in mainstream media and, more specifically, in this genre. Of course, this show is not the only narrative to include central gay characters, but it is perhaps one of the most memorable.

Tanya Huff is once again pushing against representation norms with Tony Foster, a gay wizard detective starting with *Smoke & Shadows* (2004). We also see the return of Henry Fitzroy, the bi-vampire, from the Vicki Nelson series, as Tony's part-time lover and guide in the world of the supernatural. Still, each time a series successfully represents gay communities it is notable, specifically because there are so few examples (although there are more than I've listed here). *Lost Girl* (2010-2015), a show with a twist on the occult detective genre that includes a secret world of Fae living among us, features a variety of LGTBQ+ relationships without naming them as such, and thus, making them all the more natural for not needing to be labeled. With only one regrettable transphobic episode, the series stands out as a sex-positive series that celebrates love and normalizes sexual fluidity. In fact, these stories reflect how the long running series *Supernatural* (2005-2020) struggled to deal with queering their canon, suggesting that there is more demand for stories that don't center cishet white dudes than mainstream audiences realize.

More recently, we have Lucifer Morningstar in the TV series *Lucifer* (2016-2021), based on the graphic novel series (which is, arguably, not an occult detective narrative), as he solves mundane crimes using his supernatural abilities, not unlike Liv Moore in *iZombie* or Diana Marburg with her palmistry. Although Lucifer in the show is a white male and hetero-passing, there are several moments throughout the series that feature his more fluid sexuality, including waking up in bed with both a woman and another man and having bacchanalian parties that, it is assumed, are nothing short of the orgiastic. It is also assumed that Maze, his demon companion, is not limited to heteronormative experiences. Both of them openly discuss and practice kink. What this does is make otherness, particularly sexual preferences, cool, even if it is within the framework of a hetero romance. The suave devil thinks social norms are lame and so should the viewer. Although some queer reviewers have balked at the idea that the devil is associated with queerness, I tend to read his sexual fluidity in more generous terms: Lucifer Morningstar is the light bringer, the bringer of enlightenment, someone who is a threat to the social norms simply because he embodies progressive, enlightened ideologies.

But representation is also about more than placing people of color, LGTBQ+ characters, those with disabilities, and other historically marginalized identities front and center in the narratives. It's about normalizing otherness more generally, including less visible forms, like trauma. This is not to diminish the importance of centering visibly othered bodies in the genre. Rather, it's about understanding that historically marginalized identities and generational and ancestral trauma are often inextricably linked which is why we need more narratives that explore these issues in a variety of contexts. The occult detective genre is prime for exploring the horror of trauma and how it indelibly scars survivors, not just through their experience but also through how they are often silenced. The supernatural becomes a metaphor for the proverbial demons and monsters we fight – the things 'normal society' wants to pretend don't exist.

Take the show *Haven* (2010-2015), for example. It's about a small town whose residents have unexplained powers called the Troubles. They're the B movie metaphor for generational trauma. Nobody talks about them, and the silence surrounding the Troubles is just as deadly as what happens when they leak out into the town. Some people don't even know about their family secrets – whatever abilities get passed on to the next generation – until they are literally triggered by a traumatic event. For a show that is conventional in many other ways, from the primarily white, hetero, cisgender cast, it deals with issues of generation trauma, and the silence surrounding it, with surprising psychological clarity. Audrey Parker, the main protagonist, is recovering from her own sci-fi version of ancestral trauma and, as a result, becomes not just a psychic detective, but a trauma specialist, talking to people and helping them find solutions to managing their pain and healing from their past. As any survivor knows, and as this show highlights through the various powers and psychical phenomena of the town's residents, trauma never goes away. It is contained, managed, and worked through as each character understands their family history and then learns to avoid the things that could trigger an episode.

Then there is Daniel Jose Older's short story, '*Magdalena*', from *Salsa Nocturna* (2016). Although the story is riddled with ghosts and literal ghostbusters who are also ghosts, they are not the monsters. Sure, some of the supernatural entries in the stories are, such as the parasites feeding on the children in a daycare center. But the other monster in the story is all too human – and more terrifying because of that fact. Magdalena's sexual abuse is never directly depicted on the page, but the reader knows immediately what her father did. The supernatural ghostbusters in this story are forces of good, eradicating spectral parasites that would sap innocents of their life force. This is more prominently illustrated in the ghostly friend who saves Magdalena from herself and, through radical empathy, offers some semblance of hope for a young woman with a history of trauma. Again, it is the unspoken in the story that is the most haunting. Like *Haven*, where everyone knows about the Troubles but nobody speaks of them, '*Magdalena*' grapples with the silent terrors of domestic abuse. Of course, the power of these stories is that, in the very act of telling them, survivors of trauma cease to be silenced, just like the spirits in a Vera Van Slyke tale. Monsters are exposed. Healing begins.

More inclusive stories continue to be hallmarks of the genre in its contemporary form. The genre has seen the likes of John Linwood Grant's Mamma Lucy, a black conjure woman in 1920s America doing her best to keep the darkness at bay; Valjeanne Jeffers's Mona Livelong, a steamfunk occult detective; P. Djèlí Clark's 1921 steampunk alternate Egyptian detectives; and *SLAY: Stories of the Vampire Noire* (2020) an anthology which showcases the vampires of African Disapora – and often the occult detectives that cross their paths.

Then we've got Maggie Hoaskie, a Navajo monster hunter in Rebecca Roanhorse's *Sixth World Series* beginning with *Trail of Lightning* (2019), a half-dead resurrected inbetweener, Carlos Delacruz, in Daniel Jose Older's *Bone Street Rumba Series* starting with *Half-Resurrection Blues* (2015), and so many more. Roanhorse's and Older's works are even more important because they are by authors of color writing about their own lived experiences within those cultures, not just white authors writing characters of color (although we have to be careful about how we frame lived experiences… not everyone can be a monster hunter in real life!). Each and every one of these narratives demonstrates that the liminal space othered bodies occupy can be empowering, transformational even. A genre that started as socially privileged people exploring the outer limits of the social periphery has turned on its head to examine the world through the lens of that periphery. The social margins, in other words, the fringes of society, are where we can best explore and celebrate our shared humanity.

We see this growing emphasis on inclusion in contemporary monster-hunter stories most prominently in a comparison between the two *Charmed* TV shows. The first series (1998-2006) feature witch sisters Phoebe, Piper, Prue, and later, Paige, as they fight warlocks and demons. It's a study in white feminism – they are empowered, yes, but there is a noticeable lack of regular minority characters in the show, suggesting that representing white female empowerment trumps other forms of representation. The minority side characters are often either the villains or victims of the week, clearly used only to uphold the kick-ass power of these white women. Throughout the series, there are consistent references to patriotism – the God Bless America mug they drink from, the American flag on the fridge, even in the stars and stripes outfits Phoebe has worn. Several episodes have clear patriotic threads, usually centered on soldiers, and Piper can often be found wearing a silver cross around her neck. These little details all add up to one big picture: The women are witches, sure, but they aren't evil. In fact, they love America! And they are God-fearing citizens! Just look at Piper's religious crisis when she realizes she is a witch in the first season for evidence of that. So, the only way the show can celebrate their magical differences is by making other parts of their personalities as conservative as possible. They become safer, more sanitized, their witchcraft diminished for the way it is suppressed by the normalizing parts of the narrative.

The reboot of *Charmed* (starting in 2018), however, is powerful in its complete rejection of social norms and toxic white patriarchal constructs that hurt not only minorities, both natural and supernatural, but also those privileged enough to benefit from those systems. The very first episode tackles issues like the #MeToo Movement, mandatory consent, and intersectional identities (although some would say it's a little on the nose). Mel is both Latina and gay, Maggie and Macy are Afro-Latina, but with very different relationships to that identity, proving that minorities, particularly those with similar cultural backgrounds, are not monoliths. Relationships to race and culture are often singular experiences. Mel likewise never has a formal coming out, at least not that we see – she was raised in a house that made her feel comfortable being who she is. The show then places its own version of brujeria front and center in the narrative and doesn't apologize for featuring a cast that celebrates brown woman magic. Even their explorations get more complex as the sisters realize that their magic has been westernized when they meet their Puerto Rican cousin, Josefina (notably one of two trans characters introduced that season). They even include spells in Spanish, de-centering Western culture further.

Although the later seasons show how they struggle to naturally include issues like micro-agressions in the workplace, queer and intersectional identities, and white privilege in seamless and meaningful ways that go beyond performative gestures of inclusion and representation, the show illustrates how the genre is currently grappling with centering historically marginalized identities in these stories in ways that aren't tokenizing, preachy, or signaling their progressive 'virtue'. Admittedly, it is for this reason that the original *Charmed* series, while flawed, holds up better than the reboot. The original series tackled important issues like non-traditional families, returning to college after a hiatus as a 'non-traditional student', how having children changes a woman's personal and professional life in a way that men don't experience, and a myriad of other issues, including breastfeeding in public. And, while the agenda was primarily a white feminist one, they were consistent in tone and style to grapple with these in a way felt real and relatable. If the reboot stuck to a similar tone or even had clearer tie-ins to the original show, they might have been able to explore intersectional feminism in more impactful ways.

The *Charmed* reboot could likewise haven taken cues from the first season of the short-lived *Sleepy Hollow* (2013-2017), which was one of the first popular mainstream monster hunter shows that centers othered bodies, primarily black characters, in a genre that typically views otherness as evil. Although the later seasons did not do justice to Abbie Mills or the original narrative, that first season pushed back against old toxic genre tropes and offered empowered, hopeful narratives for BIPOC characters that meaningfully confronted America's history of racism but didn't wallow in trauma narratives for its black leads.

Still, the *Charmed* reboot has its smart *Sleepy Hollow* moments. For example, it is both humorous and satisfying that their Whitelighter, Harry, is the token white regular in the series (just like the resurrected Ichabod Crane in *Sleepy Hollow* originally played second fiddle to Abby at first), a role they challenge as they try to figure out if he is a toxic threat or powerful ally for them as women of color and witches. He has to earn their trust, respect, and later, love. His privileges never entitle him to any of those things. The reality this show lays bare is that these brujas can't afford to play nice, unlike the original charmed sisters. Their identities as women of color will always make them transgressive, and no amount of normalizing other aspects of their identities will change that. The only solution is to reject institutionalized racism and be forceful in their radical magic.

So many new stories continue this pattern of rejecting normalizing characteristics in favor of unapologetic resistance and social justice. *Occult Detective Quarterly* (now *Magazine*) has upheld its agenda to include stories about 'investigators from every creed, colour, and culture', not to mention gender, sexuality, and expression on the human-supernatural spectrum. We've seen Native American cops, trans rune-readers, half-Punjabi psychics, black detectives in 1970s Harlem, gay Edwardian psychologists, and detectives from all over the world, including Australia, South America, Japan, and Africa, to name a few. Even better, these characters are never separated from the regular cast of the more traditional detectives like Carnacki and Holmes. They coexist together in a mish-mash of supernatural investigations, further normalizing otherness.

It is noticeable, too, that more representation needs to happen across the genre. Creating more space for Own Voices writers, those underrepresented authors who are writing about characters that share their lived experiences, is essential to fostering inclusivity within the genre. Similarly, Vicki Nelson is one of the few characters with disabilities and, while some stories have characters whose powers might be a metaphor for neurodiversity, I look forward to reading more stories that place those differences front and center. There are undoubtedly other forms of representation that need to be discussed, ones that my own privileges make me less aware of. I look forward to learning and reading about those too. However, I have no doubt that we, as lovers, readers, and writers of the genre, will continue to expand our own explorations of humanity, the supernatural, and the normalization of the unknown and otherness.

In the end, the best parts of this genre, and the occult detective archetype, don't just grapple with the paranormal, but perhaps the even more inscrutable concept of what it means to be human... even when someone is a ghost, werewolf, or technically undead. And of course, any connoisseur of the genre knows that the real monsters out there are the limiting beliefs that dehumanize otherness.

THE MYSTERIOUS GESTURE

RHYS HUGHES

A Nathan Gesture Adventure

He was crouched over the crystal ball on his desk. In the depths of the orb he saw nothing, but that was good, he wanted to empty his mind. To stare into the void was always soothing. It was how the occult detective Nathan Gesture recharged his soul for the next adventure. His thin lips curled in a meaningless smile and his eyes glowed.

There was the stamp of feet on the stairs and the door flew open. With a face dripping sweat, his chest heaving with effort, the loyal servant who had been Nathan's constant companion for almost two decades waved the newspaper he clutched in his left hand.

"Something very peculiar has happened," he said.

Nathan blinked slowly, roused himself from his meditation, struggled for several moments to orient himself in relation to his surroundings. But his voice was both precise and elegant.

"Summarise for me, if you would, Jubjub, my man."

"Yes, sir. One moment..."

"Catch your breath first, by all means."

Nathan betrayed no impatience. This particular scene had occurred in his apartment too many times already. A new adventure had come to him while he relaxed. It was always the way.

Jubjub finally held high the newspaper and said:

"A fiendish and cunning murder! The magnate Burton Fisk was found dead in his bed this morning with the arms of a bronze chandelier twisted around his neck. The police have arrested Burton's butler who they insist is the culprit. They add that he is clearly a genius of crime who somehow has managed to escape detection until now."

"Have they linked any other crimes to this butler?"

"None, sir. But Inspector Mimsy has declared that the murder was so clever that it couldn't have been committed by a novice. Thus the butler is an experienced villain. That's logic, sir."

"Faulty logic," responded Nathan. He sighed and then stood up. With a yawn he asked, "Is the name of the butler given?"

"Tumbrel, sir," said Jubjub.

"And the police station where he is held?"

"Ditchwater, sir."

"Then let us repair hither!"

"Why? Has hither broken again, sir?"

"Indeed it has, Jubjub."

"I will fetch my tools, sir. It'll take a jiffy."

"No need for a jiffy. A screwdriver and spanners ought to be enough and maybe a small hammer."

"That's what I will use then, sir."

Nathan nodded and regarded the bicycle that stood in a corner. He had no patience with people who called their machines by names that required a capital first letter. He saw only a bicycle, a modified tandem in fact, not a living being, and *hither* should be written in lower case throughout. On the other hand, he disliked those riders who neglected to name their trusty mounts at all. Balance was important.

Yes, when riding a bicycle, balance was a key factor.

Jubjub was an expert mechanic and with his tools he soon repaired the faulty gears. Then he helped his master carry the tandem out of the room, down the stairs and onto the pavement.

"You know the way to Ditchwater, Jubjub?"

"I do indeed, sir."

"Then let us set off with no more ado!"

Nathan mounted his comfortable saddle in the front and rested his feet in the stirrups. Jubjub took the hard seat behind and began pedalling. The tandem had been constructed by the servant in accordance with Nathan's specifications. The rider in the front had no need or opportunity to pedal. All the work was done by the rear fellow.

As they picked up speed along the road, Nathan opened the hamper in the basket in front of him. It was always kept stocked for emergencies. It was full of cucumber sandwiches on this occasion. Rubbing his hands in delight, the occult detective extracted one and crammed it into his mouth, then coughed crumbs when they went over a bump in the asphalt. Jubjub was a very careful cyclist but these roads were in an awful state. That was the fault of the city council, of course.

Twenty minutes later they pulled up outside the police station. Nathan was on friendly terms with all the most important police chiefs in the city and Inspector Mimsy was well-known to him. Nathan had solved dozens of cases that the police had assumed were already solved. Nathan Gesture was both loved and feared by the police.

"Lock up *hither* and follow me, Jubjub, my man!"

Nathan entered the station.

He was welcomed by the officer on the reception desk, who said with a tolerant laugh, "We were expecting you to turn up. But you are wasting your time. This is an open and shut case."

"Kindly inform Inspector Mimsy that I wish to see him."

The officer reached for a telephone.

"The inspector will be happy to meet you. Please go to his office. You know where. It's in the usual place."

Jubjub entered the station. Nathan turned.

"On second thoughts, remain outside, Jubjub. I don't think you will be of much use to me in his office."

"Very good, sir. Shall I take your cane, sir?"

Nathan gazed at the stout cane he carried in one hand and frowned but then he said, "No need, Jubjub."

The servant bowed and reversed outside.

Nathan had a strange feeling that he would need his cane, but for what purpose he couldn't guess. He strolled along the corridors, turned bends, skipped up flights of stairs. Then he reached Inspector Mimsy's door and rapped on it with his cane. Might *this* be the reason he required this thick length of wood? Surely nothing so trite!

"Come in!" bellowed a voice.

Nathan pushed open the door and strolled inside.

"Aha, Mr Gesture!"

"Forgive me for intruding, Inspector..."

"No need for apologies. It is always very interesting to hear anything you might have to say. You have come because of the Burton Fisk case, but I can assure you that the butler Tumbrel was responsible for his cruel and horrible death. I worked that out with my intellect. Reason is the only tool that is permissible to the detective of the modern age. I respect you, I admire you, but I believe your successes so far to be flukes. Please take a seat and I will explain everything."

"Thank you but I already have many seats at home."

"Then stand on your feet!"

Nathan smiled down at the seated Mimsy and saw a smug expression that had never been there in any of their prior meetings. The police were very sure of themselves this time.

"I will listen to what you tell me," said Nathan, "for the newspaper's description of events lacks detail."

"Naturally. Now listen carefully. Burton Fisk was very rich and very eccentric. Everyone knows this. He was also extremely clumsy, so much so that his butlers (of whom Tumbrel was only the latest in a long line) had to continually provide him with shouted instructions to prevent him from injuring himself. For example, when walking along the pavement, his butler of the moment would cry, 'left' or 'right' to ensure that he took a detour around the approaching lamppost."

"Otherwise he would walk straight into it? That is intriguing. He had a lack of coordination. Neurological?"

Inspector Mimsy shrugged. "Who knows?"

"His butlers were his navigators as well as his servants?"

"It would appear so, Mr Gesture."

"Very well. But how does this relate to his death?"

"I'm coming to that. Tumbrel was the only witness to his death but he refuses to confess to being the murderer. No matter! We have gathered an impressive amount of evidence that will serve to convict him in court. He claims that he was going about his normal early morning duties when his master called out the word 'tiramisu'. Nothing strange about that. Burton always shouted out what he wanted for breakfast and it would be brought to him by his butler on a silver tray. Usually he asked for 'toast' or 'baked beans' or 'soup' or 'grapefruits'."

"But this morning he craved tiramisu!"

"Yes, it is a type of trifle made with sponge and sherry."

"I know what tiramisu is!"

"Of course. You are a man of the world. Forgive me."

"You are forgiven. Proceed."

"Burton called for tiramisu and Tumbrel asserts that he had to go out to purchase one because he didn't know how to make the dessert himself. When he returned, the house was silent. This was strange because Burton liked to sing at the top of his voice while waiting for breakfast. Tumbrel then conveyed the tiramisu to his master's door. He knocked but received no answer. He knocked several times."

"Did the tiramisu wobble when he did the knocking?"

"I believe so, Mr Gesture."

"But did Tumbrel say anything about it?"

"Yes, he stated that it wobbled."

"Then he is telling the truth. No man could invent a detail like that. It is a detail that a liar would overlook."

"Ahem! If I may continue with the account? Thank you. After rapping on the door a dozen times, Tumbrel finally decided to enter without being given permission. He was aghast at what he saw. He dropped the tiramisu in his fright and it blobbed all over the expensive carpet (and was trodden deep into the pile by my constables when we arrived on the scene). There on the bed lay the corpse of Burton Fisk!"

"And Tumbrel has never deviated from his story?"

"Not once, I'm afraid."

"What does that say to you?"

"That he is a very bold and dangerous criminal."

"A mastermind of evil?"

"Yes, Mr Gesture. That is exactly right."

"And yet he wasn't the master in that house. He was the butler. It will surely be better to describe him as a *butlermind* of evil? Assuming that he really did murder Burton Fisk, I mean."

"He murdered him. There is absolutely no doubt."

"Please continue with your tale."

"The corpse of Burton Fisk was a horrible sight but what was striking about it was the fact that the chandelier was no longer hanging from the ceiling. It was on top of the body of the murdered man and its four arms had been bent out of shape. They were now twisted around his throat and they had strangled him to death."

"This chandelier normally hung over the bed?"

"Directly above him, yes."

"So it might have fallen on him?"

"Yes, but that wouldn't explain the twisting of the bronze arms about his throat. They required human agency."

"Is Tumbrel a strong man?"

"Not at all. He is weedy. You may see for yourself."

"You will take me to his cell?"

"Later, yes. He is a weakling, a reed of a man."

"Then how was he capable of bending the chandelier's arms? Surely this is the flaw in your argument?"

"Ah, that's the clever part. Burton was strong."

"A magnificently strong man. Yes, I have heard that said about him. I still can't fathom how the fact of his physical power proves that Tumbrel is a murderer. But tell me about the tray."

"The butler's tray, you mean?"

"Yes. After Tumbrel dropped the tiramisu on the floor in fright, what did he do with the silver tray?"

"It was found bent out of shape on the bed."

"How very intriguing!"

Nathan Gesture pondered deeply and he tapped the end of his cane on the open palm of his left hand. The resultant soft rhythm seemed to upset Inspector Mimsy, who scowled and grated his chair leg on the uncarpeted floor. At last he was unable to restrain himself.

"What are you thinking?"

"I'm speculating as to how such a weak man could bend the arms of a chandelier around the neck of a strong man. I want to know your solution to this riddle before I tell you mine."

"This is what happened, Mr Gesture, and I worked out the truth using reason. There is always a logical explanation for everything that happens, no matter how bizarre an event might seem at first. Burton Fisk was both eccentric and clumsy. He had conditioned himself to follow the directions called out by his butlers without question. Tumbrel went out for tiramisu but he had been planning to kill his master for many months. He knocked on the bedroom door and when Burton called for him to enter he did so, deliberately spilling the dessert on the carpet. Burton's attention was thus distracted for a few vital moments."

"But distracted for what purpose exactly?"

"It enabled Tumbrel to fling the silver tray like a rectangular discus at the chandelier, knocking it down onto Burton, without the magnate being able to take evasive action. It fell on him and stunned him. Then Tumbrel sprang forward and shouted out words and these words murdered Burton as efficiently as a knife or gun. He cried, 'pull' and 'push' and his master instinctively did as he was instructed."

"You are suggesting that Tumbrel used Burton's own strength against him? That he tricked his master into strangling himself with the metallic arms of that greenish monstrosity?"

"It is hardly an eyesore, Mr Gesture. It's a handsome chandelier that I would be proud to have in my own bedroom. Furthermore it has an origin that is interesting and pertinent."

"Oh? What might that origin be?"

"Tumbrel said that Burton bought it in a peculiar shop in some area of the city he had never visited before. A few days later, his master attempted to find the shop again but couldn't even locate the street. No sense of direction at all. This proves he truly was a clumsy man, the sort of useless fellow who really could throttle himself accidentally."

"I see. There are other explanations for the fact the shop had vanished.

No matter. Be assured that I used the word 'monstrosity' deliberately but please continue with your account."

"Tumbrel pretended to help his master free himself from the weight of the heavy chandelier. Burton thought that the commands 'push' and 'pull' would enable him to remove it from his body, but in fact Tumbrel fooled him into twisting the arms in the wrong direction. A brilliant crime! Now you understand why I called the butler a malign genius? It all fits together perfectly. The case has been solved."

Nathan slowly shook his head and pursed his lips.

"May I see the accused?"

"Yes indeed. Follow me. He is in the holding cell on this floor. He has tea and biscuits. We are not barbaric."

Inspector Mimsy led the occult detective out of the office and down a short corridor. He opened a sturdy door with a large key and they entered a small room with a barred window set high in one wall. On a chair sat an extremely thin man with a cup of tea balanced on one knee. His knee was trembling and the tea was spilling. The biscuit was balanced on the other knee. He was weeping and his copious tears partly helped to refill the cup that was losing tea through spillage.

"You are Tumbrel, I assume?" asked Nathan.

"I am, sir," came the answer.

"You are an innocent man. I know this and I will prove it. Answer just one question. What did you do with the tray?"

"I flung it at the chandelier, sir."

"Do you see? He admits his guilt!" chortled Inspector Mimsy.

"Wait!" barked Nathan, then he returned his full attention to Tumbrel and asked, "When you threw the tray, was the chandelier on the ceiling or was it already resting on your master?"

"It was on his body, sir. I opened the door and saw what I thought was a giant green spider. I was so shocked that I let the tiramisu slide onto the floor. Then I rallied myself and hurled the tray at the spider with as much force as I could muster. It bounced off because the creature was actually a bronze chandelier, not an arachnid."

"Thank you! That is all I needed to know."

Nathan turned to the Inspector.

"Do you have the chandelier on the premises?"

"Of course. It is evidence."

"Take me to it please."

Inspector Mimsy was flustered but he did as Nathan asked. They left the cell and strolled along another corridor to a room where exhibits were stored. The chandelier with its twisted arms lay on a table. Nathan studied it closely and then he visibly stiffened.

"Do you know what this is?" he asked the Inspector.

"Yes, it's a bronze chandelier."

"Unfortunately, it is not. It's something much worse. Bronze objects often turn green with age, but not this kind of green. This is a different shade entirely. Tumbrel is innocent and must be released at once. The real murderer is right here before us."

Inspector Mimsy arched an eyebrow. "The chandelier? You are telling me that Burton Fisk was murdered by an inanimate object with a mind of its own? A malicious light fitting?"

"It is *not* a chandelier!"

"What is it then?"

Nathan circled the table, never taking his eyes from the object. With a stamp of his foot he cried, "Tiramisu!"

And it came alive...

The chandelier untwisted its bent arms and jumped up. Now it was no longer a chandelier but a hideous little monster with four green limbs and an evil face. It opened a mouth full of fangs and cackled. Then it bent its legs and prepared to spring at Nathan.

But the occult detective was faster. He stepped forward and struck the creature with his cane, with the silver head of his cane. The thing became a chandelier again and lay silent.

Inspector Mimsy's eyes were bulging. "What the hell happened? How and why did that awful thing—"

Nathan smiled. "It wasn't a chandelier but a goblin. The particular tint of green was the clue. It is a green associated only with goblins, actually with only a very specific subspecies of that mythical monster, namely the wild Celtic goblin of ancient times. What happened this morning is much simpler than what you supposed."

"Please tell me everything, Mr Gesture."

"I won't tell you everything, because that's a lot of things, including every fact known to the human race, but I will explain the events of this case in the order they occurred."

"I will settle for that," said Inspector Mimsy.

"Good. Tumbrel told the truth at every point. It was just an unlucky coincidence that Burton chanced on the one shop in the nation that sells petrified goblins. A petrified goblin looks a lot like a chandelier and it's easy to mistake the one for the other. A clumsy man is even more likely to do so. Burton bought the object and had it hung on his ceiling directly above his bed. It was inert and harmless up there. But magic words can bring petrified goblins back to life."

"How does a goblin become petrified?"

"Geological processes are responsible. Sometimes one falls into a tar pit or a peat bog and over many centuries he is compressed and stiffened. But there will always be a magic word that can loosen his limbs and start his heart functioning once again."

"And 'tiramisu' is that magic word? How odd!"

"Not quite. The magic word is probably something like 'tir-na-nog', which is an ancient Celtic word, but this petrified goblin had been immobile for so long and was so impatient to come alive again that the first syllable was enough to awaken it. Burton's raucous singing had already loosened the screws that held it to the ceiling. Now it simply writhed and completed its liberation. Down it fell onto him."

"And strangled him with its real limbs?"

"Yes! Then Tumbrel came into the bedroom and flung his tray at the goblin, thinking it was a spider. The tray was *silver*. We all know what effect silver has on monsters and spirits. The impact petrified the goblin again and once more it looked just like a bronze chandelier, but with its arms twisted around Burton's neck."

"Just now, when you also shouted 'tiramisu'?"

"I freed the goblin again, but the end of my cane is also silver. That's why I struck at it without delay."

Inspector Mimsy wiped his face with a handkerchief.

"Mr Gesture, I am ashamed..."

"Don't be. You are a man and like most men you believe that behind every supernatural event there is a rational explanation. But in fact it's the other way around. Behind every seemingly logical phenomenon there is a ghost or a ghoul or a werewolf."

"I don't know what to say. I am in your debt."

"Most occult detectives seek to debunk the supernatural, to show that a haunting or a possession in fact has a scientific rationale. I am the only one who *bunks reason* and proves that the supernatural explanation is the right one. It is correct every time."

"Tumbrel will be released immediately. Is there anything Ditchwater Police Station can do for you?"

"Nothing. I have everything I need."

"Money? Toffees? A siren for your bicycle?"

"I am not a materialist."

"How about a basket of bananas?"

Nathan was tempted. At last he said, "Why not?"

"Excellent! We confiscated them from a smuggler only yesterday. Eat them with yoghurt in the morning."

"I believe that I shall."

"The creamier the yoghurt, the better."

"I will accept your advice."

Inspector Mimsy nodded and extended his hand.

Nathan Gesture didn't shake it.

Instead he flapped his arms, stood on one leg, contorted his face into a mask of madness, poked out his tongue.

Inspector Mimsy was baffled and alarmed.

"What does that mean?"

"I don't know," Nathan admitted, "but it was nice."

"A mysterious gesture!"

"Yes, I guess you could say I am."

"Very well, Goodbye. I will never forget what you have taught me on this latest occasion. Never!"

"Yes, you will. You always do," laughed Nathan.

Inspector Mimsy chuckled too.

Nathan turned and strode out of the building.

Jubjub was waiting for him.

"Take this basket of bananas, my good man."

"I can't hold them and pedal at the same time, sir. I need to hold tight to the rear handles of the tandem."

"Then wear the basket on your head like a hat."

"Very good, sir. Where to?"

"Home, of course! I miss my crystal ball."

Nathan mounted his saddle and threaded his feet into the stirrups and Jubjub began pedalling. The basket of bananas on his head attracted the stares of pedestrians. But Nathan was deep in thought. At last he sighed and asked, "Do you think I'm mysterious? Do you fear me? Be honest, Jubjub, my man. Do you dread me?"

Jubjub was panting with effort. His words came in gasps. "I... I... I... I... I... like you very much," he rasped.

This wasn't an acceptable answer to his question but Nathan decided to let it go. He closed his eyes and thought about how everything that happened was because a ghost or spirit or demon was responsible. Reason and logic were illusions. Nothing was natural.

Back in his apartment he stood in front of the mirror. Then he gripped a stray lock of the hair on his head and tugged hard and the mask that was his head came off with a squeak. A grimacing skull with red eye sockets glared back at him from the glass.

Another adventure was over. It was bedtime.

AN ISOLATED CASE

ROBERT RUNTÉ

Rolland judged the on-screen caller to be in his late fifties, perhaps even a youngish mid-sixties. The white hair and beard probably accounted for assuming him more aged, with the generally dapper grooming and attire suggesting that he retained his vitality. The floor to ceiling wall of books in the background hinted at education and wealth, but of course that could as easily have been a Zoom option. (Rolland's own customized background showed a colorized photo of Sam Spade's office from *The Maltese Falcon*, though he had in fact been seated out on the balcony when the call came in.) The subject's nervousness, however, could not be in doubt. His head and eyes were in constant, twitchy motion as if trying to guard against an attack that could come from any direction. It made Rolland uncomfortable to watch.

"How can I help you, uh, Mr Wilcott?"

Wilcott jumped as if tasered. "How did you know that?" he demanded. "Who I am?"

Rolland pointed at his screen. "It's written under your image on Zoom. You no doubt see my name similarly supplied on your own screen?"

"Oh. Yes." Wilcott rocked back in his chair as if overwhelmed by it all. "Of course. Sorry."

Rolland waited for Wilcott to state his business, but instead the man flung up his arms as if to fend off some unseen object flung at his head from off camera.

"Are you alright, Mr Wilcott?" He manifestly was not, but not all of Rolland's clients were aware they were behaving oddly.

"What?" Wilcott looked back at the screen and lowered his arms, awkwardly trying several positions before settling on arms crossed tightly over the chest.

Rolland had already opened a case file, titled it 'J.C. Wilcott' and now typed (below camera view) 'arms crossed in defensive/self-hug posture' into the *initial contact* box.

"I was given your card," Wilcott said, looking down and left, as if watching for something there; or perhaps avoiding eye contact. "Discreet enquiries, I was told."

"Yes?"

"That you were prepared to make house calls?"

"Ah. Normally, yes. But as it's the start of corona season…"

"Yes, yes, I'm well aware. Why we're all here. At the house. We're all completely fine. In terms of corona. Effie's got a slight cough, but we're quite sure it's nothing. No chance of it being the corona, at any rate. But, we're still in lockdown, you see. Can't leave here to come there. We need you, therefore, to come here. Please."

The 'please' slipped into a definite tone of desperation. Rolland sensed it was not a word Mr Wilcott was accustomed to using.

"But then, I'd be stuck there, wouldn't I?" Rolland pointed out. "Three weeks quarantine."

"Oh. No problem at all. Plenty of room. Rooms. Chef does a nice dinner. And let's say a fifty percent bonus for the inconvenience?"

"A tempting invitation, Mr Wilcott, but I take self-isolating seri—"

"Triple your fee for, uh, danger pay."

Rolland paused, tempted, before saying, "Why not let's start with my regular fee first and see what we can accomplish online?" Rolland adopted what he thought of as his confident, reassuring smile.

It was not returned. "You have to be here. You have to experience it first-hand."

It, Rolland thought. *Interesting.* "I rely primarily on interviews to identify and resolve issues," Rolland explained. "There's little advantage to my being physically present."

Mr Wilcott snapped up straight in his chair and slammed his hand down on the desk hard enough for the laptop to jiggle the picture. "No! You have to be here or you won't… you won't believe me."

Rolland's smile became more genuine. "Rest assured, Mr Wilcott, whoever gave you my card knew what they were doing. I have already deduced that you are dealing with a poltergeist. Things flying about the room at random, bookcases crashing down, lightbulbs exploding, that sort of thing. Am I right?"

"You think it's a ghost?" Wilcott expression was equal parts disdain and frustration. His arm grew large in the screen as he reached forward to terminate the call. "This was a mistake."

Rolland waved his hands in his *stop, calm down* gesture. "Not ghosts! Poltergeist phenomenon have nothing to do with spirits."

The arm paused, still blocking the screen. "What, then?"

That was a bit more delicate to explain. "It's complicated. I assure you there is a perfectly straightforward and scientific explanation. I would prefer, however, to conduct my investigation without prejudicing the findings by expressing my suspicions prematurely."

The arm came down and Wilcott's face reappeared.

"You think you know what this is, though? You can end it?"

Roland nodded reassuringly. "Money-back guarantee."

Rolland's real intent, of course, was to draw the phenomenon out as long as he could, the better to study it. But poltergeist phenomena were always fleeting; taking credit for when it faded financed his studies.

"Very well," Wilcott sighed, and sat back. "Ask me anything."

Rolland shook his head. "I need to start with whatever children are in the house. Anyone aged ten to fourteen. A twelve- or thirteen-year-old is best to start with, if you have them."

Wilcott frowned as he processed the odd request. "There are no children in the house."

Rolland shrugged. "Well, the adolescents, then."

Wilcott frowned. "My sons are in their late thirties and childless."

"The servants' children?" Rolland hazarded.

"There is only chef, and she hasn't brought her daughter. There is no one in the house under thirty-three."

"Ah," Rolland said. Unusual, but not entirely unheard of. Fordor himself had noted that menopause offered hormonal imbalances as nearly significant as puberty, and had speculated that the right emotional context might well give rise to poltergeist tendencies. "Women in the 45 to 60 range?"

"My wife Effie. But as mentioned, she's a bit under the weather. I'd rather not disturb her."

That was interesting! Menopausal *and* a virus. Triggering changes in the epigenome, perhaps? This might well be the breakthrough Rolland had been waiting for.

"I'll keep the interview to 45 minutes," Rolland offered as if that weren't standard. "A brief conversation might be diverting for her."

"Very well." Wilcott sighed and pushed himself up out of the chair. "I'll take you to her."

The camera view dipped down abruptly, then went to black, as Wilcott closed his laptop. Rolland took the opportunity to reheat some tea in the microwave as he relocated to his home office.

The picture came back on to reveal a woman in her late fifties, coughing into her elbow. She was in her bathrobe, sitting up in bed, bars of an old-fashioned brass bedframe just visible in the background. The sound was off, and for a moment Rolland was able to take in the bare walls, the absence of other furniture, the stark emptiness of the bedroom, before an arm in Wilcott's suit came in from the side to switch the settings. The sound came back on as Mrs Wilcott appeared seated in an elegant parlour, her robe transformed into a stylish pantsuit.

Mr Wilcott seated himself beside her on the 'settee', though of course the cushions sank more like an over-burdened mattress. Rolland would have preferred to interview Effie alone, but recognized that wasn't going to happen. Had he been physically present in an actual sitting room, Rolland could have manoeuvred Mr Wilcott to the other side of the door without Wilcott quite realizing what was happening – but one had to make do with what was possible during corona season.

"Mrs Wilcott?" Rolland began. "If I could just get your maiden name for my records before we start?"

Rolland proceeded to take a full genealogy, partly to put the respondent at ease by anchoring the interview in the mundane, but mostly because Rolland was still trying to nail down whether there might not be a genetic component to any poltergeist phenomenon. Where once he would have jumped right into questions about manifestations, he had learned to get the background details first, there being no motivation for clients to cooperate with his research once the phenomenon had stopped.

"Thank you. And now... when did you first notice something out of the ordinary?"

"When we first arrived. John," Her wrist folded backwards to indicate her husband, "had let us all in the front door and was punching in the code for the alarm, when – this will sound ridiculous – when the living room bookcase came out to greet us."

Rolland blinked. "It *spoke* to you?" That was new!

Effie gave a little laugh which morphed into a long bought of coughing. When she could breathe again, she shook her head. "It didn't speak. I just meant it came all the way out from the far wall of the living room into the entrance hall where we were. About eight meters. It happened very fast, like it was running out to see who was at the door. And then halted abruptly, as if at the sight of us."

"I see. And how large is this bookcase?"

"Not large. About the size of a person. A family heirloom. It's beautifully made. It was in my bedroom when I was a girl, so I've kept it with me."

"And how did this make you feel?" Rolland asked.

"How do you think?!" Mr Wilcott interjected. "Nearly gave me a bloody heart attack."

Rolland froze Wilcott with a glance, turned back to Effie expectantly.

"Well, it startled us all, of course. A bit of a fright that way."

"Besides startled, then?" Rolland probed.

"Well... I suppose I was a bit disappointed I'd have to clean up the mess. I mean, when it came to an abrupt stop, all the books continued on. Like it was throwing up, scattering books across the hall like projectile vomit. I thought to myself, I can get the boys to carry the case and books back into the living room, but I'll be the one having to arrange them properly on the shelves again."

"Before that," Rolland pushed.

"Before?"

"Did you feel assaulted? Threatened?" Rolland pressed.

"I suppose not. It's silly, but as a child I always fancied that bookcase a bit of a guardian. It's ornate, and at night, in the dark...well, there's a bit of face in the scrollwork. You know how that is, I'm sure, when you're a child and it's dark: suddenly your best blouse and a couple of pillows on a chair look like some monster in your room. The bookcase was always there to protect me."

"I see. And then what happened?"

"Things started flying around," Wilcott said, intruding again. "Ornaments at first, then a couple of the smaller paintings. Every bulb in the chandelier exploded, one by one. They'd wait till you thought it was over, and then the next one would pop. Piano took a swipe at me. The worst was when a kitchen drawer flung itself out onto the floor, and the knives came out after me."

"You're anthropomorphizing," Rolland said, pointing a reprimanding finger at Mr Wilcott. "That's as silly as ghosts."

"Felt personal," Wilcott grumped. But he stayed quiet as Rolland turned back to Effie.

"Did you have –" Rolland almost said "Covid-27" but stopped himself in time –"your cold before or after arriving at the house?"

Effie smiled as if recognizing his near faux pas. "It's all right. It really is a cold, albeit a bad one. I had Covid-25 two years ago, confirmed. We're told that likely gives me useful resistance to this new one."

Rolland acknowledged this with a slight nod. "So, before or after you arrived?"

"I would say after the chandelier, but that was the cough. I remember having remarked to John as we were walking up to the house that I had a headache and would lie down."

Rolland nodded absently, trying out different timelines. If her confirmed coronavirus had triggered the epigenome somehow, then the arrival of a novel corona might bring out a unique response. In pubescent teens and menopausal women.

There had been an upsurge in poltergeist activity back in 2020, but Rolland had assumed that had been an artefact of the first lockdown: more families with puberty-aged kids stuck at home, amping up both the interpersonal friction and the opportunities for observation, under conditions of general stress and anxiety. But what if the virus itself had played a role? Not just attacking T-cells, but somehow triggering innate psychic abilities?

"I take it the house is not your usual residence?"

Effie nodded. "We felt staying in the country would make lockdown feel more like a vacation. And the house is considerably larger than our place in the city, so a bit more space to spread out in."

Spread out in was interesting. Perhaps tensions within the family?

"And your sons joined you?"

"Complained endlessly about the isolation last year," Wilcott explained. "I suggested they join us at the house this time round. Visit with their mother."

Their mother? Not us?

Effie tilted her head and smiled at the memory. In his notes, Rolland categorized her expression as *regretful* rather than *fond*.

"You were all looking forward to a little family time?"

Effie's expression tightened.

Apparently not.

"Until the house started trying to kill us," Wilcott grumbled.

Rolland turned to Wilcott. "Again, anthropomorphizing. I assure you the phenomena are neither conscious nor threatening. Actual injury in these cases is extremely rare."

Wilcot and Effie exchanged a look that Rolland had difficulty interpreting. Unless...

"*Has* there been an injury?" Rolland asked.

"Ms Hillcrest, my secretary," Wilcott confessed reluctantly. "A bust flew at her head, knocked her down. Sent her to hospital."

"A mild concussion," Effie clarified. "Nothing serious. It was plastic. Just a toy." She turned to Wilcott. "If you tell people 'a bust', they'll think *life-size* and made of *marble*."

"But your secretary came to the house?" Rolland asked Wilcott.

"Dropping something off?"

Wilcott looked uncomfortable, cleared his throat. "No. I had asked her to stay at the house with us. I still have my responsibilities, of course, and Ms Hillcrest is invaluable."

"She'll be returning to your house when she's released from hospital?" Rolland asked.

"No!" Effie said, too emphatically. She seemed to recognize how that sounded, tried to spin it differently. "I've told my husband he can't ask her to return to work until she's fully recovered. She'll be staying with her own people for the duration."

"I couldn't ask her to come, the way things stand." Wilcott's gesture took in the whole of the house, the poltergeist... Effie. "Certainly not after the incident with the kitchen knives."

Rolland thought he saw the general outline of things. But to be sure, he asked, "Have either of your sons, or the cook, been bothered by the phenomenon?"

"Bothered? Of course we're all 'bothered'," Wilcott huffed. "The boys are worried for their mother. Chef threatened to quit. I had to triple her wages while we're here; organize a company scholarship for her daughter. You can't imagine what it's been like."

Actually, Rolland could imagine it very well. He pictured himself there with all his equipment, tracking Wilcott, recording each and every incident. But with Ms Hillcrest out of the picture, the situation would likely defuse before he could get down there, even if he were prepared to break isolation. He'd have to be satisfied with just the interview data.

"I meant, anything thrown directly at them? Exploded around them. That sort of thing?"

"No," Effie said firmly. "That has not happened."

"Chef has nailed the drawers in the kitchen closed," Wilcott clarified. "And the boys have retired to their separate rooms, moved anything that could be thrown or otherwise dangerous out into the common areas. Take their meals alone in their rooms. We daren't even risk tea together. It's worse for them than if they'd stayed in their flats."

For the record, Rolland asked Effie, "Your room is similarly bare?" though he already knew the answer.

"At my husband's insistence," she confirmed. "I would have preferred staying in our room."

"Couldn't risk it," Wilcott said. "This morning, a pillow tried to smother me."

Unbelievable control! Rolland reconsidered the decision not to go in person. With effort, he refocused on the interview at hand.

"But you don't feel threatened at all, yourself," he asked Effie.

"No. Not really." She looked at her husband, hesitated. "I mean, I'm frightened for my husband, of course, and it's all been terribly upsetting, but... I don't think the house is angry at *me*."

Rolland sat back in his seat. Well, that was all perfectly clear.

"Feels personal," Wilcott muttered again.

"And at Ms Hillcrest," Rolland said aloud, before his filter could stop him. *Damn.* He glanced at Effie, who was glaring at him. It was almost as if she were consciously aware of her control. Unheard of, but if there were even the slightest possibility...

"Ms Hillcrest being felled was the final straw," Wilcott said. "Once the ambulance had left, I realized steps must be taken."

Rolland nodded absently. "I'll take a detailed timeline in a moment."

He paused, considering a possible experiment.

"I wonder, Mr Wilcott, if the family has considered returning to the city. Simply leaving the house."

"No!" Effie said in a tone that brooked no contradiction. "I cannot risk breaking isolation." She coughed dramatically.

"Just your husband, then," Rolland proposed. He had hoped to demonstrate that the phenomenon followed them to the other residence, but showing Wilcott was free of it when out of range of his wife would do as well.

"No," Effie said again. "I will not allow him to be away from me."

Rolland raised one eyebrow at her vehemence.

"What if something were to happen when he was alone in the city?" Effie said more calmly. "I would never forgive myself."

Not 'happen *to* him', Rolland noticed. Effie was undoubtedly concerned that Ms Hillcrest, or some other stand-in, might 'happen' if Effie didn't have eyes on Mr Wilcott.

"But, damn it, man," Wilcott exploded. "What's causing it? You said not ghosts. You can't tell me there's a scientific explanation for surprised bookcases and flying cutlery. It's all such... *nonsense!*"

Rolland nodded sympathetically. For a man like Wilcott, 'nonsense' was the worst possible expletive. But the question placed Rolland in an awkward position. He desperately wanted to follow this case in depth, but the phenomenon – or Wilcott's deep denial – would almost certainly have evaporated before Rolland could get there. And he had a moral responsibility to Wilcott's safety.

Effie started another coughing fit.

His attention thus drawn to her, Rolland turned, mindful he also had to respect the subject's priva—

Her face had turned a deep red, the veins on her neck standing out rigidly. Rolland recognized at once it was not from coughing. It was clear from her expression that Effie did not want him to answer her husband's question.

My god, she does know! Here was an unparalleled opportunity...

"Um," escaped Rolland's mouth as it tried to keep talking to Wilcott whilst his brain worked through the implications of a fully aware, adult poltergeist.

There was a *thud* behind Rolland. He glanced 'round to see his copy of the *Encyclopedia of Psychic Science* on the floor. He spun round again to see Effie's unambiguously threatening expression.

Conscious control at a distance! My god!

Rolland felt the adrenaline pumping through his body as excitement vied with terror for his attention.

"Perhaps," he ventured, "if Mrs Wilcott would be so good as to—"

Effie frowned. There was another, louder crash behind Rolland as the entire contents of his bookcase piled up behind his chair.

"What was that?" Wilcott demanded.

"Sorry." Rolland waved vaguely at his surroundings, which showed to his viewers as Spade's office. "Renovations next door."

"Look," Wilcott said, reaching into his jacket pocket for his phone. "I'll text you your full fee right now if you just tell me what you know. Suspect, at any rate."

"Uh..." Rolland went blank, as terror definitely got the upper hand.

There was a *thump* and *clatter* from Rolland's kitchen as if the silverware drawer had been pulled out too far and fallen to the floor.

"A crack in the space-time continuum," Rolland improvised hastily, watching for Effie's reaction. "A completely random outpouring of energy into our world, that consequently pushes objects around, overloads circuits. Absolutely random. No pattern at all."

Wilcott frowned. "How the devil am I supposed to deal with... with a broken universe, or whatever you said.

Effie also frowned. It was a "*watch yourself!*" kind of frown.

Rolland licked his lips at he tried to invent an answer that would satisfy Wilcott without triggering Effie.

"You plant an aerial in the yard to draw off the energy?" Rolland tried.

Effie tilted her head slightly as she considered the suggestion.

"What kind of aerial?"

"I'll email you the design," Rolland's promised. He'd cobble something together. Simple enough for Wilcott and his sons to manage, but complicated enough to look sciency. As long as it drew their attention away from Effie, the true source.

"And that's it, is it?" Wilcott asked.

Effie gave her head a nearly imperceptible shake.

"Well..." Rolland kept talking as he tried to interpret Effie's lead. "That should do to drain off the energy from the house during lockdown. Keep things quiet."

Effie's frown deepened.

"But the thing is," Rolland continued, feeling his way, "you've got to break your, um, entanglement with the spin-network octonions that have broken through and are affecting the Lorentzian quantum gravity of the external dimension."

"What?" Wilcott demanded. "That's gibberish."

"That's quantum mechanics," Rolland replied, confident that his stringing random terms together was no more gibberish-sounding than actual quantum mechanics. "The practical outcome of which is that, after lockdown is lifted, you and Mrs Wilcott — just you two, your sons don't seem to be entangled — should get as far away from here as you can. New Zealand, say."

Effie's expression turned thoughtful as she considered the suggestion.

"*New Zealand*?" Wilcott asked, incredulous

"We could make it a vacation, John," Effie said, laying her hand on his arm. "We haven't had a proper vacation in years."

"I can't just pick up and leave. I have businesses to run!"

"You could still Zoom into the office a couple of hours each day," Rolland suggested, watching Effie's reactions to see if this compromise would be acceptable.

Effie gave Rolland a curt nod.

Reassured, Rolland pressed his point with Wilcott. "A forced vacation would still be less disruptive than drawers full of knives coming at you."

Wilcott rolled his eyes, but ended with a defeated sigh. "I suppose I could learn to love Zoom."

Effie's gave Rolland a look. The books behind his chair stirred as if arising from a slumber.

"You'd have to limit your Zoom exposure," Rolland added, hurriedly. "We don't know if entanglement is reinforced through, uh, photon tunneling. A couple of hours per day at most."

Another eye roll and sigh from Wilcott. "Very well."

Effie appeared satisfied. There was a slight plopping sound as Rolland's books settled back on the floor.

Rolland tried to maintain an expression of bland scientific beneficence as relief flooded through him, followed closely by disappointment that he wasn't going to get a chance to document any of this.

Effie's head tilted again, as if considering Rolland. "Perhaps," she said at length, "perhaps when we return from New Zealand, you could come 'round for a quick check-up. To make sure we're entanglement-free."

Generous! "Yes, of course," Rolland said at once. "I am at your service."

Effie nodded as her eyes locked on to his: *Yes, you are.*

PAUL STJOHN MACKINTOSH

Two Terrific Tudor tours de force

A review of *The Dee Sanction: Adventures in Covert Enochian Intelligence*, by Paul Baldowski, from Just Crunch Games; and *Magonomia: The RPG of Renaissance Wizardry*, by Andrew Gronosky, Christian Jensen Romer, Timothy Ferguson, Tom Nowell, Vesna Gronosky, from Shewstone Publishing.

I don't know whether it's something to do with The Tudors and all those historical dramas on Netflix, or with Enochian emanations from the 29th Aethyr, but Tudor occult investigations seem to have been quite the thing lately. Here we've got two splendid ones – both covering the same period and broadly the same theme, but very different in flavour as well as system.

The Dee Sanction won the Best New RPG judges' award at UK Games Expo. Paul Baldowski already has a major presence in the investigative/horror end of the RPG community thanks to *The Cthulhu Hack*, his delightfully rules-lite Lovecraftian take on the quintessential streamlined OSR clone ruleset *The Black Hack*. (For non-gamers, what that rigmarole refers to is the Old School Revival movement in RPG gaming, away from gargantuan and massively detailed rules, towards slim, streamlined systems that hark back to the simplicity and straightforward fun of roleplaying's early days.) And *The Dee Sanction* applies a similar approach to the world of Renaissance wizardry.

The Dee Sanction has one of those brilliant one-sentence premises that practically guarantees a game's success out of the box: What if convicted Elizabethan sorcerers were given the option to work for the Queen's secret service, ferreting out spiritual and sorcerous threats to the Realm for Cecil and Walsingham, instead of burning at the stake? Immediately, you can imagine the period espionage atmosphere of dark, smoke-filled rooms; cloak-and-dagger conspiracy; and burned, desperate agents living on borrowed time, kept around for only so long as they're useful to the powers-that-be. And if you can't whip up a rip-roaring game scenario around that premise, well, I despair of you.

The titular Dee Sanction is the secret (and fictional) codicil to Queen Elizabeth's 1563 Act Against Conjurations, Enchantments and Witchcraft, granting convicted traitorous and felonious sorcerers a reprieve - so long as they work for Francis Walsingham and Dr John Dee, On Her Majesty's Secret Sorcerous Service. The rules emphasize, though, that the poor player-character protagonists aren't Tudor James Bonds or Modesty Blaises, with wands instead of Walthers - they're more liable to be poor ignorant dabblers in the occult, gifted (or cursed) with a slight sensitivity to the supernatural, and desperately outclassed by the forces they run up against. As the rules state, they're Vulnerable, Expendable, Amateurs, and Only Slightly Supernatural. The game system divides their attributes into three basic Resources (Physicall, Intellectuall, and Supernaturall), plus Abilities, Favours of the Angels, and various other qualities. Game mechanics are handled through a typical RPG range of dice, from four- to twelve-sided, as well as (optionally) a deck of cards.

The rules are definitely detail-light as well as, well, rules-lite. There's no extensive history of Elizabethan England, and the core rulebook only runs to 68 pages. That said there's already a slew of adventures available, thanks to a phenomenally successful Kickstarter campaign. Foes are liable to be Redcaps or Devil Dogs as often as they are wicked Spanish sorcerers with dark designs on Gloriana. Most of the adventures tend to be written as far more investigative than confrontational: given the relative vulnerability of the PCs, that's certainly just as well, and that's definitely the direction that the system is slanted.

Magonomia is a voluminous (385-page) book, built on – and including – the Fate system. For the non-gamers among us, Fate is a fast-moving and very

versatile story-focused game system built on a core mechanic of four six-sided dice (each marked -1, -1, 0, 0, +1, +1), giving a possible range of rolled outcomes from -4 to +4. It's often used to run very content-lite games, but in this case, I'm glad to cite the opposite: *Magonomia* is an immensely detailed dive into Tudor society, politics, folklore, and above all, sorcery and witchcraft. The game's premise is that it is the RPG 'of Renaissance wizardry. The player characters are wizards whose magic is based on authentic sixteenth century folklore.' It has one of the best recreations of authentic historical magical traditions that I've encountered in years of gaming, well tailored to the Fate system. The magical Sciences are divided into five schools: the Science of Alchemy, the Science of Astrology, the Science of Sorcery, the Science of Theurgy, and the Science of Witchcraft. Each has its own dedicated progression scheme and style of play, with all kinds of possibilities for character development, from flying wizardry to a career of drudgery waterproofing the gunpowder in the Queen's galleons.

Obviously, the premise of this game is very similar to *The Dee Sanction*, but players have a great deal more latitude in their choice of career – Queen's Agent is just one of the options. It is also heavily slanted towards magicians as characters, but there is more than enough detail on other pursuits, including the martial discipline, to allow players to run characters who never pick up a wand. It certainly has a vastly greater depth of period detail than *The Dee Sanction*, with exhaustive guides to both mundane and enchanted Albion, creatures and secret societies, and so on. It's also beautifully produced, with parchment-tinted pages adorned with both Tudor and original artwork.

Gamers will and should follow their own preferences when it comes to choosing between the two games – if there ever is need to choose. *The Dee Sanction* is low on prep and high on atmosphere, though the actual level of immersion in the game and the period may vary. *Magonomia*, meanwhile, is immensely rich and deep, as well as drawing on a really well-proven game system with many other resources available for it. *The Dee Sanction* might be better for more casual gamers who prefer short-play sessions and one-shots; while *Magonomia* will likely suit deeper and longer-term campaigns drawing heavily on the historical and magical lore of the period. Either way, would-be Elizabethan elucidators of esoterica are exceptionally well catered-for at present. So, by God's grace, play a set, that shall strike a crown into the hazard!

A Universe of Gaming Reopens

A review of *Basic Roleplaying Universal Game Engine*, written by Jason Durall and Steve Perrin. Published by Chaosium.

Connoisseurs of roleplaying game lore and general corporate awfulness will have no doubt followed the debacle of Wizards of the Coast's controversial changes to D&D's OGL, where the inheritors of the *Dungeons and Dragons* franchise managed to piss off practically the entire RPG community by modifications to the time-honoured Open Gaming Licence (OGL). Previously, this governed open access to a slew of roleplaying games, not just D&D, as well as third party content written for that game. Wizards of the Coast later walked back the revisions, but the damage had already been done. Gaming companies worldwide have switched to a new Open RPG Creative License (ORC), which crucially contains the important wording 'irrevocable', so that rights to publish, once extended, cannot be withdrawn.

First beneficiary of this new licence out of the gate is the *Basic Roleplaying Universal Game Engine* from Chaosium. Basic Roleplaying (BRP), for those few who don't know, is one of the longest-established roleplaying systems on the market, dating back to the earliest foundations of the hobby. It underpinned *Call of Cthulhu*, the investigative horror roleplaying game par excellence, probably second only to D&D in terms of popular culture influence. BRP has stayed around the market as the foundation for numerous other games over the decades, and Chaosium has now given it a new lease of life in this edition, governed by the terms of the new licence. In principle, Chaosium has jumped the gun a bit with this edition. The ORC Licence has still not been completely finalized. That said, the wording is held online , and any final changs are unlikely to make any difference to the actual content of this book, merely governing the terms under which it can be shared and used.

The book is a pretty lavish production, boasting the best of Chaosium's artwork, so it's worth clarifying exactly what we're talking about here. As confirmed by Chaosium, the text dealing with rules mechanics, which pretty much covers the entire contents of the book, is free to copy and reuse, provided it is also licensed under the same ORC terms. Copyrighted and trademarked material that is actual creative intellectual property, such as the pictures in the book or references to still in-copyright Cthulhu Mythos IP created by modern writers such as Ramsey Campbell, is not available under these terms. But you're still getting an entire RPG mechanical system, based on one of the oldest platforms in the book, and incorporating decades worth of refinements and improvements. Budding RPG creators can take the rules right out of the book and base their own settings on them, which is precisely the point.

As this should make clear, you're not getting an immediately playable game out of this book. There's no single setting or context to guide gameplay. As DIY kits go though, this is pretty much a complete chassis and powertrain, needing only some styling and bodywork. Some creators might even feel a little overwhelmed. There are options to cover every period from prehistory to the far future, and every genre from sorcerers to superheroes. There are power scaling mechanisms from gritty and low tech to superhuman. there are systems for Magic, superpowers and PSI. and critically, all this stuff has been tested and proven in various incarnations over the decades. it's backwards compatible with much previously released material. Some readers may balk at seeing pikes and plasma rifles bracketed in the same system, but you certainly can't criticise Chaosium for trying to cram the quartiest of quarts into a pint pot.

Some have criticized this edition for missing the opportunity to completely revamp the system and bring it up to date with innovations in gaming made since its inception. My experience is that we're talking about differences in style as much as differences in maturity. Yes, there have been developments in gaming systems since BRP was first formulated, notably the *Powered by the Apocalypse* approach where the Game Master never rolls the dice and events happen only in response to player actions. The back-tobasics Old School Revival gaming movement in RPGs came along in response to the huge complexity of some systems, and these days you can get some games with rules just one page long. There are completely different systems that offer more of a narrative vs. simulationist game style, to use one of the dichotomies that have grown up in the RPG community, but simulationist games are still what many players are looking for. And a simplified version of BRP wouldn't necessarily be BRP, and give the same player experience. *Call of Cthulhu* in its current 7th Edition is far more dense and complex than BRP, but that hasn't held back its current storming popularity. Presentational complexity is not the same as mechanical complexity, and much of the apparent complexity in BRP: UGE consists of optional bolt-on parts that don't affect the core. The book could arguably have spent more time explaining how to put its different parts to work, and how to trim or tweak them, but I can't say I feel shortchanged by the result. Those who already own its predecessor, the so-called *Big Gold Book*, perhaps won't need to buy this; those who don't certainly will want to in preference to the BGB. That said, the production values of the new edition are streets ahead of the BGB, and I can see many BRP grognards wanting to upgrade for that reason alone. As for game creators, if you want to make anything in the BRP system compatible with the new ORC, you need to use these rules.

Since this text is all ORC, it may well be made available in free forms later, including online, just as many other previous games and systems have posted their system reference documents online. Chaosium staffers have specifically stated that there will be text-only versions available free to use in due course. But honestly why wait? The book is gorgeous - and hugely inspirational. The BRP UGE is complex only in the ancillary detail added to fit it to your period and setting of choice. The basic game mechanics remain simple, elegant, intuitively understandable, tried and tested, and very familiar. Anyone who's familiar with RPGs as a whole knows exactly what they're getting with this. It's not ideal for all types of games, but it's still perfect for many, and many gamers' point of reference for all RPG systems. Even for people who've never played RPGs before, it's the kind of system that will instantly jog their memories with references and examples they've heard about. Personally, I've written games in numerous different systems, old and new, and I'm still defaulting to BRP. The ORC initiative is massively worth supporting across the board, and with this release it's got a flagship product it deserves. This is an essential buy for anyone seriously involved in the RPG creative sphere - and 100% recommended for anybody who just wants to have a damn good time.

The Excavation at Hob's Barrow – A guest review by Davide Mana

The Excavation at Hob's Barrow, by Cloak & Dagger Games, is published by Wadjet Eye Games and is available on Steam and GOG.com for Windows, Mac and Linux systems.

A form of interactive storytelling that became popular in the late '80s/early '90s, point and click adventure games included best-sellers *The Secret of Monkey Island* (1990) and its successors, *Indiana Jones and the Fate of Atlantis* (1992), and *Grim Fandango* (1998). Using their mouse, players would lead the main character of the story through a series of places and events, interacting with characters, collecting clues and solving puzzles to reach the resolution of the narrative.

This form of gaming was considered by all means extinct by the dawn of the 21st century, yet recently we have seen a resurgence, in part fueled by nostalgia. Many small games, often financed through crowdfunding, reprise

the look & feel of those older games while adding some new twists to the mix. One of such games is *The Excavation at Hob's Barrow*, launched in September 2022 by Cloak and Dagger Games, and nominated for the Game of the Year award by PC Gamer magazine.

In *The Excavation at Hob's Barrow*, we follow young and independent Thomasina Bateman, a Victorian-era 'barrow digger' following in her antiquarian father's footsteps. A letter from a mysterious Mr Shoulder brings her to Bewlay, a village in the Yorkshire moors that is the location of the titular Hob's Barrow, an unusual burial mound.

Thomasina is therefore an occult investigator, and her mission will require observation, problem solving and exploration skills. Over a few days, Thomasina will meet and interview the locals,try to locate the barrow, and then set up an excavation. But strange doings are afoot in Bewlay, and a general atmosphere of secrecy is weighing on the community. Encounters with sinister villagers, nightmares and visions will lead Thomasina to discover the deep connection between the barrow, the local legends and her family history. What starts as a purely intellectual pursuit – excavate an ancient burial site and publish the results – will take a personal turn: discover what really happened during the previous excavation, in which Thomasina's father was somehow involved. As the main character's goals shift, so does the tone of the story, adventure morphing into nightmare.

While graphically *The Excavation at Hob's Barrow* replicates those early '90s games, down to the big pixels and scrolling frames, story-wise the game strikes in some new and unusual directions. The story is much more adult and gruesome than the standard game fare from the '90s, and both the plot and the set-up take inspirations from such folk horror classics as *The Wicker Man* (including a local aristocrat with an interest in the Old Religion) and *Blood on Satan's Claw* (Thomasina will be staying at the Plough & Furrow Inn in Bewlay, and will visit a ruined chapel straight out of the 1971 Piers Haggard movie).

True to folk horror tropes, Thomasina will find herself surrounded by ambiguous, untrustworthy characters, and entangled in a web of ancient rituals, legend and superstitions, set on a course whose final destination is inescapable.

The writing of the adventure is very good, the dialogues are pitch-perfect, the characters are interesting and nicely characterized, and the general sense of tension and paranoia is enhanced by an interesting manipulation of the time frame: while the main plot-line is linear, we go through a series of nested flashbacks, as well as documents and letters, that deepen the background, help define the character of Thomasina, and stress the general sense of confusion, hinting at unspeakable deeds in her father's past.

Thomasina's predicament can be dire, but the game-play is straightforward and the story is as easy to follow as it is entertaining. This being a point-and-click adventure, much of the game involves exploring one of a dozen locations, looking for clues, and collecting items that will unlock the next step of the way – and while the early puzzles are reasonably easy to figure out, the later part of the game can stump the player for quite a while. The risk of spending a lot of time going round in circles is real. Still, a committed player with a modicum of experience in adventure gaming (and maybe a smattering of Latin) will work through the whole story in about eight hours. Depending on your tastes and your inclinations, this might be a little on the short side, and indeed this writer found the game highly satisfactory and fun, but some extra game time would have been welcome.

More critical is the absence of alternate endings, making *The Excavation at Hob's Barrow* a maze with only one possible way out. A choice in line with the tone and the themes of folk horror, this might turn away players looking for freedom and options in their adventures, and severely limits the re-playability of the game.

These drawbacks are more than compensated by the evocative soundtrack (by The Machine, The Demon), and by the excellent voice acting, that helps make each one of the fifteen or so main characters unique and interesting. Admittedly, the dated graphics might not be everyone's cup of tea, but once the player gets used to the anachronism, story and atmosphere will easily capture the player. One of the plus sides of the retro-style of the game is a very low requirement in terms of hardware, so that we do not need the latest in home computer technology to enjoy the ride.

The Excavation at Hob's Barrow is a self-contained story, and it is unlikely to have a sequel – but given the overall quality, it would be nice to see more folk horror/occult detection games from Cloak & Dagger.

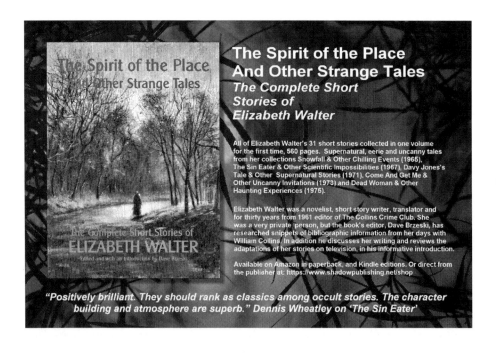

THE NATURE OF PANIC

SIMON AVERY

1

The act of taking one's life is not something one does without a great deal of soul searching, but I simply cannot live with what I did. My misguided actions seemed quite appropriate to me once. I cannot take any of it back now.

The box is buried beneath the church, but whatever it was that allowed me access all those years ago has shut me out. The ecstasy of the wild has abandoned me. It no longer loves me enough to keep me or permit me to make amends. Perhaps that is just the natural law of things.

So if I cannot rectify my mistake I cannot go on. This is my apology to Annabel, even though she will never see it, never know it, never understand what was in my heart.

I have not known peace in this life and I fear I will not know it in the next.

F.

2

His name was William Williams, but everyone called him Twicey. I met him on the last week of May. We were both out in the sunshine, picking strawberries on a farm a mile off the coast of North Devon. 469 acres, 30 fields, many of them filled with poly tunnels with 150 or so pickers inside. Romanians, Bulgarians, Lithuanians and Poles, mostly. I didn't earn as much as them. I was too slow. But that wasn't really why I was here. I got up with these young people at first light and lumbered down the raised gutters picking the best strawberries and arranging them in punnets in a trolley for eight hours a day, five days a week, May to the end of July.

Really. Fucking. Slowly.

Admittedly it was good money for a young, fast worker. You could make up to £10 an hour. Some of the payslips in peak season could be £600-700 a week. I was one of only a handful of British people here for the season. "You Brits would rather do anything else than pick crops," a kid from Bucharest had said to me one night. He wasn't wrong. Despite closing the door on the EU, we were still quite happy to expect them to serve our food, clean our hospitals, or toil in a field all day so we could have strawberries in time for Wimbledon.

"I've come to see a man about a caravan," Twicey said that day we first met. The soft, stretched out vowels were unmistakably that of a Welshman.

I was on a break. Lying in the grass with my hat on my face, sweating, my back in crisis talks with my knees. Neither of them wished to return to the poly tunnels. The long grass was cool on my skin.

I lifted the hat and squinted into the midday sun. "That'll be me, then," I said. "Do you snore?"

"Are you asking?"

"I'm asking."

"Then I'm snoring. On occasions I sleepwalk in the nude too."

"Brilliant," I said. "I'll lock my door tonight."

I liked him immediately.

Twicey was tall. Very tall. He had a bulging paunch that he seemed rather proud of. He often stood with it pushed out, like a woman braced to go into labour. Hair that had receded back to the crown of his head. He grew it long and bushy to the base of his neck. Deep, ineffably sad eyes. That first day he was wearing an out-of-shape T-shirt, a straw hat, some old jeans that he'd cut down into shorts, and some bulky and perfectly new hiking boots. In the first couple of days, I'd catch him wearing a look of faint bemusement on his face, as if surprised to find himself standing in a field picking strawberries with people half his age. Some of it, I'd later discover, could be chalked up to thirty years of light substance abuse. He'd liked to drop acid at least once or twice a month until 'the incident'. I'd only learn about that later on. But part of Twicey's mind still lingered somewhere in that uncertain state; a sort of euphoric escape hatch in the reality of things. I envied him those moments of dropping out, being elsewhere. I wanted to be elsewhere too.

After our shift ended I made room for him in the static caravan I was staying in. It was an old, ramshackle park provided for the workers. The barest minimum of facilities. Sometimes there were four or five to a caravan. There were some wild parties that kept me awake at night.

"There's some dubious stains on the mattress," I offered as we stood in the doorway of the tiny room. "I think someone felt a bit unloved and it got out of hand. Quite literally."

We turned the mattress over but we discovered it was showing us its best side already. Twicey sighed and shrugged. "It's no good," Twicey said, "we'll have to kip together." I stared at him. He winked at me. Over those six months I never did know when he was being serious.

"I could do with a pint, I could," he said finally.

We retreated to the local pub down the road. Most of the workers gravitated to the community centre on the farm after dark to down some beers and play pool, do karaoke. It wasn't really my scene. I just wanted some peace and quiet.

"Is this your first season?" I asked. We sat sipping Guinness in the largely empty pub. Every time we reached for our glass we groaned loudly and then smiled ruefully at each other.

"Never done it before, no," Twicey said. "Had to get away, you know. From life, I suppose." He smiled. "*Life*. Christ. Wasn't prepared for my back hurting like a bastard."

"It's painful for the first two weeks, but then you get used to it."

"Do you?"

"No, I just cry into my pillow at night until the sweet embrace of oblivion takes me."

"Well, there's *that* to look forward to," Twicey said, and smiled. "How about you? How long you been doing this?"

"I did it once a few years back while I stayed at my aunt's house. Nearly killed me, that first time."

We were both pushing fifty, not entirely match-fit for the job we'd chosen, both of us here for reasons that we weren't comfortable enough with each other to share just yet. But we would. Instead I told him about my aunt, one of the reasons I was in North Devon.

"She lived a couple of miles from here. Her name was Frances de la Wode."

"*Lived*?"

"Yeah, she committed suicide a couple of months ago. Filled her pockets with stones and walked into the river at the end of her garden."

"Christ. Like Virginia Woolf."

"Exactly. Frances was a bohemian in the old sense of the word. She was an artist and a writer. *And* a self-proclaimed witch."

"A *witch*?"

"Oh, yeah. People came from all over to practice magic and create all sorts of art. Mostly women. She owned this beautiful 16th century farmhouse and painted it pink. *Bright fucking pink*."

"Was she married?"

"No, she had a lover called Cecily, but she died a few years ago. Frances was alone for the last ten years or so. That's why I stayed with her on my first strawberry picking season."

"So, what, did she leave the house to you in the will?"

"No, apparently Frances didn't believe in them. My mother is dead, so I'm the administrator of Frances's estate. I'm going to spend my spare time clearing the house and try to locate Frances's daughter."

"She hasn't come forward? Not even with property inheritance on offer?"

"They were estranged from what I can gather. I met her a couple of times when we were kids. Her name was Annabel, but she ran away from home when she was sixteen. Never seen again."

"Christ. Do you know why the old girl committed suicide?"

"She left a note. It's a bit vague. I have it on my phone. Here—"

Twicey took my phone and read it a couple of times, raising his eyebrows, puffing out his cheeks, shaking his head. Finally he passed the phone back to me. " 'The ecstasy of the wild has abandoned me.' It is a bit… *witchy*, isn't it?"

I laughed. "Yes, I suppose it is. The word *eccentric* doesn't really cover it with Frances."

"What do you think the business about the box buried beneath the church means?"

"No idea, mate. I'm just the good nephew, doing his duty."

"Still…" Twicey began. I could see that look in his eye. Interest piqued.

"Do you want to come with me on Sunday?" I said finally. "I'm going down there to get started."

Buried treasure? Of course he fucking did.

3

On Saturday I drove into town for supplies. I was restless when I had nothing to do with my hands. There was no good in sitting still. I'd wasted a good proportion of my youth doing that. Now I was catching a glimpse of the old man I was becoming in the bathroom mirror, I felt like I was making up for lost years, foolish mistakes. Second-hand dreams, Ingrid called them.

Afterwards I drove the 105 miles to Clifton, an affluent suburb of Bristol that had been built with profits from tobacco and the slave trade. I drove around, trying to fool myself that I wouldn't stop this time. That I'd just keep driving. But then I found a gift of a space to park a little way down the street that Ingrid lived on; I pulled in and I turned off the ignition and sat, listening to the engine ticking and my mind beginning its familiar waltz.

Two years and I still wasn't over it.

She lived in a row of tightly packed white Georgian terraces that had seen better days. The grandeur was flaking away from the facades. There were plastic boxes filled with empty wine bottles outside every house except Ingrid's. Concrete front yards, dirty net curtains at the windows, cars bumper to bumper on the street outside.

I didn't intend to stay. I told myself that every time. Every fucking time.

It had taken Ingrid a while to get back in touch after she moved out of my house in Dorset. I hadn't realised the damage I'd done until it was too late. But then after six months she'd emailed me. She'd settled somewhere new. She was OK. Later on there were further emails, an address, a softening of tone, that old familiarity coming back. I told myself that maybe I could make amends, but I was just fooling myself; I wanted another chance. *That* old story. I'd disappeared inside myself and forgotten that her demons were worse than mine. But she'd found work at the Inland Revenue, said she was seeing a counsellor, and she was going to Alcoholics Anonymous again. She was doing well. Moving on.

So I drove out here every month or so, just to see her, to appease that old ache, the yearning to see her face, to remember how she moved, how she looked when she thought no one was watching. And I told myself this wasn't acceptable behaviour for a man of my age, that it did more harm than good. But it kept on happening because I was dumb enough to think that the *next time* would be the charm and I could finally move on. *Next time.*

She came out after half an hour. She looked well, healthier than I think I'd ever seen her. A filmy summer dress and sandals. She always reminded me of either Jean Harlow or Carole Lombard, I never could distinguish which one. That air of faded Hollywood glamour. I'd fallen for her face and stayed for the beating heart underneath, along with some stupid, misguided male idea of being able to save her. But I was too far gone to do that. We'd had a limited shelf life but we'd both tried to fool ourselves that it wasn't the case.

She was followed by a man in glasses and with longish hair, younger than me, a look of quiet composure that suggested he might be a psychiatrist or a teacher or something. They walked down the street to a yellow VW Beetle, the old kind. He tossed her the keys and they laughed. They were the very picture of middle-class contentment. They got in the car and drove away. I felt it turn my bones to lead, that keen sense of being abandoned all over again. I sat there for some time, feeling a physical revolt in my body, an urge to drive after her and fix the situation, roll the operating system back to a point where it last worked. But instead I drove away, back to North Devon, to that shabby little caravan. It began to rain on the way home. I didn't talk to

Twicey when I got back. I couldn't. I wasn't able to spill my guts in front of strangers. It wasn't how I was wired. Another misguided male vanity. So I went to bed and lay awake, listening to the rain drumming on the roof.

Almost 50. Christ, I thought. Look at you, you pathetic fucking fool. These second-hand dreams; they do you no good.

4

Frances's house had languished for years without love or attention, but even now, on a dreary Sunday morning, with rain on the ground and the sky a sunken slate grey, it still stood out in the lonely landscape, bright and pink and strange. We were a couple of miles away from the farm, close enough to the coast to smell the sea in the air, hear its gentle susurration. Gulls crying out, twisting on the air currents above us.

Twicey didn't drive, didn't have a car. He'd wanted to walk and I told him not to be pillock, and *get in the fucking car*. He did, but he was a deeply reluctant passenger. I sensed there was a story there somewhere, but I could wait; he'd get to it eventually when he was good and ready. He'd brightened considerably once we'd parked and made our way down the rugged track to the door of the rambling stone farmhouse.

"Christ," he said, "look at this bloody place! It's incredible." He laughed. "And fucking *pink*!"

Even though the love lavished on this place had long expired, and all the colourful characters that Frances had attracted in her heyday were long gone, their fingerprints remained in the art on every wall, door and window. Despite that bright day-glow pink exterior, it was looking a little shabby now. The red-tiled roof was spattered with orange lichen.

"If you think this is impressive, wait until you see inside," I said.

Twicey's mouth actually fell open. The interior was a fantasia, an explosion of decorative art, ceramics, furniture, fabrics and magical ephemera. A bewildering and overwhelming display of clashing styles and vivid colours and confrontational subject matter. By the time you'd fought your way to the kitchen at the back of the house you were glad to see something normal like a sink, a cooker, a kitchen table.

The huge stained glass window on the landing caught Twicey's attention first. He climbed the first flight of stairs to study it. "Crikey, this is a bit fruity, isn't it?"

The window depicted Pan as a ravenous, insatiable god, luring three naked nymphs into the forest. He had the shaggy hindquarters, legs and horns of a goat. He brandished a florid and erect phallus. It was a vivid, obscene piece of art. Frances had enjoyed the effect it had on her more conservative guests. "Frances was attached to a sort of neopagan witchcraft devoted to Pan," I said. "My mother always tried to cover my eyes when we came down during the summer holidays," I smiled. "She was a bit touchy about gods with their wedding tackle out."

"So she brought you to a house where they practised witchcraft and all the other mad shit?"

"Well, yeah. She was my mother's younger sister. They were like chalk and cheese but my mum loved her. She wanted to see her every now and then."

Twicey nodded, came back down the stairs. He kept glancing back up at the window. "They must have been eye-opening visits, though," he said. "For a nipper, like."

"I was a kid when I was first exposed to it, so I suppose I just thought it was normal."

"What was she like, though? Frances."

"Mum always said that Frances believed she'd been born a witch. She even had slightly pointed ears and a strawberry birthmark over her right eye. She looked slightly, I don't know, *Elfin* in appearance. Anyway, all of that apparently confirmed it for her when she was old enough to read about that sort of thing.

"She was expelled from three different schools. By the time she was twelve, she decided that she wasn't going to sleep in the family house anymore, so she pitched a tent in the garden for four years and kept a pet spider called Horatio at the entrance. She'd let my mum in for awhile but tired of her eventually. That never really changed. She'd put up with me and my mum for an hour or two when we'd visit over the summer, but then she got a bit bored of talking about dad's job and our week in Margate. It all seemed like a pale substitute for a life to Frances."

"Been about a bit, had she?"

"In her time she'd been an artist's model, published stories, hitchhiked all the way across Europe to Turkey and through Iran, Afghanistan, Nepal... A string of lovers, one of them, if she's to be believed, 'a famous French actress. If there was an exhibition of de la Wode art, then you could guarantee that the police would be confiscating half of it and then trying to prosecute her for public obscenity.

"Then she came here and settled down with Cecily, a woman she'd met in Kashmir. They opened the house up to all and sundry in the name of art and witchcraft."

"But this must have been like a paradise for a young kid."

"It wasn't until I was older that I realised that Frances wasn't your usual sort of aunt. Even in the seventies, she was a bit of an anomaly, particularly out here in the sticks. She dressed outrageously, smoked in public, an unabashed lesbian, the house always filled with masses of bohemian types. I'd sometimes walk in on a circle of people while they were conducting some sort of ritual. There were people in the garden in various states of higher consciousness, dancing around stark naked. The constant smell of cannabis, obviously.

"Eventually mum would get impatient. She thought it was all nonsense. And Frances thought we were just too conventional. "Sod off home, now, poppets," she'd say eventually. And once mum had estimated that she'd done her sisterly duty for another year we sodded off back to the train station and home to Dorset."

"What about the daughter? Was this before she ran away?"

"Yeah, I saw Annabel here, but she was a shy girl as I recall. Spent most of her time in her room."

"When did it all start to go south?"

"Once Cecily died, I suppose. People stopped coming here. The party had moved on, left Frances behind. I think she felt betrayed by it all at that point."

"How do you mean?"

"I don't know. Maybe you expect all of that devotion to pay you back in your dotage. But I got the impression that she felt it had moved on, too. Like she mentioned in the note. That it had shut her out."

We spent the morning making a start on the front room, pausing every now and then for Twicey to marvel over an altar, or some magical paraphernalia, an upright piano decorated with nymphs that peered out behind a tangle of vines, an antique writing desk, a bookcase groaning under the weight of hundreds of old books. Indeed there were books everywhere, piled up on the stairs, around the fireplace, on the windowsills, beside the kitchen sink. A mass of dead plants, whose leaves had withered and turned crisp, fallen into the grubby, damp smelling carpet. It was an almost overwhelming task ahead of us. I think Twicey was already having second thoughts about the whole enterprise after the first hour. But I felt obliged to take care of the lion's share of it myself.

We ploughed into the seemingly endless stacks of papers for some clue as to the whereabouts of Annabel, Frances's daughter, but nothing turned up so by noon we decided to venture outside for a break with our flask of coffee and our sandwiches. The back garden was long overgrown, an abundance of long grass and wild flowers; a veritable riot of colour and scents. There were beautiful mosaic paths and long stagnant tile-edged pools. At the bottom of the garden, an ancient willow stooped over the river that Frances had walked into with her pockets filled with stones. We stood out there, listening to the rush of wind through the leaves, the hesitant birdsong all around us, the gentle sound of the river rippling beneath the fronds of the willow. The sun came out then and its rays glimmered through the leaves. There was a ragged, slightly faded magic here. I think we both sensed it. We didn't talk for a while.

"Are you looking for a reference to the box buried beneath the church at all?" Twicey asked. "Asking for a friend, like."

"That's all you're here for, isn't it?" I said. "Looking for buried treasure."

"I just want to know what it was," Twicey said. "What she meant."

"I'm not sure she was in her right mind at that point," I said.

"Well obviously, she topped herself."

"No, I mean a lot of what Frances said was smoke and mirrors. Words that set the tone for a ceremony. You had to *believe* it for it to be real."

"It's usually a lot of people off their cake." Twicey emptied the last drops of coffee into the river. "I know all about that. Although there's a lot to be said for altered states. Higher consciousness. I wouldn't dismiss everything she said." He smiled, dusted the crumbs of bread off his t-shirt.

Later, near the end of the day I found a letter hidden in a well-thumbed encyclopaedia of magical herbs. It was in a pile of books beside her bed. A spider was building a grand web from the bed post to the book. Twicey told me he was probably Horatio, Frances's guardian, and that I'd almost certainly pissed him off. But the letter was my first concrete lead to tracking Annabel down. It appeared to be from a local solicitor.

Dear Frances,

Thank you for your letter. I'm afraid there's not much I can add that the police haven't already told you. It doesn't sound like they were unduly concerned about your daughter's safety, and, as Annabel is now 16 we can no longer make a referral to children's services.

As long as she can show she is living in accommodation which provides a safe environment and she has a stable, respectable method of supporting herself financially, there are no legal barriers to leaving home at 16 years or older.

If, as you suspect, she is staying with the occupants of a neighbouring farm, and her welfare is not under any threat, then perhaps it might be best to give Annabel some 'space' and then try to reopen the lines of communication somewhere down the line.

Please do not hesitate to contact me if you have any further questions.

5

Marion Bryant was technically my employer. I'd only seen her a couple of times, but she was aware that I was Frances's nephew. She taken over the running of her old man's farm at the age of 21. Under her guidance, the farm had embraced new technologies and business horizons, fruit, vegetable and arable farming, sustainable agriculture. She was 46 now, had a brood of seven children, and owned farms in Kent, Herefordshire and Shropshire.

After I reached out it took a couple of days for Marion to get back to me. She came across the fields while I was on my break and offered me a few minutes of her time. She had a hard face that suggested she didn't particularly want to hear any of your bullshit, thank you very much, but then, once you began to talk to her, her features softened and her smile disarmed you entirely. We stood in the sunshine with the sound of quiet industry all around us. I was turning a good shade of mahogany after five weeks of balmy, almost Mediterranean weather.

"When you were young, did Annabel run away from Frances and come to stay at your farm?"

She gave me an inscrutable look.

"I suppose you're trying to track her down. Is she named in the will?"

"There isn't one. Do you know what happened to Annabel? It'd make my job a lot easier if you did."

She glanced away for a moment, back to the old farmhouse in the distance. Seeing all sorts of memories. "I don't suppose it makes a lot of difference after all these years."

"If I can find her, I can ensure she gets her inheritance and I can close the book on the whole thing."

"But that's just the thing," she said. "I'm not sure I'd want Annabel coming back here."

"Look, if you had your differences as kids, I'm sure a lot of water has passed under the bridge since then..."

She puffed out her cheeks and studied me again. Trying to gauge if whatever it was she'd kept to herself all these years was worth sharing.

"Come on," she said finally. "Let's go inside and I'll put the kettle on."

* * *

"Annabel ran away from home on her 16th birthday," Marion said. We were sat at the kitchen table in the old farmhouse. It was worn from years of family life. It was cool in here. A slate floor, an Aga, a multitude of small and muddy wellington boots at the door.

"She was an odd child. Not surprising, of course, all things considered. But mum and dad had a fairly good relationship with Frances over the years. I was about 8 years older than Annabel, so we weren't in the same classes at school, and anyway, she didn't exactly go out of her way to make friends. But then she turned up at our door one evening and asked if she could stay here for a while as she couldn't go home after what she'd discovered.

"Mum took her in. Made her dinner and a bed for the night, thinking she'd call Frances after an hour and let her know where Annabel was. But then over dinner she announced why she'd run away from home. She'd overheard her mother talking to some of the guests about how she got pregnant with her. Of course, my mum had wondered about that for some years, considering that Frances was resolutely gay."

"What was it Frances said?"

"She told the visitors that she had announced one day that they were to invoke Pan at the abandoned church in the forest and that she intended to demand he impregnate her."

"Right," I said. I didn't know what else to say.

"Apparently there was a ritual that Frances and the rest of the house guests took part in over several nights and days. After that Frances went into the forest and came back the next day, announcing that Pan had indeed deposited his seed in her and that she would be with child imminently. And sure enough, nine months later, Annabel was born with the same strawberry birthmark over her eye as Frances.

"My mum was horrified, obviously. She didn't believe the story, of course, but I think she decided there and then that France's parenting skills weren't what they should have been. She loved children and she couldn't abide the thought of them in distress. Annabel begged her not to tell Frances where she was. She threatened to just get on a train and see where it took her if she did."

"What did your mum do?"

"She arranged for her sister to take her. She lived in Christchurch, on a farm too. She arrived the next day and took Annabel with her."

I sensed a 'but' coming. "What happened?"

"Annabel was a wilful child. I think she took after her mother in that respect. She didn't like authority. She got into a lot of fights at school. The science hut burned down one summer and everyone was certain it was Annabel's doing.

"A couple of months after my mum's sister took Annabel in to work and live on their farm, we received the news that the farm house had burned down during the night. The entire family perished. There was no sign of Annabel's remains. But we never heard from her after that day."

The silence seemed vast. I had no idea how to plumb its depths.

"So, if she is still alive, I don't know where she is," Marion said, rising from chair. "And you're free to do what you will with that information." She led me to the door, back into the sunshine. It seemed like an unwelcome guest after Marion's story. "But if you do happen to find her, I think you'd do well not to turn your back on her."

6

I found records of the fire after some rooting around on the internet. The police made a fairly desultory search for Annabel to assist in their enquiries, but she had vanished. There was no record of them finding her. I assumed that Frances had eventually discovered that Annabel had only bolted as far as the neighbouring farm. I imagine she was also aware of the implication of her daughter's culpability in the fire in Christchurch which had claimed the family who had taken her in.

There were various search engines other than Google on the internet offering ways to pinpoint people by name, location, or place of employment. Some of them allegedly dredged through the 'deep web', picking up personal web pages, press mentions, and old and long dormant MySpace pages. I tried combining Annabel's name with various farm work permutations in the neighbouring counties; I tried lists of public records, birth, marriage and death information. I combined Annabel's name with 'strawberry birthmark', and came up with results for various groups and forums that I scoured for some kind of clue, but it was the slenderest of hopes and it resulted in nothing. I had a photo of Annabel at the age of 15 which I'd discovered slipped between the pages of another book beside Frances's bed, but nothing else of any real value that would aid my search.

Meanwhile I toiled in the fields during the day and spent my evenings at

Frances's looking for further clues to Annabel's whereabouts while I cleared her house. Twicey continued to accompany me, still hoping to find some mention of the box buried beneath the church, convinced that it would be the key to something that he couldn't put a name to. One Sunday afternoon we ventured out into the forest beyond the farmhouse and followed an ancient chiselled track, tunnelling through beeches and hazel, ferns and sycamores. The scent of summer and the earth was heavy in the air, the heat turning the leaves translucent. It felt fortified somehow, and guarded with its secrets. We stumbled upon an ancient stag-headed oak clouded with hornets and red admirals. It glistened with a bloody sap that was clearly irresistible to the insects. I began to hear the hum then, but didn't become completely aware of it for some time.

"This is like Shakespeare," Twicey said. "You know. *William* Shakespeare."

I smiled. "Yes, I think I've heard of him. Go on then, amaze me."

"Well, you know, in his comedies, like *Midsummer Night's Dream*, his characters go off into the wildwood for growing and learning. *Changing.* That's what the forest is all about. Finding yourself by getting lost. It's a bleeding paradox, ain't it?"

"Fucking hell, Twicey."

It was the hum and murmur of life in microcosm. In that hot, scented stillness I saw the delicate little forget-me-nots poking their milky blue flowers into sunlit patches, and the violet hellebore raising spikes of pale, greeny-mauve flowers from purple coloured leaves. I could feel a pressure building in my head as my awareness of it grew. I heard the sound of insects beneath my feet like a massed whisper implying a gentle madness if I succumbed. The smell of hide and flesh and sex. I was suddenly overwhelmed with ecstatic emotions. It took my breath away and I wilted. Twicey was behind me in an instant. "*Easy* there, boy," he said.

"Christ," I said. "Can you hear that. Can you *feel* it?"

"I think you've been out in the heat too long, sunshine," he said gently.

After a rest, we spent another hour hunting, but we didn't find the church. It felt like the forest was keeping its cards close to its chest.

7

"Why don't you drive, Twicey?" I asked one night. We'd retreated to the desolate train station close to the farm. Saturday night. The young folk were living it large. We just wanted peace and quiet. I don't think I ever saw a train pass through that station. It was little more than a tin shack with some old timetables pinned to the walls, a low bench on the narrow platform. We'd taken a pack of craft ales and worked our way through them.

I didn't expect to get it out of him, but perhaps I'd convinced him of my nature, that if he couldn't trust me, then there was no one else. I never heard him talking to friends or family on the phone and he generally deflected questions of that kind.

"I was on my way home to Gloucester on New Year's Eve. This was about eighteen months ago," he began. "6 p.m. Dark already. Coming back from St Ives, where my brother lives."

He paused, put the bottle of beer down between his feet, stared emptily at it for a moment. "I was about ten miles south of here. Someone flashed their lights at me. He thought I had my main beams on, but I didn't. I flashed him back to prove it. That split-second between the flash and the impact was infinitesimal. I caught a glimpse of an old man's face. Just a brief look of *utter* surprise. And then there was the sound of the impact. It was so fucking *loud*. No chance for me to react, or brake or swerve.

"By the time I was out of my car, I could hear myself shouting 'no', over and over, utterly fucking hysterical. When I saw him lying there I knew it. Life had changed. Just *changed*. I had something in my mouth. I spat it out and realised it was glass. Fragments of it from the shattered windscreen. My legs gave way. I realised that there were other people around me. A coat on my shoulders. The police came. They had me in the back of their car. I blew into a bag. They swabbed my cheek, checked my phone to see if I'd been texting at the time of the accident. I gave them a statement. I could barely sign it, my hands were shaking so much. But I was clean that day. I hadn't done any kind of drugs for at least eight months prior to this." He glanced at me like a cornered animal.

"My brother arrived and took me back to his house. He had to pull over halfway back so I could puke my guts into a verge. I lay in the guest room that night, going over and over it. The next day the police called to say that the old man hadn't made it through the night. His name was Albert Deakins. So I was a killer. I kept going through the day, trying to rewrite it in my head.

"Anyway, half-way into the new year, I started to function again. I had some therapy. A lot of crying. Started panicking in enclosed spaces. That fucking caravan terrifies me sometimes."

"It's not just you. Some of the stains in there scare me too."

He laughed.

"So I got signed off work. Post-traumatic stress disorder. The inquest came around. 'No blame should attach to the driver.' I tried to start to drive again after that, but I kept having panic attacks. I felt like I was in limbo, like I couldn't start living again. Finally I put my house on the market. Then I quit my job. I had money saved to keep me afloat. Started travelling around on the train. And then I ended up here. Almost the scene of the crime. I found out where Albert Deakin's family lived. Ten miles down the road. I want to go and see them, talk to them, but I get a bus there and I seize up. Can't do it. More panic attacks. Terrified of their reaction when they see the man who killed their dad, their husband."

"You weren't to blame, mate. The inquest proved that."

"I know," Twicey said. He angrily cuffed the tears out of his eyes. "But *still*."

8

One evening after a day in the fields watching the heat shimmer on the horizon, I went back to Frances's cottage and found a key entirely by accident. It was wedged between a pile of books that were warped out of shape with damp on a window ledge. It had a little keyring on it that read: SAFE.

"Fuck *me*," I whispered to the encroaching darkness.

I called Twicey and told him what I'd found. He appropriated a bicycle and covered the two miles in record time. He arrived at the door doubled over with his hands on his thighs, panting heavily. I thought he was going to have heart failure.

We spent the evening turning the house upside down. We looked behind books, checked for false stair treads, false-bottom drawers, behind cabinets and pictures. Eventually, after three hours we found a loose floorboard in Frances's bedroom and uncovered the little safe. As we pulled it out of its dusty hidey-hole, I thought Twicey was going to puke with excitement. He'd seen too many films.

He was a bit disappointed when all I pulled out of the safe was a sheaf of papers inside an A4 manila envelope. I spread them across the kitchen table and I could hear our held breaths, the ticking of the clock on the mantelpiece.

"Christ, what *is* this?" Twicey said, his interest piqued again. "It looks like a file from a private investigator."

It was. There was a sheaf of surveillance photos and a written report compiled by a private investigation firm offering a tracing service. It was seven years old. With their private databases and various tracing techniques, they'd found Annabel within 14 days for a fairly agreeable fee. There were some further reports culled from a variety of news articles from papers in Bristol, Bath, Swindon, Winchester and Southampton suggesting a multitude of suspicious incidents where people had lost their lives in fires and domestic accidents.

"Is this implying that Annabel is responsible for all of these episodes?" Twicey said.

"Certainly seems that way," I said. At some point the dark had stolen across the overgrown back garden and into the house. I heard that humming sound again, more like a machine under the earth, or a mass of insects. It had arrived with the darkness.

"You can handle talking to her on your own then, sunshine," Twicey said. He said it lightly, but I think he meant it.

9

I called the number listed by the private investigators, but I got no answer. Called it again on my break and then again when I got back to the caravan. Nothing. She could have moved on; this address was seven years old. But it was the first concrete bit of information that I had, so I clung to it and rang the number several times during the course of the evening. Still no joy.

Despite his initial reluctance, Twicey agreed to accompany me the following evening after work. The address was in Bath. A 120 mile journey. We packed some sandwiches and made up a flask of coffee and hit the road at six in the evening, the sun falling in the rear view mirror, flashing on the windscreens of the oncoming traffic. Twicey tried to keep himself distracted, either with a newspaper, or the radio, or rooting through the assorted CDs scattered around the footwells of my old Volvo. I drove as carefully as I could in deference to an event that had shattered his life into pieces. We'd had to pass near Albert Deakins's house on the way, and I could see him turning brittle with the psychic trauma of it all. I tried to distract him by telling him about Ingrid, about how we'd met. She'd lived upstairs from me in a converted Victorian townhouse in Hastings. We'd been two people who had sex with each other before anything more serious presented itself. Ingrid was an alcoholic. She'd been through years of abuse and shattering mental illness. She'd tried to commit suicide one night and I got to her just in time. We saw something in each other that we'd done our best to run away from all those years; I think I'd fooled myself that I could keep on saving her, and in the process it would heal my own wounds. I'd lost Emily, my wife to leukaemia; it had sent me running away from life, from any kind of responsibility. I'd lived cheaply, from one day to the next. By the time I ended up in Hastings, I suppose some part of me was already trying to repair things; looking for people who'd find the healer in me.

But some things, some people, can't be healed. Ingrid was one of those people, and I was another. Some things are broken for good. You just have to find a way to get up and put one foot in front of another and appreciate the small things, little kindnesses, decent people. Sometimes you have to travel so far for those things, for people like Ingrid, for people like Twicey, but it's worth it.

"And you keep going up there, just to see her?" Twicey said. We were stuck in a traffic jam on the A39.

"It's like an addiction," I said."Withdrawal symptoms. I just crave being able to see her."

"Does it help, having seen her with a new chap?"

"No, of course it doesn't. I'm aware of the folly of it all, Twicey. I'm almost fucking 50. I should know better. I should *act* better."

"It's technically stalking, mate. It's *well* out of order."

"Yes, *I know*."

"*Alright*. Touchy. I think you've got to let it go, mate. She's moved on. Show her some respect."

I nodded. I knew all this, of course. I didn't want to hear it, but I *needed* to.

It was dark by the time we arrived in Bath. Having visited the town before, I was expecting to rock up outside a row of elegant, golden-coloured Georgian terraces, but I was disappointed. It was on the outskirts, near a pretty rough looking estate where the kids roamed around looking distinctly feral. We parked across the street and I turned off the engine. The house was a shabby Victorian terrace split up into flats. There was a row of recycling bins lined up outside, broken glass glinting under the streetlights, a couple of cats screaming at each other.

"Go on then, our son, what are you waiting for?" Twicey gave me a push.

"I'm trying to decide what I'm going to say," I said, rather feebly.

"You've had 120 miles for that!" Twicey said. "Just ask her if she's a *firestarter, a twisted firestarter*. See if she's killed anyone lately. Go on, don't be shy."

As it turned out, there was still no one home. I rang the bell a couple of times, then quickly cupped my hands and peered into the window. Just a plain sofa and carpet, nothing on the walls, no TV. I trotted back to the car.

"Stakeout, then?" Twicey said. "Just like in the films. We should have doughnuts."

"She probably doesn't even live here anymore," I said, unwrapping the sandwiches. "It's been seven years."

We sat there for a couple of hours. It was after ten when Twicey noticed the woman come walking down the street. "*Eh, up,*" he said. "Look at her face."

"Strawberry birthmark," I said. "Fucking hell."

There was no doubt that this had to be Annabel. We watched her let herself into the house and then I got out of the car. I didn't feel especially comfortable confronting a lone woman like this, but if she *was* dangerous in any way, ideally I wanted her on the back foot. I was ashamed at how tight my chest was as I approached the door, how loudly my heart was beating.

I was both disappointed and relieved when Annabel answered the door. She was a slight woman with fiery red hair, skin like porcelain, freckles across her nose that suggested the adolescent she'd been when she'd run away from home. A little of Frances's overbite. That strawberry nevus that dominated how people looked at her. Usually they faded by the time a child reached puberty, but if it didn't there are removal options for adults to minimise its appearance. Clearly it didn't concern Annabel. Her hair was tied back in a rough bun and she looked up at the stranger at her door without any kind of discomfiture.

"Annabel?" I said.

She held the door between us. She'd taken off her shoes. Her clothes were quite plain. She didn't seem to have anything to hide. "Yes," she said.

"I'm here about your mother," I began.

"My mother?"

"Yes. Frances de la Wode. I'm afraid she died in January. I'm sorry."

She looked bewildered. "I'm afraid you're mistaken. My mother was called Kate and she died when I was a little girl."

The complexion of the exchange changed subtly. "Are you absolutely sure?" I said, and realised immediately how ridiculous that sounded. "She had a farmhouse in North Devon."

Nothing. "I'm afraid you've got the wrong person." She made to close the door.

I wasn't sure how to proceed. Then I remembered that I had a photograph of Annabel when she was 15 in my pocket. Her mother was in the picture too. I took it out and showed it to her. She stared at it for a good long while. "That *is* you, isn't it?"

She smiled stiffly. "That girl certainly *looks* like me, but it isn't. I don't recognise that other woman."

I was wrong-footed, unsure how to proceed. I glanced desperately back at Twicey. He grinned back at me with his thumbs up.

"Look, I know this is a bit strange, but can I come in for ten minutes? You can bring a neighbour down if that would make you feel safer."

"That's quite alright," she said. She stepped aside and opened the door. "Come in."

The flat was as sparse as that first glance through the window had suggested. There was no character to it. No books, no pictures on the walls, no photos on the mantelpiece. It was as if she'd just moved in, or was about to move out. I sat down opposite her. She hadn't turned any lights on, so the streetlights provided diagonal bars of light across the room. Annabel sat in shadow and pressed her knees together, her fingers linked, her manner quite relaxed, quite still.

"You say that your mother died when you were a child?" I said.

She nodded. "My father brought me up alone. He was a diplomat. He worked from various embassies and consulates in Paris and Vienna and Cairo."

"That must have been quite a colourful childhood," I offered.

"It was beautiful. We met all sorts of wonderful people. We spent one weekend with Salman Rushdie, another with Prince Charles and Princess Diana. They were such lovely, fascinating people. Once we flew to Basra in a military helicopter." She smiled in the gloom at the apparent lucidity of her memories. "Sometimes people thought daddy was a spy. But he wasn't."

"Is he retired now?"

"No, he died when I was 21."

"I'm sorry," I said.

This was ridiculous. I couldn't decide if I'd made a huge mistake, or she was a fantasist, perhaps a split-personality. The silence stretched between us then, and I felt a blankness creep between my thoughts and my mouth. I heard that humming sound from the forest begin, like the pulsing of an imminent migraine in my skull.

"Look, I'm the administrator of Frances's estate. I'm her nephew. I'm clearing her house now. She had a daughter called Annabel. I met her a couple of times. She'd be my cousin. She ran away when she was 16 and worked on a farm in Dorset..."

The woman didn't respond. I couldn't see her face, couldn't discern if any of these darts were hitting the board. I'd realised that I could smell something. It was an odour that was both unpleasant and simultaneously alluring. A musky, heady scent, like the hide of a wet animal, and raw, naked arousal. The humming in my head was growing, like a vein throbbing in my temples. I was feeling off-balance and at the same time, unaccountably filled with lust. I sat forward, trying to conceal a sudden, wholly unwelcome erection.

Annabel didn't move, but she gradually seemed to swell in the darkness, become more than she was. A vast, feral thing, made out of the wild. I was sure that I could smell the odour of the wood, of cool shaded spaces, of its green depths, of the scent of stagnant pools and the earth, freshly broken up beneath my feet. A shaggy hide and the snort of nostrils, of flesh and secretions.

"Would you..." I began and immediately forgot what I'd intended to say. I wavered in the dark for a delirious moment; I could barely see her outline. "Would you agree to a DNA test? I'm not... I'm not disputing that you are who you say you are, but... I need to... resolve this."

It was all I could do not to fall to my knees and crawl across the room, to bow my head and offer myself to whatever lived inside her. But she hadn't even moved. Finally she shrugged and said, "Of course."

That was enough. I struggled to lift myself into a standing position. She led me back to the front door. I trailed after her like a naughty schoolchild. My head was spinning, split in two. The crisp night air revived me slightly, and I swam frantically towards it. I hovered at the threshold, between one world and another, turned back to her. She was the same slight woman with her hair tied back, barefoot, delicate features. I coloured. "Leave it with me," I heard myself say. "I'll be in touch with the arrangements for the DNA test."

I was in the car. I couldn't remember even crossing the street. I was breathing heavily, sweating like I'd just done several laps around the block.

"Have you got a *boner*?" was the first thing I heard Twicey say. And then, "What the *bloody hell* have you been up to in there? You've been gone for an hour and a half."

Christ, I thought. What the *fuck*?

10

Litha. The summer solstice. Longest day of the year and the apogee of the light. The sun is at its zenith and the fires which are lit to celebrate it cast shadows which will lengthen in the following months. Although there were all kinds of nationalities assembled here at the farm, they'd decided, with

Marion's consent, to celebrate midsummer with a fire on the nearby hill. There was a celebratory atmosphere in the campsite. Some of the girls walked around wearing white and flower garlands on their heads. A bunch of lads went skinny dipping in the river. There was music everywhere. They started drinking early (again, with Marion's consent).

Twicey and I hung around the camp for most of the day, retreating in the afternoon to the caravan for Twicey to cook chili while we listened to Alice Coltrane CDs. Frances's house was mostly cleared by that time. Some antique book dealers were going to turn up in the next couple of days to give me a price for her collection. I was still waiting to hear back about Annabel's DNA test, still a bit shaken by our encounter.

"I've had an idea," Twicey said, after we'd eaten.

"Oh yeah," I said. "Should I brace myself?"

"Probably, but hear me out first."

"Go on then."

"I've been thinking about Frances. About that box buried under that church in the forest."

"Mate, *it's not there*," I said. Although according to the maps and the research we'd done, it *did* exist. The Church of St Mary, apparently both devoutly religious and wildly pagan in design. A royal forester who'd commissioned the church in 1130 had most probably been on a pilgrimage to Santiago de Compostela in Spain, picking up tips on architectural design. "We've looked three times. Fuck knows why we can't find it." Although this kind of anomaly was seemingly more and more commonplace to me.

"From what I've gathered about Frances is that a lot of her workings, her rituals were about altered states of consciousness," Twicey said."Whether that story about getting up the duff with Pan is bullshit or not, she spent a couple of days with her acolytes on the ritual. Magic isn't about escaping into a dreamworld, or into other dimensions, it's about new ways to see our existing world."

"What's your point. Twicey?"

"My point is we don't see the world, we see our *perception* of the world. It's about more than the bricks and mortar, the cars, the houses. It's about seeing beyond that shit and finding all the layers of history, the memories and stories. Murders and love affairs, the people who've passed through. These maps—" Twicey gathered them up off the table and screwed them up, chucked them out of the open door. "We have to let go of the maps and just *drift*."

"And how do you propose we do that?" But I knew what was coming.

He took the blotting paper of LSD out of his pocket and placed it on the table where the maps had been a moment ago. "150 micrograms for you, 500 for me. Boom! Off we go."

"I don't see what good it would do," I said. "I've seen people on acid. They're all over the bloody place."

"Well that's why we focus our energies first on what we intend to get out of the working."

"The *working*?"

"Just listen. We devise an *ad hoc* ritual, a sort of summoning. I saw them in Frances's books. Look, I copied one down." He produced a creased piece of paper and flattened it out so I could read it. "I half-inched some incense to burn too. We make an altar in the forest and say those words, ask for guidance from Pan, tell him what a stand-up geezer he is and then take the acid."

I looked out of the caravan at the fire they were building on the hill. It was a soft, balmy afternoon. An air of the last day of term. Most of them wholly unaware that they were participating in a watered down pagan ritual. I was momentarily concerned that I might come out the other side of the experience changed and then immediately realised that it would probably be a good thing if I did.

"Fuck it," I said finally. "Why not?"

11

Twicey had done his research, I'll give him that. He found a clearing in the depths of the forest with a giant beech which had collapsed under the weight of its own branches. It would act as an altar. He explained what we were going to do. He'd cribbed bits and pieces from various books in Frances's house and then pieced them together with research on the internet.

"Every magical act must have a purpose, a pattern and a perimeter," he said. It seemed slightly absurd hearing a man in a beer-stained Cocteau Twins t-shirt talking gravely about magical invocations. "The *purpose* is a clear statement of intent at the beginning of the working, the *pattern* is the structure of the words, movement, offerings and incense and flowers and fruit. The *perimeter* is the limitation, the physical circle or the period of time the working takes."

We'd brought a few punnets of strawberries with us and picked a handful of wild flowers on our journey through the forest – buttercups, ox-eye daisies, meadowsweet and forget-me-nots. It seemed like a paltry offering for the god of the wild, but I suppose that wasn't the point. We took the acid and Twicey began the ritual. He'd told me that we had a good half an hour to an hour until we'd feel the full effects of the LSD. It would give us sufficient time to complete the ritual. The birdsong was like a massed choir in this clearing. I kept looking up into the branches wound together above us, thinking that something was already here, waiting for us to say the right words.

As it turned out we both felt a bit silly, kneeling at our makeshift beech altar and reciting the words that Twicey had written out. But he was adamant that we take it seriously. Perhaps the words were less important than the *intent* of the thing. We burned the incense and asked for Pan's guidance to the church, to some sort of revelation. We had no sense of a perimeter; the entire forest was our circle, so we abandoned that idea and hoped for the best. We meditated in the clearing, eyes closed, gradually tuning in to the silence beyond the birdsong and the creatures creeping through the trees, the bending of branches, the hiss of wind in the leaves that made it sound like distant rain. I kept waiting for the acid to take effect, my limbs gradually becoming loose, my attention both specific and diffuse at the same time. I could hear the beating of my heart, so loud I thought I might choke on it, and then the merest rustle in the trees nearby almost overwhelmed me with fear. I thought I'd open my eyes and there he'd be, half-man, half-goat, his shaggy hide and his horns, snorting with displeasure at these two chancers who should have known better.

At some point we were taking our shoes and socks off, rolling up our jeans. There was no water nearby, but we followed the flinty track out of the clearing and deeper into the wood as if it were a river. Carefully lifting our legs, one in front of the other. Suddenly every rise seemed like a mountain. I found a glade thick with herb Robert, wood avens and blue bugle, another mossy old beech whose trunk had split with top-heavy mushrooms, half rotten with water curling from it. I stared at them for a long time, or perhaps I just passed through. I had no idea. Things weren't making any sense. The world was gently spinning out of orbit. I climbed a tree and stared down. From this vantage point, I caught a glimpse of someone stumbling around in ever-decreasing circles until he fell on his side and began to laugh. I could hear a humming noise begin. Once it began it was all I could think about. It drowned out the distinctive sound of chiffchaffs in the branches, high above me. I clambered back down and glanced around, trying to locate its source. I couldn't hear my heart anymore. Just the sound of that insistent hum. It had dogged me, taunted me, and now I believed that it was leading me

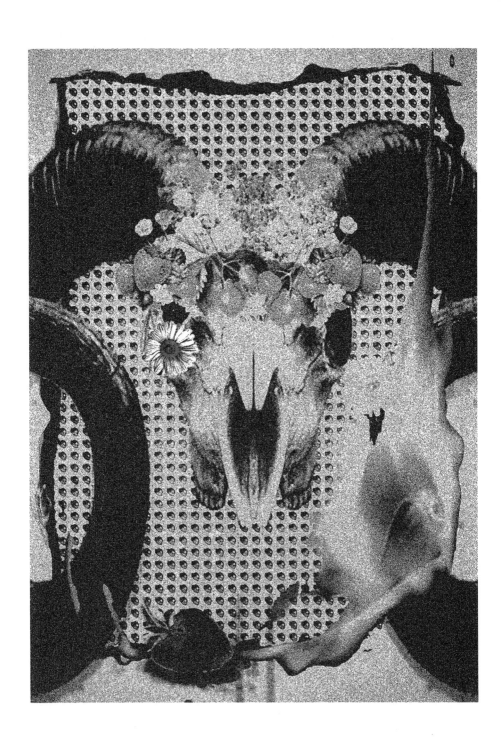

somewhere. A drone, made of the sounds of the earth, scurrying insects, the wind through the leaves, bees humming at pollen, the smell of the feminine. A surfeit of the senses. The quality of light changed as I delved deeper into the forest. Everything was imbued with a delicate golden light. Everything revealed itself to me then. The world wasn't what I thought it was. I wasn't the man I thought I was. There was in that moment some kind of enigma that was simply yearning to be revealed to me. I felt that yearning somewhere deep within me. A remnant of Frances's golden years here in this forest; the vestiges of that earlier matriarchal culture that she'd fostered at the cottage and here in the wilds of the wood. It was imbued in everything. I was swimming through time, in the abode of the Goddess. The world was transformed. I wanted to get lost and exist in this moment forever, away from the noise and harm of the real world, that *other* world. I could feel the layers of memory, peeling away; I followed in their footsteps to a door that had been closed to us thus far. I heard Twicey stamping loudly through the undergrowth behind me, then staggering to a halt. The humming fell away at the source and we stood, awed in a clearing where the sun lit everything from above in a hazy golden glow. Past, present and future were all the same. I was dimly aware that it was all perceptual distortion and synaesthesia.

Had Pan led us here? I don't know, but our offerings of wildflowers and strawberries were strewn across the clearing. I felt the soft flesh of the fruit, bursting beneath my bare feet. It was silent now. Just the sound of our hushed breaths. The Norman church had been all but claimed by the forest. The roof had caved in and one of the walls had crumbled where an incongruous carob tree had collapsed against it. White admirals congregated around the olive and pomegranate trees, the orchids and hyacinths at the entrance. The flicker of their black and white wings in the latticework of light was mesmerically beautiful. There were red sandstone carvings of beasts with elastic limbs and dragons entangled in savage tendrils of foliage. A sheela-na-gig, displaying her scalloped sexual parts with gusto above the entrance. Vines climbed across the walls, heavy with purple grapes. We hovered at the threshold, aware that everything was changed and ripe with immanence. A huge olive tree had burst through the centre of the church, its roots pushing through the stone where the nave, chancel and apse had been. The windows were long gone.

Twicey was somehow ahead of me. He'd fallen to his knees at the thick roots of the olive tree and had begun to dig with his bare hands. He seemed divinely inspired. For a long time, I couldn't recall who he was or why he was here. I was watching someone else, moving slowly around the perimeter of the church. I didn't see him as much as sense him. The weight of him, the sheer *immensity* of his presence. Neither man nor beast. I heard him snorting and panting, could smell the flesh and damp fur, the scent of sex in the air around us. I was afraid of him, aware of my physical arousal, that basest of desires that man would never entirely slough off. Pan stood for panic. But I was still in the world. If everything was familiar, then surely I wouldn't come to harm. Everything was the same, I thought; everything was transformed.

Twicey was laughing then and his hands were filthy with earth. He had a box in his hand, wrapped in polythene. I laughed too and ran away from there, out of the church and into the forest.

He found me later, *much later,* curled around a tree, my eyes wide open. I remembered it getting dark and wandering, lost around the forest, looking for Ingrid in every clearing. That familiar desolate ache swelling in me. And then finally, listening to the dawn chorus just as the first light glimmered through the branches. It was a cacophony; a symphony of beautiful, uplifting song. I think I wept at it. But at some point I'd wandered to the back of my mind and couldn't find my way back. Twicey knew the way. He brought me back to the caravan, and my bed. I slept for twelve hours straight.

12

By the time I woke, most of the workers had already departed and the camp was a desolate place. I walked around when I got up, eager to reassure myself of its normalcy, that the foundations of my life were still the same. It was reassuring and disappointing in equal measure. Afterwards I went back to the caravan. Twicey was still in bed. I could hear him snoring through the paper thin walls. The box he'd dug out of the earth in that place in the forest sat on the table, its lid open, the contents spilling out. I stared at them for a moment, then made some coffee and sat down to study at it all. It didn't take long to see what it was, what it represented. Ostensibly it was a box of Annabel's things. A bracelet with her initials on it. A ribbon with some of her hair tangled in it. A toothbrush. Photographs of the sixteen years she'd spent with Frances. A worn teddy bear. A dress, neatly folded. Each of these objects seemed to be imbued with a weight that couldn't entirely be explained. I suppose it was residual magic, evaporating into these prosaic surroundings. Placed on top of these things were objects that wouldn't have made a whole lot of sense to Twicey when he'd unwrapped them, but I understood them immediately. Photographs of Paris, Vienna, Cairo. Maps, train ticket stubs, a model of a military helicopter, paperwork from a diplomat's office, a tatty paperback of the Satanic Verses and a chipped old mug commemorating the marriage of Charles and Diana. There was a sheaf of handwritten history there too, with just enough detail provided by Frances so that Annabel could fill in the gaps. An old life erased, a new one conceived.

Twicey and I talked it through when he woke later. Frances had used the private detective to track Annabel down and to confirm that her daughter had grown up wild with the nature of panic in her bones. She hadn't wanted a reunion; all she'd wanted was to excise her history in the hope that it might set Annabel on the straight and narrow. Replacing it with a brittle backstory, a flimsy fantasy. The romantic allure of the diplomat's daughter. The immorality of the act was staggering, and, I felt, the equal of Annabel's suspected crimes.

But that magic was spoiled now. I suspect the spell had been broken as soon as Twicey had unearthed the box. Annabel called me two days later but I missed it, so she left a 'message. The DNA check had of course, proved that she was indeed Frances de la Wode's daughter. But with the spell broken she'd already remembered. It was a short and bitter message. She didn't want anything from her mother, didn't want to hear from anyone associated with her. I later discovered that she'd hanged herself in that bare little flat on the outskirts of Bath. It seemed like a cruel but inevitable final chapter to a life.

On the day we left I offered to drive Twicey to finally visit the family of Albert Deakins, the man he'd accidentally killed. He was reluctant, but I could tell he was finally ready for me to persuade him into it. That morning he emerged from the caravan wearing a purple corduroy blazer.

"*Really*?" I said.

"What?" he said. "It's my best bloody coat."

We loaded the car with our possessions and left the camp. Twicey didn't say much. He was shaking by the time we arrived at their door. Fearful of the family's animosity; after all, he was the man who'd killed their husband, their father. But his fear was unfounded. They welcomed him with so much kindness and empathy it was he who wept first. Albert's wife and her two grown-up daughters showed Twicey photographs, told him how his work in anthropology had taken him around the world. He had a passion for be-bop jazz and gardening. He had been filled a sense of urgency to live life, even at the age of 76. He couldn't bear to be sitting still for long. They asked Twicey about himself. They knew he hadn't been speeding, or drinking, or otherwise distracted when the accident happened. I waited in the car while Albert came to life for Twicey. No longer just the face that had haunted him all this time, no longer merely a death, a statistic: he became a man who'd lived life to the full, a man who, his family reassured Twicey, would have forgiven him.

Afterwards we drove to the cemetery where Albert was buried. Twicey went to his burial plot, under the shade of some trees and said what he needed to say. To apologise.

Then we went home.

13

The act of forgetting is not something one does without a great deal of soul searching, but it's clear that something has to change.

I didn't drive to Bristol to see Ingrid again. It was shame that kept me away rather than anything more laudable on my part. Instead I sat in my house by the sea and watched the leaves turn and the days get shorter. I've tried to tell myself that I was nothing more than a chapter in the book of Ingrid's life. She'd folded down the corner there once, but now she's moved on. New stories, new lives.

It's like going cold turkey. I wake up sometimes in the night, convinced I can hear that drone, made up of the sounds of the earth, the bees humming, insects swarming and leaves rustling overhead. The air tainted with the smell of heated flesh and musky hides and sex. The suggestion that I have not learned anything from that afternoon lost inside the forest, in the abode of the Goddess. The growing certainty that something has always been waiting for me in the aching darkness of my own nature.

Finally, today, I went around the house and gathered up all of Ingrid's things that remain. I haven't touched them since she left in the vain hope that eventually she'd return and need all of these things again. Photos of us pinned to the fridge, a hairbrush with her hair wound around it, an old pullover, a paperback, a few other things. I don't need all of it. It's *the purpose*: this statement of intent; *the pattern*: my account of a summer of strawberry picking and house clearing and friendship; and *the perimeter*: somewhere that I won't stumble upon again.

This is my working.

I've put Ingrid's things in a wooden box. I'm going to seal it up and take it somewhere far from here. It's a line in the sand so I can move on. I don't need a new history, just a door to a better day, to wiping the slate clean. I'm thinking of Annabel taking her life because it was no longer hers to keep; and Twicey at the graveside, trying to let go of guilt and being allowed to see his way clear; and Ingrid, on the cusp of something new and good for her. I'm thinking of all of us, locked in our own private, wounded trajectories. These second-hand dreams. They do you no good.

I'm going to bury that box deep, where no one can find it. And then I'm going to walk away and forget.

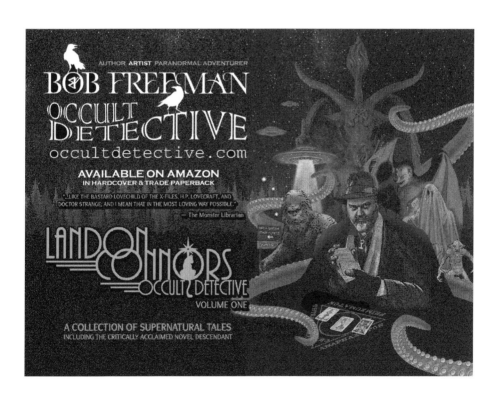

Title: The Curious Affair of the Missing Mummies
Author: Lisa Tuttle
Publisher: Jo Fletcher Books
Format: Paperback, Kindle
Reviewer: Dave Brzeski

The classic occult detective story was actually inspired by that stalwart denier of the supernatural, Sherlock Holmes, in that it was Arthur Conan Doyle's Holmes stories in *The Strand Magazine* that set the style for the regular series of detective stories, featuring the same lead protagonists. Add to this the contemporary fashion for short ghost stories in back then, and it's inevitable that some authors would eventually combine the two concepts.

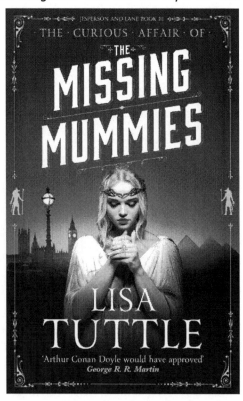

The best known examples are probably William Hope Hodgson, who brought us the adventures of *Carnacki, the Ghost Finder* in the *Idler Magazine*, and Algernon Blackwood, who went directly to book publication for the first five of his six stories of *John Silence, Physician Extraordinary*.

This almost inevitably lead to a still commonly held opinion that this sort of amalgam of detective

206

fiction and the supernatural only really works well in the short form.

Of course there have been an awful lot of novel length occult detective tales since then, but I rather think that Lisa Tuttle has finally blown that particular belief out of the water with this 420 plus page novel. It's true that the adventures of Jesperson and Lane were introduced to the World in two novelettes – namely *'The Curious Affair of the Deodand'*, in *Down These Strange Streets*; and *'The Curious Affair of the Dead Wives'*, in *Rogues*, both edited by Gardner Dozois and George R.R. Martin.

The Curious Affair of the Missing Mummies is actually the third novel in the series. There was no way I had time to read the first two before writing this review, but I confess that I couldn't resist reading the two shorter works.

While they provide a good introduction to Jasper Jesperson and Aphrodite 'Di' Lane, I can happily report that it's not necessary to read these stories first, any more than it is to read the first two novels.

It's a complicated affair, involving Fairly inconsequential Egyptian trinkets, and papyrus scrolls and eventually a mysterious mummy, stolen from the British Museum, a woman who claims to be reincarnated from an ancient Egyptian priestess, who may, or may not be a charlatan, and a fairly irritating young woman, who latches herself onto Di.

For the most part, any supernatural elements are kept fairly vague in what could be simply a mundane series of crimes, albeit possibly perpetrated by some dodgy cult, or other. Whether, or not they stay vague throughout I'll leave to you to find out when you read it.

While the concept of the hero, and his assistant, who chronicles his adventures is hardly uncommon I fiction, I found Jesperson and Lane refreshingly different. At no point did I get the impression that Miss Lane was in any way less intelligent, less capable than Jesperson. They make a great team, but she could easily carry a book on her own.I will certainly try to find the time to read the first two books. Highly recommended.

Title: Grimoire of the Four Imposters
Author: Coy Hall
Publisher: Nosetouch Press
Format: Hardcover, Paperback, Kindle
Reviewer: Anthony Perconti

Coy Hall's *Grimoire of the Four Imposters* is a collection of six self-contained (yet interconnected) stories that make up a mosaic novel. The titular 'four imposters' comprise the meat of the book, with two flanking tales serving as thematic bookends. The focus of this novel is an exploration of a mythic and highly elusive tome of spells that is just as fluid as the arc of history. Hall, a history professor by trade, utilizes the focal point of the alchemical McGuffin as a means to examine a specific historical period. Set in and around the late 17th Century, *Grimoire* acts as a dark mirror, reflecting back a turbulent and violent era of human history. The novel is replete with warfare, colonial exploitation, religious fervor, sectarian violence and paranoia. In Coy Hall's vision, history itself, is the hungry maw that consumes all it encounters. The supernatural elements found in *Grimoire* reflect the fears and concerns of the historical populous: where malign, soul corrupting entities are never far away and God harkens back to his Old Testament roots. A time when Enochian adepts could transcend the boundaries of life and death and a fear of the dark is not only warranted, but essential. *Grimoire of the Four Imposters* is a cosmic horror fiction of the Pre-Enlightenment Age.

In the book *'Note'*, the author states: "Dr Toth speculated that, relative to the individual reading the grimoire, the imposter stories always take place around 400 years in the past." This bit of troubling information immediately puts the reader in a state of disorientation. How can a section of a historical volume, irrespective of when it is being read, *always* take place 400 years prior? Professor Hall then goes on to say: "If an attempt is made to decode *Grimoire of the Four Imposters*, exercise proper caution. The translation is new to this edition." Following in the footsteps of various literary tricksters (the likes of Italo Calvino, Jorge Luis Borges and Gene Wolfe, come to mind), Coy Hall inserts himself in the narrative as the latest translator of the tome. This sneaky move on the author's part only enhances the reader's state of confusion and unease: what exactly am I getting myself into?

The four imposter stories that comprise the grimoire are all set in and around the world of the late 17th Century, across various locations. Three are set in and around Europe: Germany, the Carpathian Mountains and England, while the fourth is based in (I suspect,) The Lesser Antilles. It is through these stories that Professor Hall paints a portrait of a world that engages with the supernatural on a regular basis. A world where these encounters are simultaneously miraculous and terrifying. We are given a glimpse of specific, discrete worldviews. It is fascinating (and quite telling) that the supernatural aspects of the three European branches of the grimoire are somewhat antagonistic (or at least opaque) with its relationship to humanity. The magic and the 'miraculous' that are on exhibit are fraught with aspects of body horror and metaphysical danger. When bargaining with these higher entities, the ante is always in human lives and souls.

Hall weaves a retelling of the old Wandering Jew legend ('The Orb of Wasp and Fly, Being a Psalm of the Malformed Mind'), a scholar bargaining for a book of spells from a powerful aristocrat ('The Nightshade Garden') and two itinerant German executioners plying their services in an unsettling English village ('Sire of the Hatchet'). These tales are a disquieting mix of folk or rural horror blended with cosmic horror ("A fetus of roots, Hutter thought. An abomination").

Professor Hall portrays a Europe that is in the midst of a cataclysmic transition. These three tales offer the reader a glimpse of a war-torn continent (The Thirty Years War, The Siege of Vienna), where religious (and ethnic) strife is de rigueur. The Islamic Ottomans, fundamentalist Puritans, Protestants and Catholics are in open conflict over ideological supremacy and of course, resources. This transition is also echoed in the arts and sciences as well, in an inexorable shift from superstition to rationalism. Where Cassini and Flamsteed are mapping the heavens and such luminaries as Papin, Siegemund and Coronelli are expanding the boundaries of their given disciplines. This fraught relationship with the supernatural is counterpoised in '*The Third Imposter: The Brine of Bone Alchemy*'. The Carib people have a traditional pantheistic accord with Lonu. Like Cesar, this seabound deity is given his due (in human sacrifices) in exchange for its protection. When a castaway band of Frenchmen encounter Lonu forged simulacra, their slim hope of rescue is extinguished. '*The Brine of Bone Alchemy*' had a paranoid tenor to it, that was to me, highly reminiscent of the classic 1956 film, *Invasion of the Body Snatchers*.

The novel concludes with the extended coda, '*An Encounter in 1724*'. In this tale, the descendants of key characters from the opening chapter ('*An Encounter in 1690*') take center stage. Doctor Bela Toth (the nephew of occult scholar Dorin Toth of '*The Nightshade Garden*') and Thomas Fretwell travel from London to the city of Nottingham, with the hopes of rescuing the ever elusive and mysterious *Grimoire of the Four Imposters*. These two empathic characters are compelled by a seemingly sinister force in retrieving the enigmatic tome. "Bela Toth closed his eyes and kept them shut. He was too frightened to look, and each moment he didn't look it became more impossible to do so... A lone finger of bone, covered in a rime thick as that on the windowpane, grazed the nape of his neck." This chilling passage harkens back to those Victorian practitioners of the ghost story. Professor Hall can certainly write creep inducing passages that would give M.R. James and William Hope Hodgson a run for their money.

The climax of *'An Encounter in 1724'*, culminates in the subterranean tunnel network beneath Nottingham Castle. It is at this point that the two companions descend into a version of the underworld, a 'lung of Hell', where sorcerous practitioners can mold the twin forces of life and death to suit their purposes. "Vegetable life was not a conscious existence, but it manifested worms and provided something of a pincushion for slivers of memory. A few nerves burned until the soul departed the shell." Fretwell and Doctor Toth (like his uncle before him) are in essence avatars of the Prometheus archetype. These individuals abhor the loss of knowledge, any knowledge (human or otherwise) and they are willing to make personal sacrifices in order to ensure its safety. Or as Toth succinctly states, "We mustn't destroy knowledge that has come before us. That was the folly of the Dark Ages. Consider the sources of your neglect. Think of your John Dee. Why is he dismissed only two centuries after Elizabeth admired him? Why is Michele Nostradamus forgotten? What of Paracelsus?" As Neal Stephenson extensively explored in *The Baroque Cycle*, Professor Hall also delves into the shift from an earlier age to a newer transformative age. But I would contend that Hall's characters, especially the likes of the Toth clan, Lady Sarkozy, Thomas Fretwell and Lady Willoughby are more interested in a synthesis of systems, rather than the old ways (natural philosophy) being entirely subsumed by the new (empiricism). The preservation of *all* knowledge is a paramount concern to these individuals.

Like the contents of the grimoire in question, I am being deliberately nebulous and uncommunicative when it comes to the various whys and wherefores of the book's plot. My experience (and advice) with *The Grimoire* is just to go with the narrative flow and enjoy the ride: all the while remembering to pay attention and take note of character names. This is a sneaky book brimming with alchemically self-aware automata, body horror infused sorcery, occult scholars, pagan gods, spectral apparitions and several quests in search of tomes of power. Professor Hall has crafted a wonderful Gothic cabinet of curiosities. This book is the perfect combination of the classic frame narrative, cosmic and folk horror, and philosophical digressions, infused with a heavy dose of moody atmospherics. *Grimoire of the Four Imposters* 'reads' like a classic Hammer or Amicus horror film, by way of Mario Bava. Turn down the lights, stoke the fireplace and pour yourself a strong one. This is the perfect Halloween season read.

Title: The Promise of Plague Wolves

Author: Coy Hall
Publisher: Nosetouch Press
Format: Paperback, Kindle
Reviewer: Anthony Perconti

Coy Hall's follow up to 2021's *Grimoire of the Four Imposters* is an impressive work of the supernatural investigator subgenre. Hall regales us with another 'translation' (from the original Latin) of a manuscript dating back to the late seventeenth century. *The Promise of Plague Wolves* sees Doctor of Theology and member of the Order of Saint Guinefort, Dorin Toth in his first book length adventure. It is my sincere hope that *Plague Wolves* is the opening salvo in a long running and successful series.

In the year 1686, Toth is dispatched by the Bishop of Graz to investigate strange goings on in the pox-ravaged Styrian highlands. Much to the chagrin of Toth, the meddlesome and vain Doctor Kaspar Groza is also assigned to the case: the pair have a strained mutual history. Suffice it to say, there is no love lost between the two men. The epicenters of the bizarre phenomenon emanate from the neighboring village of Drunstall and the chateau Karnstein, some two leagues distant. Hammer Films aficionados will get a kick of this not-so-subtle reference. It certainly put a smile on my face. Dorin Toth is accompanied by his constant companion, the cranky greyhound Vinegar Tom. Like Toth, Tom is also a (very active) member of the Order of Saint Guinefort (and with very good reason- a simple Google search on the saint will shed much light for any inquiring minds).

I am reminded of the works of the great Robert E. Howard, as it pertains to Toth's nature as an outsider character. Like Conan and Kull that came before, Dorin Toth is met with constant distrust and suspicion, even though his motivations are benevolent. His Romani heritage is front and center for all the world to see, as a symbol of personal pride, while the untrusting and insular world that Toth navigates always looks askance at the learned master of the arcane. "You would've been halted at the gate two years ago. You would have been turned back, Master Toth, letter or not. No Jew or gypsy was allowed here then."

Plague Wolves is incredibly well researched (and well written) historical fiction, that leans heavily towards the supernatural. But don't worry, the late sixteen-hundreds had plenty of terrors emanating from the natural world to go around. Hall's descriptions of late-stage pox victims (and those that have succumbed to the disease), in certain parts of the book, made me feel downright queasy. To say nothing of the repulsive Burke and Hare like duo of Grau and Toader (along with

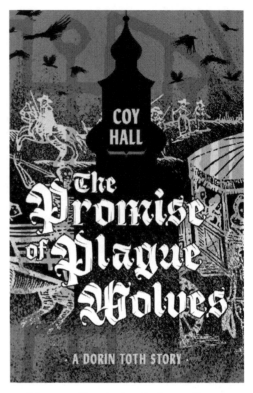

their unnatural offspring). In a sense, this travelling pair of changelings are the titular wolves that haunt the Styrian Wood. But as the novel progresses, we are introduced to a darker, more malevolent (and exponentially powerful) entity that is responsible for the strange goings on. An entity that requires a compact with *le meneur de loups*.

Plague Wolves had me turning those pages, well into the wee hours of the night. It is a book brimming with intrepid, yet very human heroes (Toth, Annalise), boon companions (Tom and Basina), shocking denouements and dark wonders. Am I being intentionally vague? Yes, absolutely; part of the fun is the journey of discovery that Hall parcels out like breadcrumbs, to readers.

Fans of John Silence, Thomas Carnacki, John the Balladeer and Jules de Grandin will find much to love with this novel (Toth is a nice addition to this pantheon of worthies). The same goes for fans of well researched historical fiction. Coy Hall pays loving tribute to the greats that came before, while carving his own unique niche in the occult detective genre. *The Promise of Plague Wolves* is a bravura performance. I look forward to reading the further adventures of Dorin Toth and Vinegar Tom.

Title: The Evil Within (Dark Devon Book One)
Author: S.M. Hardy
Publisher: Allison and Busby
Format: Paperback, Kindle
Reviewer: Rebecca Buchanan

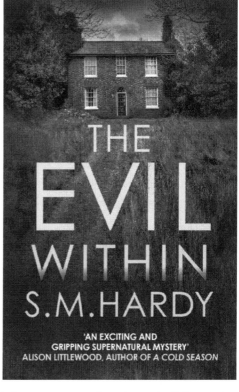

Bereft and feeling lost after the death of his fiancee, Jim Hawkes leaves his high-stress, high-pay finance job in London and rents a vacation cottage in tiny Slyford St James. But the village is not the quiet retreat he was expecting. A series of strange deaths – beginning with that of the little girl who once lived in the very same cottage – have left their mark on the community. And then there are the sounds coming from the attic. And the barking dog that he can never find. And then someone tries to kill him... Can Jim uncover the truth before the murderer finishes what they started?

I love paranormal mysteries and occult detective stories, but the description of *The Evil Within* left me uncertain where it fell on the spectrum between mystery and straight-up horror. The answer, I discovered, is that Hardy has taken elements of both genres, as well as bits of psychological and crime thrillers, and mixed them all together. The result is an unsettling, spooky mystery that moves inexorably from the mundane to the fantastic, from the humdrum to the horrific. The evil that Jim faces is both human and more-than-human, and his allies in uncovering the truth are likewise both human and not.

And it's a good thing for Jim that he does have allies. He's a rational, down-to-earth sort who has little patience and no use for 'woo-woo'. But when he arrives in Slyford St James he discovers that everything he thought he knew about himself and the world is wrong; and that is an upsetting, unsettling discovery that nearly sends him flying back to London in a panic.

But he has Jed, the local handyman, and Emma, a wealthy woman who herself is an outsider to the village. Both are psychics who recognize Jim's awakening gift and urge him to use it to solve that series of strange deaths.

And when Jim does decide to dig into matters... well, no spoilers.

The Evil Within is the first book in the Dark Devon series. It is a highly engaging mixture of the traditional English village mystery with ghosts and psychics and a ruthless killer who will stop at nothing. The creeping sense of dread and the slowly mounting tension kept me turning the pages until the end.

Title: The Miskatonic University Spiritualism Club
Author: Peter Rawlik
Publisher: Jackanapes Press
Format: Paperback
Reviewer: Dave Brzeski

I first discovered H.P. Lovecraft in my early teens, and soon became a huge fan. I quickly developed the technique of scanning through horror anthologies and novels, searching for text in italics, which seemed to be the easiest way of finding references to the Cthulhu Mythos. I came to read authors like Graham

Masterton, and F. Paul Wilson, simply because they slipped sly references to Lovecraft's Mythos into their novels.

Eventually, like so many, I became jaded. I became heartily sick of Lovecraft pastiches. There were simply too many of them, and they were for the most part formulaic. I reached the stage where a reference to the *Necronomicon* would be more likely to put me off reading a book than anything else.

There are exceptions, though – a handful of authors who can still breathe new life into an old concept. Peter Rawlik is most certainly one of them.

There's a review by Shaun Hamill

on the back cover blurb, that nails the description of this novella so perfectly that I may as well just quote from it...

"Imagine Nick and Norah Charles (from the *Thin Man* films) up against cosmic horror, Lovecraftian lore, and traditional Christmas ghost stories, and you're not far off."

Rawlik doesn't shy away from haunted house clichés, such as the aged caretaker, who won't stay in the house after dark, but he very knowingly uses them to set the scene for private detectives, Megan Halsey-Griffith, and Robert Peaslee (Lydecker wasn't really in any condition for field work), people who are intimately familiar with Lovecraftian horrors, but who absolutely do not believe in ghosts, to take on their latest case.

It was just a babysitting job, they were told. All they had to do was make sure that a small group of students managed to keep out of trouble, while they investigated the supposedly haunted Crag House.

Rawlik loves crossovers, so it was no surprise to find various haunted house stories were referenced in a Christmas Eve ghost story-telling session in a manner that suggested they had their roots in legend, rather than novels. Actually, some of them may well have, before they became classic haunted house novels.

You should be getting the impression by this point that this little book packs in more fun than it's reasonable to expect in under one hundred pages.

It's also contains lots of beautiful full, and double page illustrations by Dan Sauer. Sadly, my one complaint is that the print on demand production standards weren't really good enough to present the artwork as well as it should have been, which prevented the book from being the thing of beauty it might have been. This is an issue we're well familiar with at ODM, but sometimes simple economics has to win over quality.

The next book in the series, *The Eldritch Equations and Other Investigations*, at close to 250 pages, promises much more quality material to get ones teeth into, and it rides high on my TBR pile.

DESCRIBIN' THE SCRIBES

MIKE ADAMSON holds a Doctoral degree from Flinders University of South Australia. After early aspirations in art and writing, Mike secured qualifications in both marine biology and archaeology.

Mike has been a university educator from 2006 to 2018, has worked in the replication of convincing ancient fossils, is a passionate photographer, master-level hobbyist, and journalist for international magazines.

Short fiction sales include to *Metastellar, The Strand, Little Blue Marble, Abyss & Apex, Daily Science Fiction, Compelling Science Fiction* and *Nature Futures*. Mike has placed stories on over 220 occasions to date, totalling well over 1.1 million words.

His single largest creation is the science fiction opus *Tales of the Middle Stars*, of which there are currently almost sixty completed stories ranging from flash to novella length, detailing the great adventure of the human colonization of the stellar neighbourhood in the centuries ahead. Forty of these tales have been published to date, in many different international venues. Forthcoming projects include novels in the science fiction and mystery fields.

Mike has begun to carve out a reputation in period mystery, especially brand new Sherlock Holmes adventures, appearing with a variety of publishers, particularly Bellanger Books, from which his first Sherlock Holmes novel has now been released.

You can catch up with his journey at his blog *The View From the Keyboard*: http://mike-adamson.blogspot.com

SIMON AVERY has been published in a variety of magazines and anthologies over the past 30 years, including *Black Static, Great British Horror 4* and *The Year's Best Dark Fantasy and Horror*. His novella *The Teardrop Method* was shortlisted for the 2018 World Fantasy Award. A collection, *A Box Full of Darkness* and a novella *Sorrowmouth* are available from Black Shuck Books.

'*The Nature of Panic*' features the same unnamed protagonist from a previous story, 'Songs for Dwindled Gods' in Occult Detective Quarterly #4. Simon is currently in the process of compiling a number of stories with this character for a collection, as well as a new novel.

His blog can be found at: https://simonaveryblog.wordpress.com

PAUL 'MUTARTIS' BOSWELL is a self trained artist, illustrator and screen printer creating weirdo drawings, freaked out creatures from other dimensions, sculptural mutations, and occasionally wall scrawlings. influenced by nature, the supernatural, weird and strange literature, primitive musics, obsolete technologies and the human psyche.

Emerging from Rural Somerset Mutartis Boswell presents us with a mixed up twisted world where the likes of freakish anthropomorphic creatures stalk apocalyptic landscapes co-existing with lost technologies, which have mutated and taken on a new life. Boswell's weird and wonderful visions are fueled by a powerful imagination, a soup of the mind whose ingredients range from a childhood brought up on comics, old horror movies, sci-fi, northern European folk tales, weird 1970s kids TV, and Punk Rock to name but a few of his influences.

More recently he has been screen printing in his home print studio using ethical materials, which has enabled him to put his work and ideas on garments and limited edition prints.

www.instagram.com/mutartis/
boswellart.blogspot.com
boswellart.bigcartel.com/

BROCI is a Finnish illustrator and comic artist who specializes in dark fantasy and horror inspired illustrations.

Her portfolio site is at https://www.broci.net/

DR MARIA DEBLASSIE is a native New Mexican mestiza bruja and award-winning writer and educator living in the Land of Enchantment. She writes and teaches about spooky stuff, romance, and all things witchy. She is forever looking for magic in her life and somehow always finding more than she thought was there. Find out more about Maria and conjuring everyday magic at www.mariadeblassie.com

JOHN PAUL FITCH lives in Western Australia with his wife and children. His debut collection – Diabolique – was released in 2022 by Hybrid Sequence Media. https://hybridsequencemedia.com/product/diabolique/

BOB FREEMAN is an Occult Detective, author, artist, and game designer. His lifelong passions for mythology, folklore, magick, and religion has led him to become a respected lecturer on the occult and paranormal phenomena. *Landon Connors*, an omnibus of his Occult Detective fiction, is available on Amazon. Watch for *Vampirella: Dead Flowers*, written by Freeman with Sara Frazetta and artist Alberto Locatelli, and *Fire & Ice: Miniatures Adventure Game*, created by Bordermen Games, in association with Frazetta Girls, Bakshi Productions, and Dynamite Entertainment. Freeman lives in the haunted hinterlands of Indiana with his wife Kim and son, fantasy author Connor Landon Freeman.

Bob can be found online at occultdetective.com, bordermengames.com, and youtube.com/@occultdetective

NANCY HANSEN has been an avid reader and prolific writer of fantasy and action/adventure fiction for over 30 years, and is the author of many novels and short stories. You can find various examples of her work at Pro Se Press, Airship 27, Mechanoid Press, Flinch Books, Wolfpack Publishing, Occult Detective Magazine, and Tule Fog Press. In 2022, Nancy was honored and humbled to accept the PULP GRAND MASTER AWARD from Airship 27's Pulp Factory Awards committee.

Nancy has an Amazon Author Page at https://tinyurl.com/vwncsmub

Some of her books are also available on Barnes & Noble online and Smashwords. She has an infrequently updated writing blog at http://nancyahansen.blogspot.com/ and can also be found lurking on Facebook/Meta and Twitter/X.

Nancy resides on an old farm in beautiful, rural eastern Connecticut with an eclectic cast of family members, two rambunctious kittens, and one very beloved and incredibly spoiled elderly dog.

RHYS HUGHES was born in Wales but has lived in many different countries. His first book was published in 1995 and since that time he has published fifty books and hundreds of short stories. He is currently working on a collection of linked crime fiction stories called The Reconstruction Club. His work has been translated into ten languages.

STEVEN PHILIP JONES writes novels, graphic novels, audio scripts, non-fiction books and anything else anybody needs him to write. If it involves words, he's happy. More of Steve's occult detective stories have appeared in such titles as *Arkham Horror: Secrets in Scarlet, Sherlock Holmes and the*

Occult Detectives, Sherlock Holmes: Adventures in the Realm of Lovecraft and *Dracula Beyond Stoker.* Steve's other credits include the novels *King of Harlem, Henrietta Hex: Shadows From the Past* and *Lovecraftian: The Shipwright Circle*; the comics series *H.P. Lovecraft Worlds, Nightlinger* and *Wolverstone and Davis: Street Heroes*; the graphic novel adaptations of *Bram Stoker's Dracula* and the films *Re-Animator* and *Invaders from Mars*; and the nonfiction titles *The Clive Cussler Adventures: A Critical Review* and *Comics Writing: Communicating with Comic Books.*

Steve graduated from the University of Iowa where he majored in Journalism and Religion and was accepted into Iowa's prestigious Writers' Workshop MFA Program.

You can check out Steve's website for his latest news and musings as well as to watch trailers for his comics and novels: http://stevenphilipjones.com/. You can also join the Steven Philip Jones, Writer page on Facebook at: https://www.facebook.com/stevenphilipjones/.

MICHEALE JORDAN was born in LA, educated in New York, and lives in Cincinnati. She's worked at a kennel and AT&T, at a Hebrew School and a church. She's a bit odd. Now she writes, supervised by a long-suffering husband and two domineering cats. (She also makes pie).

She's written two novels,

Mirror Maze (https://www.amazon.com/dp/B0CFCYN87H) and *Blade Light* (https://www.amazon.com/dp/B0C5GJL51W).

Her website, **www.michaelejordan.com**, is undergoing reconstruction (a complete mess) but just grab a hard hat, and come on in.

"M.J." is an American video content creator on YouTube and an avid reader of vintage horror fiction. Her channel, *Reading This Life*, has operated since 2021 and slowly gains a loyal following. The channel features videos of book reviews, book hauls, and community hijinks. Her piece in this issue is her first review article, ever.
Check out her BookTube channel here: https://www.youtube.com/@M-J

NACHING T. KASSA is a wife, mother, and writer. She's created short stories, novellas, poems, and co-created three children. She resides in Eastern Washington State with her husband, Dan Kassa.

Naching is a member of the Horror Writers Association, Mystery Writers of America, and The Science Fiction and Fantasy Writers Association, She is head of Talent Relations at Crystal Lake Publishing and was a recipient of the

2022 HWA Diversity Grant.

You can find her work on Amazon. https://www.amazon.com/Naching-T-Kassa/e/B005ZGHTI0

STEFAN KELLER can be found here https://pixabay.com/users/kellepics-4893063/

PAUL STJOHN MACKINTOSH is a Scottish writer, poet, journalist, RPG creator and media professional.

Born in 1961, he was educated at Trinity College, Cambridge, and currently lives in France.

His published work includes novels, short stories, collected poems, ghostly ballads, and several RPGs.

Details are online at www.paulstjohnmackintosh.com

ANDY PACIOREK is a graphic artist and writer drawn mainly to the worlds of myth, folklore, symbolism, decadence, curiosa, anomaly, dark romanticism and otherworldly experience, and fascinated both by the beautiful and the grotesque and the twilight threshold conciousness where these boundaries blur. The mist-gates, edges and liminal zones where nature borders supernature and daydreams and nightmares cross paths are of great inspiration.

Online bookstore: http://www.blurb.com/user/store/andypaciorek
FB Page: https://www.facebook.com/TheArtofAndyPaciorek
Tumbler: https://andypaciorek.tumblr.com/

ROBERT RUNTÉ, PhD is Senior Editor with EssentialEdits.ca and freelances at SFeditor.ca. A former professor, he has won three Aurora Awards (Canadian SF&F) for his literary criticism and currently reviews for the *Ottawa Review of Books*. In 2018, he inherited the incomplete manuscripts of the late great Canadian SF&F author Dave Duncan to finish and publish, the first two of which are forthcoming from Shadowpaw Press and Tantor Audiobooks. Robert's own fiction has been published in over fifty venues and several of his stories have been reprinted in 'Best of' collections such as *Canadian Shorts II*. You can see Robert in a two-minute video about acquiring and developing books at https://youtu.be/v-vO6fHzxMg?t=67 or listen to his thirty-minute speech on English teachers, fan fiction, and the future of publishing at https://tinyurl.com/35kf3x45. He can be found on Facebook at dr.robertrunte and he blogs at http://sfeditorca.blogspot.com/.

He lives in Lethbridge, Alberta, with his wife, two daughters and three dogs.

JOE TALON grew up in a small village in West Somerset, England. Joe has always loved the soft hills and deep combes explored during a childhood spent wandering about the countryside, haunted by the possibilities of the otherness existing in the world. The quiet seconds after a footstep is heard on a stairway, but no one is there. Or a shadow passes a window and it makes the heart pound – just for a moment.

Joe's first love, writing, combined these two passions, giving birth to the Lorne Turner series. Together they weave stories of mystery, crime, suspense, and the supernatural. Joe's protagonists are broken men, who rely on the teamwork of strong women to help solve the paranormal, the murderous, and the plain weird.

Joe's home life is dominated by six rescue dogs, avoiding the heat of a Spanish summer and loving the warmth of the winter mountains.

With a strong fan base, a stream of five star reviews, and being an Amazon Best Seller, Joe Talon's series, The Lorne Turner Mysteries are gathering high critical acclaim.

Joe Talon Author Amazon Page: author.to/JoeTalonBooks

Joe Talon Author BookBub Page: bookbub.com/authors/joe-talon

Joe Talon Website: joetalon.com

Printed in Great Britain
by Amazon

43264611R00126